"Get out of my head!" Kane growled

He wrestled against the forces assailing him. The other entity—a shadowy form zooming between Kane's view of the world and his embattled mind—looked over its shoulder at the ongoing struggle.

Kane heard a voice no human on Earth ever had. It was deep, rumbling, pervasive. It might have been male, but there was an odd quality to it that seemed almost sexless. "Your friends are going to die." The vibrations of those words burrowed deep into him—like termites chewing through the heart of a tree.

Kane writhed in the smothering grasp of his opponent.

"You're going to shoot them," the shadow taunted. Kane's right arm tore free from the engulfing mass of darkness, and he reached out, fingertips brushing the icy flesh.

"I'll rip you out of my skull first!" Kane bellowed. "I'll shred you into ribbons!"

D1115893

Other titles in this series:

James Axler
Outlanders®

SHADOW BORN

A GOLD EAGLE BOOK FROM
WORLDWIDE®

TORONTO • NEW YORK • LONDON
AMSTERDAM • PARIS • SYDNEY • HAMBURG
STOCKHOLM • ATHENS • TOKYO • MILAN
MADRID • WARSAW • BUDAPEST • AUCKLAND

Recycling programs
for this product may
not exist in your area.

First edition August 2014

ISBN-13: 978-0-373-63883-3

SHADOW BORN

Copyright © 2014 by Worldwide Library

Special thanks to Douglas P. Wojtowicz for his contribution
to this work.

Printed in U.S.A.

Where force is necessary, there it must be applied boldly, decisively and completely. But one must know the limitations of force, one must know when to blend force with a maneuver, a blow with an agreement.

—Leon Trotsky,
1879–1940

The Road to Outlands—
From Secret Government Files to the Future

Almost two hundred years after the global holocaust, Kane, a former Magistrate of Cobaltville, often thought the world had been lucky to survive at all after a nuclear device detonated in the Russian embassy in Washington, D.C. The aftermath—forever known as skydark—reshaped continents and turned civilization into ashes.

Nearly depopulated, America became the Deathlands—poisoned by radiation, home to chaos and mutated life forms. Feudal rule reappeared in the form of baronies, while remote outposts clung to a brutish existence.

What eventually helped shape this wasteland were the redoubts, the secret preholocaust military installations with stores of weapons, and the home of gateways, the locational matter-transfer facilities. Some of the redoubts hid clues that had once fed wild theories of government cover-ups and alien visitations.

Rearmed from redoubt stockpiles, the barons consolidated their power and reclaimed technology for the villes. Their power, supported by some invisible authority, extended beyond their fortified walls to what was now called the Outlands. It was here that the rootstock of humanity survived, living with hellzones and chemical storms, hounded by Magistrates.

In the villes, rigid laws were enforced—to atone for the sins of the past and prepare the way for a better future. That was the barons' public credo and their right-to-rule.

Kane, along with friend and fellow Magistrate Grant, had upheld that claim until a fateful Outlands expedition. A displaced piece of technology…a question to a keeper of the archives…a vague clue about alien masters—and their world shifted radically. Suddenly, Brigid Baptiste, the archivist, faced summary execution, and Grant a quick termination. For Kane there was forgiveness if he pledged his unquestioning allegiance to Baron Cobalt and his unknown masters and abandoned his friends.

But that allegiance would make him support a mysterious and alien power and deny loyalty and friends. Then what else was there?

Kane had been brought up solely to serve the ville. Brigid's only link with her family was her mother's red-gold hair, green eyes and supple form. Grant's clues to his lineage were his ebony skin and powerful physique. But Domi, she of the white hair, was an Outlander pressed into sexual servitude in Cobaltville. She at least knew her roots and was a reminder to the exiles that the outcasts belonged in the human family.

Parents, friends, community—the very rootedness of humanity was denied. With no continuity, there was no forward momentum to the future. And that was the crux—when Kane began to wonder if there was a future.

For Kane, it wouldn't do. So the only way was out—way, way out.

After their escape, they found shelter at the forgotten Cerberus redoubt headed by Lakesh, a scientist, Cobaltville's head archivist, and secret opponent of the barons.

With their past turned into a lie, their future threatened, only one thing was left to give meaning to the outcasts. The hunger for freedom, the will to resist the hostile influences. And perhaps, by opposing, end them.

Prologue

Neekra dreamed of ages past, her memories stretching far back through the delirium and pain of the orichalcum scepter jammed through her avatar's torso. She sought escape from the incalculable energies held within the unstable alloy scorching through her hijacked cellular structure. The superstring biological computers that she'd molded into her core, powerful transmitters that allowed her incredible telepathic ability and the power to sculpt human bodies as if made from clay, misfired and shuddered…

But she fought for her consciousness. She still could find a back door, a way to escape the dissolution of the lost fragment that had managed to escape from where the rest of her body was imprisoned.

"It's the only way we will ever be free," a voice whispered in her ear.

She felt the strength of a lover's hands running down the length of her body, warm whispers brushing her earlobes. Was this a dream, a fevered remnant of a time when she was merely Annunaki and not the being she sought to return to in resurrection?

Then she was tumbling, careening across her own time line, before her father, Enlil, burdened her with the horrible task as punishment for her all-too-human weakness…

…and there was Neekra, bastard child of Enlil, kneeling on the hard floor, her legs curled beneath her shapely thighs, her chin touching her chest, eyes closed.

She didn't dare open them, even as her father paced in front of her, his ponderous tread shaking the ground for emphasis. Enlil reached down, hooked her chin with a crooked forefinger and drew her to look up at him.

"Open your eyes!" At the sharp command, her eyes popped open and she looked Enlil in the face. He was tall, magnificent, clad in a simple silk sash adorned with a gold chain as his belt. Muscles rippled beneath his fine-scaled skin; Enlil would have been an inspiration to the greatest human sculptors.

As divine as his appearance was, he was also a commanding force, his voice cementing her in place with its deep, vibrating tone.

"Sweet child," he whispered, a hiss with all the warmth of an Arctic wind. "You disappoint me."

"I'm…I'm…so sor…" Neekra began.

His fingertip touched her lips together, cutting her off. Neekra was so frightened, even the urge to shiver cowered somewhere between her shoulder blades.

This has to be memory, she thought, and for a moment, Neekra was confused at where that realization came from. *This is just a fantasy, a delusion created by my suffering.*

I have not feared Enlil in millennia, came the conclusion.

And almost as if the Annunaki overlord had overheard the defiance she'd displayed twenty-five centuries hence, Enlil wrapped his long fingers around her throat and neck, craning her head up.

"I can smell the stink of his sex on you," Enlil growled.

"I can explain…" Neekra's younger-self sputtered, not daring to break her stare from his.

"The explanation is simple, my little girl," Enlil huffed. He slid his fingers through her crimson-streaked black locks, claw-like nails scratching along the back of her head.

There had been times when such a caress might have been the beginnings of rough intimacy between herself and the god of her world. Now she felt menace in his clutch. Electric bolts of pain sparked through his nails.

"Please…"

He hurt you, but don't give him that satisfaction, Neekra thought. *Don't let him have his victory in seeing you cry.*

Yet Neekra's memories had been cast in stone. She could not change that past, that history, and she could not alter the memories that stuck in her brain.

Enlil's revenge was as unspeakable among the Annunaki as it would be with any less evolved, so-called barbaric race. It was his manipulations, his cruelty that nurtured Neekra into what she was, what she had grown to be. That hate had poisoned her, blackened her soul so that thousands of years could not erase the fury she felt toward her father.

Perhaps she could have found a better way out of the hell she'd been stuck in, a better mentor or lover, a better teacher, someone who could have laid the groundwork for redemption. She'd seen those things inside of Kane's mind, and the minds of others who'd opposed her spawn, the darkness with which she infested the world. Rather than giving in to hatred for an abusive, sadistic father, she could have found worth in making her life better, making the world better. She could have rebelled like her half sister, Malesh, and fought for independence against the global order that their fouler kin had wrought upon humanity.

Instead, Neekra took solace in the arms of Negari, the Igigi whose affection and intimacy had drawn the wrath of Enlil.

Negari had promised her gifts and talents that would make Enlil tremble before her, rather than lord over her. Work was being done across the planet, on the opposite shores of a mighty ocean, far beneath the waves at one of the deepest realms yet known to the Annunaki. There, in experiments shielded from the rest of the world by six thousand feet of water, 191 atmospheres of pressure, they had discovered a form of life that made even the mightiest of the overlords tremble. Even Enlil himself could not survive the bone-crushing pressures of one and a quarter tons of weight per square inch.

And so Neekra crawled forward in time, further along the path she'd already endured, fully aware that in this fever dream, time passed much more swiftly than in the real world, where Kane and Nehushtan had impaled her, attacking her avatar's cellular structure with energies equivalent to the output of a dying sun.

Through her continued psychic retreat, she arrived at the night when Negari caressed her ravaged form, working with healing technologies that could negate the torment that Enlil used as his signature on her flesh. The puckered skin, the torn muscle knitted back together. Neekra still felt the rent wounds in her spirit. Even Negari could do little for that, but as he nursed her injuries, kissed and comforted her, gave her tenderness, he whispered of the wonders that they had discovered within the protein structure, a living virus that had brought madness and devastation across the lands of Sumeria until the overlords combined their might to stop it.

"It's magnificent," Negari whispered. "It's one consciousness, a complete mind in each strand of complex molecules, smaller than a single chromosome, yet able to tap into immense knowledge."

"How can that help us?" Neekra asked. Her injuries faded, and a warm sensuality bathed her entire body, cellular regeneration within the "healing coffin" having an effect on sexual desire.

"It means we can shed these bodies," Negari said. "And

if we wished, we could become one being, or we could exist among the teeming millions of apes sprawled across the face of this planet. Or even further."

Neekra raised an eyebrow, and Negari answered her curiosity with first a kiss. "We could become the totality of the Annunaki race. They would become puppets, marionettes on strings of self-replicating protein that would infest them."

"That sounds…tedious," Neekra responded. She brushed her lover's cheek.

"It seems like it would be, but the samples we captured, isolated down at the Tongue, they don't show that feeling of limitation," Negari said.

"Of course not," Neekra stated. She smiled. "It's trying to seduce you. Trying to let it into your brain and then to escape. Father has done everything in his power to limit its existence, yet…"

"Yet he still makes us toil, unraveling the secrets built into it on an atomic scale," Negari responded. He rose, then gently lowered himself between her open thighs. His hands cupped her face tenderly, his emerald eyes meeting her crimson gaze. "I can advance us without letting the totality loose on the world, without having it infect us. We would be ourselves, mightier than anything this world could hope to contain."

Neekra reveled as Negari put his words aside and utilized his tongue and lips for other, much more pleasurable things. His kisses, his nibbling of her newly revived flesh provided an escape from the agonies inflicted upon her, at that time from the rage of Enlil, and outside of the memory, from the assault of Kane.

The time of needles came up next, after years of Negari's experimentation. He'd isolated the particular protein chain that could be turned into the base root of a world-encompassing hive mind. The first experiment was on himself, and slowly the natural telepathy of the Igigi race became stronger. Within him, the proteins reproduced, growing, laying the groundwork of sheathing along his nervous system, which acted as the conducting antenna coil for his thoughts. As soon as that happened, he reached out to Neekra.

He spoke to her, mentally, without outside Annunaki technology, reaching blindly around the globe, over a mile of ocean water or, even more impressively, through the crust of a planet.

That night, Neekra's body came alive with the touch of a lover who no longer needed to be in the same room. Neekra cried out, thrashing at his ministrations, biting down hard on her lip to prevent her uttering his name.

Still, she was found out. She was cornered, quizzed, whipped and battered by an enraged Enlil.

Negari had gone too far, committed himself to an experiment, become something that was greater than Enlil, and this was a world where *none* could be greater than he. He had not crossed a universe to become the second-best in his own Olympus. He was to be Zeus, the mightiest of the mighty, yet Negari dared to slap their leader in the face.

Igigi had been meant to be the servant class—never mind that Neekra was the result of Enlil's night with one of those serfs.

"What is good for you, Father, is forbidden for me?" Neekra gasped, stretched against the wall, naked and helpless. She wouldn't shrink, not even as vulnerable as she was now.

Enlil pressed against her. "You act as if I care what happens to you."

Then Enlil showed Neekra exactly how much he "cared" about her, brutally, slowly grinding her cheek against the wall with his forearm as he drove into her again and again. All he was doing was stoking the fires of hatred, the hunger for revenge that would cross centuries unabated, growing only in depth of spite and disgust.

Soon, Neekra whispered into the ear of her younger self, something that did as little for the remembered image as if she'd given promises to a baby photo of herself.

The dream broke. A little bit of vision was still left in the dead eyes of Gamal, and she saw collapsed figures all about her. She'd gone to full armor in an effort to protect herself, her "piggyback brains" from being assaulted by the humans who caught on to how she'd reconfigured the man's body to accommodate the telepathic organs, the biological computer that granted her the seemingly impossible powers necessary to shake the world.

No one around her was conscious. She tried to move, but all around her was crust; her flesh turned to ash with black, ugly sap crawling from cracks in her surface.

Don't have long, she thought. *Nehushtan will awaken the least injured with the least energy first, then tap into him.*

Neekra stretched to reach for one of her spawn. Some must have been left alive.

And there were. She could feel two of them, staying deep in the rubble of crypts that had been struck by grenades and bullets. Those two hid, knowing that there would be others to come to her aid immediately. Neekra had programmed them that way, making certain she had a backup plan in case things went to crap.

They had gone beyond crap. The spark of life in the carcass she inhabited was fading fast, and as she did a mental inventory of herself, she saw the deterioration of the protein strings that made up her "telepathic antennae"— the webbing of natural materials that turned her into a living psychic transmitter, able to manipulate thought as well as cellular structure. The protein "biocomputers" also could create the telekinetic fields that gave her superhuman strength and durability far beyond even her father's brute force at his prime.

She pushed out a blackened polyp of tar, separating cracked chunks of Gamal's ashen corpse. Gamal had been one of the people she had been drawn to, three charismatic figures who would be attuned to her, to be her pawns. Neekra's body was somewhere, operating on autopilot, chosen by Enlil to be the guardian of the tomb of Negari, her lover. Neekra was an excised intelligence, her lobotomized body an engine of destruction whose sole purpose was the death of anyone foolish enough to attempt a rescue of the Igigi who dared to ascend to unearned godhood.

Whether Neekra's wandering ghost was an afterthought, or a callously calculated punishment, she knew she was a nomad. She was an infection, capable of only infesting one host at a time. To find that host, she was limited to a psyche that could handle the power of her mind and spirit; otherwise she would burn him out, but it still needed to be a mind that she could overpower.

Now, all she had for a body, for a means of travel, was the combination of two blobs of semisentient snot that she'd birthed from Gamal's body. She could last in them for a while, but it was nothing like she could do with a host such as her last one.

She injected what little of herself was left into their cytoplasm, mixing with them, letting the two amorphous entities unite. They each had undamaged protein string centers—four, in fact—which she laced together into a matrix that could sustain her until she could recover.

With that, the blob carrying her consciousness stretched out pseudopods, latching on to imperfections on the ground, swinging itself along, making for the corkscrew that would lead her to the surface.

The light-sensitive sensory organs in the membranes of her host body cringed at the overabundance of sunlight, even though dawn wouldn't break for another five minutes.

All she needed was to scurry to a thicket of thorns, burrow under the sand and wait.

Hiding was her only solace, at least until she could find someone, something.

And then it would be a game of catch-up.

Kane and Durga had been put on a trail now. They had been after her hiding place. There, they would subdue her body and then attempt to destroy it. But by battling her, they would loosen what bonds held Negari in place.

Doing that would free him, and if Neekra had caught up by then, she'd retrieve herself and awaken as she was meant to be.

She crawled under the graying, ever-lightening sky across the arid dirt toward the dry grasses of the tree line.

A scaled foot set down in her path.

It was Durga. He'd vowed to destroy her, and now she was vulnerable to him. The mega-cellular form she was trapped in couldn't withstand the deadly venom he stored in his fangs. He had used enough to blind her previous avatar, but…

"Don't cringe from me," Durga spoke gently.

He knelt before her on the dirt and reached out, cupping her balloon-like form.

"You and I have a journey to complete," he whispered, cooing to her as if she were a baby, scooping her up and cradling her in his arms.

"Come now, darling," Durga said to her. "We have to find your tomb."

Confused, weak, unable to communicate for the moment, she was wound in a blanket that prevented her from stabbing Durga's skin with cilia, tiny little barbed stingers that could suck the blood from his flesh. The blanket protected her primitive visual stimulus organs, though, and concealed her from the burning heat of the sun.

She now rested in a bucket seat and heard the rattle then rumble of an engine firing to life. They had been in a jeep belonging to the Panthers of Mashona, the militia run by her old host, Gamal.

"Tell me where to drive, my sweet," Durga whispered. Except it wasn't a whisper. He was contacting her with his thoughts.

Neekra thought back to the pain and fire of the staff within her torso, a reminder of another era when the ancient artifact was used to send her to flight. When Suleiman Kahani battled the thing within the crypt after it had slain the slavers.

Neekra recognized what her father had wrought from her and recognized landmarks about her. Her battle with Kane had been the final key to remembering where she and her lover had been interred. Neekra, at Durga's mercy, passed on that information.

She prayed that she would not regret this decision.

Chapter 1

Kane made certain that there was nothing left down below in the necropolis. For the past two days, his friends had been prisoners down there, captives of the two beings he searched for traces of. An apocalyptic battle with one of them had ensued after her erstwhile companion seemed to turn on her, warning Kane about his plan about destroying their alliance and the avatar of their ally.

The *her* was Neekra, a bodiless entity who had taken possession of a militia warlord by the name of Gamal. Neekra's power was such that she was able to turn a tall, muscular, powerful man into a crimson-skinned goddess full of voluptuous curves and able to give "birth" to amorphous spawn. Those things she created had been the basis for vampire mythology, semiliquid entities that inserted themselves into corpses, wearing their carcasses like suits of meat. Neekra, or her issue, had been around the world, creating a universe of mythologies surrounding the walking dead, but here, in Africa, was where she "lived." When Kane came to Africa, summoned by an artifact that had been ancient in the time of Atlantis and was attributed to King Solomon of the Bible, Neekra sought him out and psychically attacked him and the one Kane learned later was her ally.

Neekra's psychic imprisonment of Kane was a testing of the waters. Kane shuddered at the thought that instead of the warlord Gamal, it could have been him, his physique telekinetically sculpted, organs reattributed and external appearance mutilated until he became the same rust-red feminine goddess who sought domination of the necropolis.

Neekra's host was nearly invulnerable, ignoring grenade blasts and bursts of full-automatic gunfire directly into her face. Yet she wanted Kane and others to hunt for her prison, the place where she'd been interred for dozens of centuries, mind and flesh amputated from each other.

Gamal's body had only been destroyed by the combination of the venom that was innate to a race of pan-terrestrial humanoids called the Nagah and the burning energies within the staff once wielded by Solomon and Moses. Neekra's host was reduced to ash, tar-like blood turning the collapsed mound into what Kane's dear friend Grant called "a greasy smear."

Kane poked and prodded at that smear. Although no sign of animation was left within the ugly concoction, Kane felt no relief. He had encountered another goddess who had survived the destruction of her body, taking root to reincarnate in the bodies of three young women. Neekra's thousands of years of existence had influenced stories of night terror around the globe, so the death of one body wouldn't stop her. They'd put her down, but still someone else was looking for that body, that tomb she sought.

That *someone else,* the same man who wanted out of the alliance, was Prince Durga, exiled regent of the underground Nagah city-state of Garuda in India. Durga, like all Nagah, was a humanoid, an upgrade of humanity created by an ancient alien entity named Enki, a member of a race called the Annunaki, who had been involved with another superhuman species, the Tu'atha de Danaan, in manipulating humanity and its rise to power on Earth.

The Nagah had been human, with additions of cobra DNA, skillfully crafted by the benevolent Annunaki, to create a benign, hidden race.

The Nagah survived skydark in their underground city of Garuda, but not without some losses. The small nation-state finally, after centuries, made its presence known to Kane and the other explorers of Cerberus. What could have become a wonderful alliance turned to tragic ashes as Durga chose that moment to make his bid for sole leadership of the pan-terrestrial society. Allying with gods and men, Durga launched a civil war, and had not Durga greedily varied from his plan and sought out superhuman power for its own sake, he might have succeeded. As it was, Kane and his allies ended that war, but not without loss of innocent life in addition to the destruction of human and Nagah co-conspirators.

Kane had thought that Durga was dead, killed in a fuel-air explosion, but the same technology that made the prince into a living force of nature spared him, just barely. As he plotted revenge against his former bride, now the matron queen of the Nagah, he traveled across the Indian Ocean to Africa, seeking a cure for his crippled condition, as well as means to renewed power. Part of that power was discovered in an army of cloned beasts, with physical might to rival a bull-gorilla, bat-like wings and a taste for human flesh. Those hybrid mutants were known as the Kongamato, but Durga's control of the animals was usurped by a warlord of the dreaded Panthers of Mashona, an outlaw militia who ruled the lands to the west of Harare and Zambia, the same Gamal who "donated" his body to the she-devil Neekra.

Durga hadn't only relied upon the Kongamato, apparently. When Kane assailed the necropolis, he encountered a cadre of cloned Nagah, their physiques further upgraded with Igigi/Nephilim DNA to turn them into his shock troopers. Durga possessed a dozen of those clones, at least when he was alongside Neekra.

A lone figure stepped onto the dirt next to Kane.

"Grant said it was time to go. The place is wired and ready to blow," the young man said.

The six-foot, perfectly muscled Nagah clones that Durga utilized weren't the only creations the prince made. Physically, the young man, Thurpa, looked to be eighteen or nineteen, at least as far as Kane could see through his cobra-like features. Chronologically, though, Thurpa must have been less than a year old.

The Cerberus adventurers and their companions had discovered Thurpa's clone nature. He looked absolutely normal, but during Durga's struggle against Neekra, Thurpa suffered the same pain from physical injuries and psychic trauma. When the young man gripped Nehushtan, the ancient walking staff of kings and prophets, its healing power *transmitted* through him to Durga.

Even now, Kane could see the numb shock on the young man's features, realizing that any memories since before the day he met Kane and the others had been a lie, a fabrication implanted by a renegade prince whose rampage slew even his mother, the old matron of Garuda. Thurpa had thought that he could return home, but he'd never set his own eyes upon it. Rather, they had been echoes of another's mind; most likely, it was Durga's.

"How are you feeling?" Kane asked him.

"Like I should stay down here when you press the detonator," Thurpa replied.

Kane shook his head. "No. We won't do that."

"I'd been worried that I was maybe hypnotized or brainwashed," Thurpa said. "Now, I find that I'm his clone. Worse, I'm the son he always wanted."

"We don't judge our friends on the sins of their fathers," Kane told him. He rested his hand on the young man's shoulder. "You've done so much good alongside us."

Thurpa's amber eyes glistened in the backwash of light from his torch. The boy was in tears. "I've killed pretty well."

"Killed to protect, killed to liberate," Kane corrected. "And you risked yourself jumping on the back of a superhumanly strong creature to stop her."

Thurpa frowned. "I attacked her because I realized, I'm not real. I'd be no…"

Kane gave him a light tap on the shoulder. "You feel real enough to me. And you *would* be a loss. Nathan would feel alone, and Lyta looks interested in you."

"A freak in a land he was not born to," Thurpa replied.

"Her first look at her rescuers," Kane said. "If anything can make you feel good and real…"

Thurpa shook himself free from Kane's comforting grip.

"And spread *his* seed?" Thurpa asked, glaring at Kane in disbelief.

"It's not genetic structure that makes you good or bad," Kane returned.

Thurpa's glare dimmed in fire, his anger draining. Kane had seen emotional defeat on faces before. This was a crushing blow to him, and such despondence could easily lead the young man to reckless risks or an act of desperation, if not direct suicide.

Thurpa had easily earned Kane's respect for courage and tenacity. He'd also shown himself in other ways. As a Magistrate, Kane had developed a quick sense not only for danger, but also for the content of a person's character. All this time he'd spent with the young Nagah had informed him that this cobra-hooded stranger *was* someone he could trust, someone with compassion, despite the origin of his chromosomes.

"Come on, there's nothing down here except for corpses," Kane told him. "We'll go some place you'll feel better."

"I thought we had been chasing my father and Neekra to her tomb," Thurpa asked.

"It's got to be better than this. And spending time in the sun and the air will do wonders for your spirit," Kane told him.

Thurpa nodded.

The two men walked up the corkscrew ramp, returning to the surface, where the others waited.

THE FIRST SIGN that their detonation worked was a slight rumble that actually tickled the soles of Lyta's feet. The ground throbbed as a shock wave grew, and she found herself backing away from the epicenter. Ripples in the dirt rose, and then it seemed to telescope inward, rocks crashing downward. She knew that she was dozens of yards from ground zero of the blast and that the caverns below would absorb most of the concussive force of the detonation, but even so, the earth surged and heaved.

Jets of rancid air and dust blew out from cracks burst between solid rock by the shattering explosion. Clouds rose into the midmorning sky, thick and roiling, turning a sunny day to darkness. The roar of crushing rock from below fooled her, for an instant, into believing that the mother of all thunderstorms slashed down on the six people.

"Grant doesn't fool around when it comes time to blow shit up," Lyta said softly.

Nathan shook his head. "Considering what they did to the Kongamato, I'm not surprised."

Lyta glanced to one side. Thurpa stood alone, looking

down into the dirt. His interest had been momentarily snagged by the explosion, but now he withdrew back into himself and stared at the ground.

The cobra-like young man, who had shown her such care and concern a few days before, no longer let himself feel like one of the group. She walked over to him.

"Thurpa?"

Amber eyes opened, turned toward her.

"Come on, let's get going before we're wearing an inch of cemetery dust," she said, leaning toward him, bumping her shoulder against his.

Thurpa turned up one corner of his mouth. "I'll join you guys in the truck."

Lyta reached up, lacing her fingers with his. She could feel the hardness of the scales on the inner pads of his fingers and across his palm. At first, he seemed reluctant to give her a squeeze, but she pressed harder. The scale pads had been stiffer than normal skin but not sharp edged; they obviously were worn down by day-to-day operation, or maybe it was just a case of natural evolution. Pointy, jagged edges on a palm got in the way of everyday life. With too tough a set of skin on the bits that needed tactile feedback, they'd be effectively crippled, not as if it had been the scales on the soles of his feet.

He was warm, and his scales were soft and smooth. When he squeezed her fingers, managing a little bit of a smile, he was gentle. "Kane mentioned that you might be interested in me…"

"That man may be jumping the gun. I just lost my fiancé," she whispered.

Lyta quickly stood on her tiptoes, bringing her full lips close to his ear hole. "But he ain't barking up the wrong tree."

Thurpa leaned away, looking her over. "I wish that I could…"

Lyta cut him off and elbowed him in the ribs, pointing to the sky. "Looks like we're gonna get…"

"Come on!" Brigid Baptiste shouted from their pickup truck, untouched for days since the Cerberus group hid it to the side in order to ambush the militia group who had her in a slave queue.

The two ran for the truck. Nathan was in the bed, holding up a tarp. Thurpa lifted Lyta up and under the canvas, then bowed his head as dust, sand and tiny pebbles came raining down. Lyta reached out and took his forearm, pulling with all the strength of her legs to bring him up and into the truck bed. Kane also was under the canvas, helping Nathan hold up the protective tarp, while Grant and Brigid settled into the cab.

The sound of tiny objects rattled off the roof of the cap, snapping and popping on the canvas that Nathan and Kane used as an improvised umbrella.

Grant fired up the engine once most of the debris settled around them, turning on headlights and windshield wipers to see through the remaining cloud of airborne particles and to scrape layers of dirt from the glass. He looked through the back sliding window into the cab as Kane pushed the tarp back, letting the gravel spill out through the netting and the lowered tailgate. As the pickup gained speed, the gravel and dust poured as a trail behind them, kicking up a swirling cloud.

The four people in the bed of the truck immediately got to work making certain the dust was swept out. The last thing they needed was an easy way for someone to track them. Without the dust fully expunged, there'd always be something kicking off the truck, leaving a smoky trail showing recent passage and making them much more visible from the air.

So far, except for the Kongamato, Durga and Neekra hadn't shown means of aerial surveillance, but then, Durga himself had kept an Annunaki skimmer in his employ back in Garuda. If the Nagah prince had the wherewithal to find cloning facilities, a means of pumping out mutant soldiers like the not-so-bright "brothers" of Thurpa or the aforementioned Kongamato, aerial surveillance wasn't out of the question at all.

Lyta had been lucky enough not to have seen the beasts and their wing-arms with musculature and power akin to a bull-gorilla's. Blobs reanimating corpses, making them like legendary vampires in strength and agility, were bad enough. The Kongamato themselves, with their bat-wings, had been a pure nightmare.

A nightmare that she, and her three companions in the bed of the truck, kept an eye out for by scanning the skies. While Grant set up the explosives in the underground cavern, Lyta and Nathan went to work gathering ammunition and extra firearms and loading them into storage lockers on the truck. It was hard work, but preparation was necessary. They had been going up against the tomb that Neekra sought and didn't have an idea of what they could expect there.

They had picked up rocket launchers among the arsenal, though Lyta had been present when the others opened fire on Neekra's latest avatar and wasn't convinced that rockets would be enough. That feminine body, composed of no more than human flesh, ignored entire magazines of automatic gunfire and close-range blasts of hand grenades. Maybe an antitank rocket could have done some damage to that incarnation of her.

What were they going to find at Neekra's home?

What else could Durga call upon?

Thurpa looked worried, but his concern seemed to be much more than what they would run into; it was also what his role would be. The young man had learned that his presumptions of being a recent recruit had been simply an illusion, false memories entered into his mind. He had been able to transmit the healing energies of Nehushtan, Nathan Longa's responsibility, to Durga. What other controls and connections did that fallen prince hold over Thurpa?

She reached out, resting her hand on his knee. It took a few moments before Thurpa's vision focused, instead of gazing glassily at the recently swept bed of the pickup truck. He rewarded her with a slight smile, resting his hand atop hers.

"You have friends here," Lyta said.

"I know that," Thurpa replied. "Which makes me all the more worried of what I might do to you."

"We'll be expecting trouble," Kane mentioned. "We don't want to hurt you, and we know you don't want to cause us any trouble. But we can protect Lyta and Nathan if necessary."

Lyta glanced toward Kane. He was a large man, six feet in height, with powerful ropes of muscle in his upper body, akin to the musculature of a wolf. His eyes were a cool blue, and now, in the light of his words, those orbs seemed especially predatory. The warrior had done some amazing things, first rescuing her, then protecting her from the freakish amorphous blobs of Neekra, and then in subsequent battles.

She thought about how Thurpa measured up to him. The young man gave up four inches of height and thirty pounds to the explorer from America. While the Nagah had fangs and venom, and a layer of scales that might armor him somewhat, Lyta had little illusion that those would make up for Kane's greater size, strength and experience.

The hardness in Kane's gaze softened, and he added, "We won't let you hurt them or yourself."

"Thank you," Thurpa said softly.

GRANT, BEHIND THE wheel of the pickup truck, kept his voice low, allowing the Commtact on his jaw to do most of the work of transmitting sound into Brigid's and Kane's Commtact receivers. Between the jostling of the truck on the roads and the relative solitude of the pickup's cab, he knew that this conversation would be private.

"Thurpa turns out to be a creation of Durga. Maybe even a clone," Grant said, putting their suspicions on the table. "What can we do about this? And will it have an effect on us?"

"Everything we've seen of Durga is part of a long-term plan," Brigid offered. "He's not one to go for a quick partial victory."

"Except when he took a dip in the Cobra baths back in Garuda," Kane subvocalized. Grant caught a glimpse of him in the rearview mirror. He was looking toward the forest to the right of the truck, so what noises he made would be lost in the wind and the other three wouldn't see his throat and jaw move. "And he's learned his lesson from that disaster."

"Instant gratification and physical power weren't enough to protect him, nor give him the victory he sought," Brigid concurred.

"So, Thurpa, if he is a ticking time bomb, might not go off for years?" Grant asked.

"I don't think that he's a bomb," Kane's voice popped in, disembodied. "He's too valuable to Durga."

"Kane has a point," Brigid returned. "From Thurpa's account, we learned that when Neekra attacked Durga, sensory input seemed to be deferred between Durga's body and Thurpa's. When Thurpa sought the regenerative capabilities of Nehushtan, he could sense Durga also drawing strength and healing."

"So, Thurpa is Durga's means of immortality?" Grant mused. "Like an overflow valve. Things get too hot for Prince Asshole, it vents through our friend."

"On a psychic scale, yes," Brigid concurred. "The two of them have a psychic link through which they share the load."

Grant frowned, his gunslinger's mustache accentuating and exaggerating the downward bow of his lips. "So if we ever have to take down Durga, we could hurt Thurpa."

"Why have a bomb when you have a perennial human shield?" Brigid inquired rhetorically.

Kane's grumble, to Grant's ears, was indicative of a stewing, deepening anger stemming from impotence. "Not that your riddle needs answering, but he gets psychic shielding from Neekra, and he gets something that will stop us from putting a bullet into his head."

Brigid nodded. "Correct."

Grant watched the mirror image of Kane glance toward Thurpa in the back of the truck. He saw profound pain in his friend's features, that impotence toward helping the young Nagah, whose only sins had been those of his father.

"What's to say that Hannah's children aren't going to end up the same way?" Kane asked finally, looking away from Thurpa. "Durga implanted his DNA into her, giving her twins, the first and last children she'll ever have."

"Durga's a bastard, but those kids will be raised right," Grant said. "Manticor will be a good father to them."

"Will fatherhood be enough when they're in psychic contact with a sociopath like Durga?" Kane asked. "They'll grow up with what the rest of the world would think are schizophrenic delusions."

"But we'll get this information to Hannah," Brigid said.

Kane's grunt showed his frustration. "And what will that provide?"

"It will warn her of what's coming," Brigid told him.

Grant kept his eyes on the road. Even as he drove, he was trying to figure out what could mitigate any telepathic influence on Hannah's twins or on Thurpa.

"What about the control interface that Gamal used?" Grant asked. "It was a thought transmitter."

Brigid turned to him. "Use it as a signal blocker? But that was a lot of machinery. Unless it would be an area denial device. It sends out a scramble signal…but then, no one could use any natural psychic ability in Garuda."

"It'd have to be a blanket, wouldn't it?" Grant asked.

"We could try something akin to a torus defense, but…" Brigid mused. "Brain waves would have openings in areas away from the ring itself, either transmitting over the top or under the earth."

"The only way we have to protect Hannah's children is to end Durga," Kane murmured. "And if we kill Durga, what kind of harm would we cause Thurpa?"

Brigid sighed. "He said he'd be willing to sacrifice himself."

Grant's mood darkened even further, but he refused to let go of any hope. "Let's see that it doesn't come to that."

Frustrated and feeling helpless in the face of Thurpa's personal danger, Grant's stomach twisted. He needed to vent his impotence on something.

The hiss-boom of a darting rocket drew his attention from the side. Their pickup truck had passed into a sandy, barren clearing between trees, and a line of enemy trucks were parked up on a hill. It had to be the militia, the Panthers of Mashona—or what was left of them.

And there would be no mistaking Kane, a white man, or Thurpa, a human cobra, in the bed of their truck.

"Here comes shit!" Grant bellowed, tromping the gas to keep ahead of subsequent rounds of enemy fire.

Chapter 2

As soon as the wobbly spear, riding its tail of smoke and fire, hissed past the bed of the pickup truck and smashed into the ground, Thurpa grabbed his folded rifle and looked along the cottony trail back to its point of origin. He grimaced at the sight of three trucks, similar to the one that Grant and the others had procured back at Victoria Falls, except these had been mounted with machine guns and were filled with gunmen.

What do you think you are, idiot? A swordsman? Thurpa winced at his own self-reproach and snapped the stock open on the rifle.

Kane clapped him on the shoulder, shook his head.

"We're moving too fast. You'll waste ammunition!" he shouted over the roar of engines and crunching dirt kicked up by the pickup's tires.

Thurpa glanced back and heard the crackle of enemy weapons, but there was no sign of near impact. He was trained well enough to keep his finger far from the trigger, making certain he didn't inadvertently send a bullet out of his rifle. Considering the amount of jostling and physics at work in the bed of the pickup, he realized the wisdom of Kane's admonition. One bad bounce or rut in the ground, and a shot intended for one of the enemy militia could go into an ally.

They needed to rely on Grant's driving skills to make it out of this alive.

"When we slow down, then we shoot," Kane added.

Thurpa looked to Nathan and Lyta. He tried not to spend too long looking at the young Zambian woman, though she was pretty. Again, he was thrown back to when he discovered that he was a clone of the Nagah prince Durga. He'd learned from Kane, Grant and Brigid that his "father" had played upon racial purity differences among the Nagah to assemble for himself a die-hard crew, an army who would give him the strength behind his uprising.

Of course, that race-baiting, those who had been "born cobra" or had been false Nagah having been converted by the Cobra baths, was simply a means of pecking and splintering the society of the underground city of Garuda. The underground city was home to humans, "natives" and pilgrims who undertook the change in a nanotech machine bath, and as in any society with a great deal of immigrant influx, there had been the disenfranchised who felt as if they were owed something, either by their "birthright" or simply because they had toiled hard to cross dangerous borders and frontiers. As such, Durga had a means of destabilizing an otherwise rock-solid representative republic monarchy.

Blaming "the other" was one of the oldest means of gaining personal power, even with a government in which the will of the people was able to overrule and defy royal decree. Hatred was at once a means of consolidating groups and eroding the fabric of a society. Thurpa heard about the rifts within Nagah society still existing as open wounds since Durga's expulsion from the city.

The thought of Durga's nurturance of bigotry reminded Thurpa of how much he *wasn't* a product of his father's mind. He was attracted to a young human, one who didn't resemble an Indian. The African Lyta was as exotic as he could imagine. She had stated that her heart was off limits because of the loss of her fiancé, but he wanted nothing more than to protect her.

Thankfully, the pickup truck was staying far ahead of their enemies, bullets zipping far and wide, missing the Cerberus exiles and their allies. Thurpa's patience started to grow short at being a "sitting target," unable to do something to stop their pursuit. He could see that bit of warrior pride in his father, the willingness to dive head-to-head with an enemy, no matter the odds.

Kane's hand clapped his shoulder again. "Get ready!"

A jolt of excitement rushed through Thurpa. That surge of excitement told him just how true his "superiority to mammals" was. Adrenaline was a human trait, and he recalled the origin mythology of the Nagah, how Enki crafted their race from humans, adding to them the traits of the cobra and some from the Annunaki themselves. Along the way, the alien might had faded into recessive genes, but not the cobra aspects, though according to Kane and the others, maybe it was well enough that he didn't share the same genetics as the Igigi or, as they had been known to the Cerberus heroes, the mindless drones called Nephilim.

Thurpa liked his brain, liked independent thought, loved his freedom. That was what frightened him so much about being a mere clone of Durga. But that thought quickly tumbled aside. The brakes locked the tires of the pickup truck, and dust kicked up as the vehicle came to a halt at the top of a ridge. They had been looking down a slope at their pursuit, meaning that the militia had to fire uphill. It'd give them a small edge, and the barked order from Kane spurred Thurpa into action.

He took aim at the windshield of one of the approaching trucks and, from the stable platform of the tailgate, pumped every round in his magazine into the militia vehicle. After the fifth impact, a white spatter of cracked glass was visible, but he kept shooting. He fired on single shot, leaning into the recoil and allowing the barrel not to kick and rise as he poured round after round into the glass. It took him several seconds to empty out half of the magazine when Grant shifted gears.

Lyta lunged out, grabbing Thurpa by the arm to keep him from jolting out of the bed of the pickup. She had the forethought to have her knees pressed against the tailgate.

So far, things seemed to be going well. Thurpa might not have been the best shot, but he peppered the cab of one of the enemy "technicals," even as the machine gunner on the back was distracted by rifle slugs slicing through the windshield and back window into his legs. The heavy machine guns that the technicals sported might have had steel plates around the back of their frames, to protect the face and upper chest of their users, but the cabs had no such bullet protection. With their legs being torn at, any hope of accurate fire was thrown out the window.

Even so, those bullets whipped and popped through the air over their heads in the pickup's bed.

Kane surged beside Thurpa, rising to a half-standing position and snapping his arm forward. Thurpa could see a small object leave the ex-Magistrate's fingertips and knew that he was closing down pursuit behind them. The rear tires kicked up dust and dirt, creating a smoke screen, the engines throbbing just in time as the tread caught traction and the pickup truck moved over the small ridge, racing away from the militia.

Behind, Thurpa could see the concussion wave and smoke from the thrown grenade, a vomitous column that was quickly followed by the sharp crack of the gren's detonation.

"Reload," Kane ordered the other three.

Thurpa did so, depositing his mostly empty magazine and keeping it to reload later. He put in another curved stick, rocking it until it was secure in the magazine well of the rifle. Another thirty rounds ready to fly, giving their enemy a reason to slow down. He looked around, seeing that they had made a turn and watching the bend in their smoky trail, and the pickup zoomed along in the rut between two ridges.

Kane kept watch for sign of the militia bursting over the hill they'd topped, all the while keeping another hand grenade ready to throw. The small explosive might not have destroyed an enemy vehicle and its shrapnel might not have caused harm to the men in the backs of those gun jeeps, but the blast would be sufficient to slow pursuit, giving the Cerberus crew and their allies the room they needed to fall back and outmaneuver the marauders.

Kane gave the roof of the pickup a hard slap, and at that moment Grant swerved hard to the right. Nathan, Lyta and Thurpa clutched at what handholds they could find as the force of the turn threatened to send them tumbling against each other like sacks of cement. Thurpa was glad to return the favor to Lyta by cushioning her, and he also managed to lash out his hand, blocking Nathan from barking his temple against the sidewall of the truck bed.

"Thanks," Nathan muttered as Lyta was sprawled into Thurpa's lap.

"You've done far more…"

Gravity seemed to cut out from beneath them before Thurpa could finish his sentence, the pickup topping the ridge and going airborne for a few feet. Right now they were in free fall, moving at the same speed as the falling truck they rode in, so the illusion of zero gravity was strong.

In that moment of eerie physical calm, Kane threw his

grenade. His little hand bomb seemed to career wildly away from the truck, almost as if it had been flying at a right angle to where the man hurled it, but that also was an illusion. The wheels hit the dirt, and Thurpa grunted as Lyta mashed him deeper onto the floor of the truck bed, knocking the breath from him. Nathan grimaced as his shoulder struck the same bit of rail that his head nearly had been dashed against.

"Sorry!" Grant bellowed over the racket, obviously in apology for the landing after their short flight.

On the heels of Grant's shout, Kane's second grenade went off. This time, the explosion sounded louder, and the rising jet of smoke and debris from the blast was accompanied by a flaming object that tumbled end over end through the sky. Thurpa hung on, watching the trail of the burning thing through the air until he realized that it was a human arm, or what used to be one.

"Direct hit!" Thurpa shouted.

"No time to celebrate," Kane answered. "We're slowing in three."

Thurpa counted down in his mind, scrambling to his knees and bringing his rifle back to bear. The pickup's brakes squealed and dirt flew. The desert wilderness might have made things harder for Thurpa to see targets, but that worked both ways. Instead of going full speed forward, they backed at a slower speed deeper into the ever expanding clouds of kicked-up dust.

Kane had pulled his hood up and put on the faceplate of his shadow suit. The skin-tight, advanced polymer uniform had undergone several upgrades, one of the most useful being a set of high-tech optics built into the cowl's faceplate. Thurpa might not have been able to see a foot past the back of the pickup truck, but that didn't stop Kane, and he could see where the man pointed.

Backing farther into their dust trail also bought the Cerberus expedition more time. The militia opened fire at the far end of the cloud of debris, missing the pickup by yards.

"Now!" Kane ordered.

Thurpa fired in the direction that Kane pointed, pulling the trigger as fast as he could. He surely couldn't put out the amount of lead that a machine gun could in this manner, but he would make sure that his bullets were on target and not wasted. Kane himself used a borrowed battle rifle, and his training with full-automatic meant that he could control the kick of powerful recoil. Kane's rifle was louder, and from the cab, Thurpa could make out a sidelong muzzle-flash.

Brigid was using her own shadow suit's optical technologies, shooting out the window of the cab with a weapon. Thurpa didn't care what she was firing, just that what lead they threw at the Panthers of Mashona had an effect. Thurpa had seen what this militia was like when he was still beside Durga and the Millennium Consortium expedition. They had soured him on people, and the marauders only continued to make bad impressions when they discovered Lyta and the other survivors of her frontier village held as slaves.

Lyta was half starved, dehydrated, and left bloody and scarred by heavy chains. That kind of abuse turned Thurpa's stomach, especially in the light of meeting good people, like the Zambian military at Victoria Falls and of course Kane and his allies from Cerberus. When he saw the creatures who were to feed upon the Panthers' captives, his patience for them was totally discarded.

He didn't raise a finger to help them when Neekra's horrifying spawn attacked another of their units, only moving or shooting to protect Nathan and Lyta. Thankfully, in the presence of the ancient staff, they became invisible to Neekra's vampiric horde.

Thurpa wanted every bullet fired through his rifle to strike one of the Panthers and cause irreparable harm and pain to them. The militia had been the reason two city-states had come together as allies, because the Panthers of Mashona sought out technology and slaves. The marauders had been thieves, scavengers, parasites. They gave nothing to the world.

The pickup truck roared to life, jolting forward, but this time Thurpa was prepared. He'd braced himself, as had Nathan and Lyta.

"How'd we do?" Thurpa asked, seeing Kane throw one last hand grenade before they got to full speed. Kane remained quiet, but he looked toward Thurpa to acknowledge the question. Moments later, Thurpa heard the detonation of Kane's good-bye bomb. Once more, screams filled the air, and the militia continued shooting wildly.

Finally, the man in the black high-tech suit spoke. "We're doing okay."

The pickup swerved, swinging around into the tracks of the enemy vehicles. As they cut across their pursuit's trail, Thurpa glanced into the distance. No more vehicles were on the horizon, but the look he got was fleeting, and he was certain that he'd miss something. He only had his human eyes, not built-in telescopic or infrared receptors on a moon-built faceplate.

As it was, Kane didn't sound too glum, despite his conservative estimate of their success. He just kept perched in the truck bed, eyes peeled for their foes.

This explosion didn't sound as vigorous as the one that sent a flaming limb soaring through the sky. Gunfire still rattled from whichever vehicles were still in the chase.

They were not safe, not by a long shot. The battle was still to be won.

Grant shouted through the small window between the cab and the bed. "Found some tree line! Going for it!"

Kane gave his partner a thumbs-up, and once again, those in the back of the pickup truck held on for balance. Grant shifted the gears expertly, this time going for maximum traction and performance from the tires, not kicking up dust clouds to cover their tracks. As such, Thurpa was surprised to see how little a rooster tail of dirt was kicked up as he changed course. This was not to say that the transit over the lumpy ground was any smoother, but it was faster than he'd seen Grant take the truck in this car chase.

Kane patted Thurpa and Nathan on the shoulders, motioning toward his belt. Instinctively, both young men reached up and gripped the webbing tightly for support.

Once again, the Cerberus leader's big rifle erupted, staccato bursts of gunfire sizzling out the muzzle as the weight and leverage of Nathan and Thurpa anchored him enough so that he could devote both hands to controlling the weapon. Thurpa looked toward racing vehicles on their trail, watching one of them swerve off course. It teetered on two wheels, then struck a rut and went nose first into the ground. Men flew, cartwheeling through the sky and screaming as their technical flipped end over end. When the militiamen hit the ground, they didn't bounce. They burst like ripe fruit, splattering their blood in huge splashes of crimson.

Thurpa couldn't hear over the sound of Kane's rifle, but his mind filled in the ugly, crunchy and wet noises made by men striking the earth hard enough to pop them like balloons.

Kane dropped an empty magazine and fed another into his weapon before continuing to hammer away at the opposition. Because Grant was going for speed, there was a lot less variable in terms of how the truck would bounce, and Kane's short bursts compensated for recoil and amount of time on target. One of the closer enemy jeeps had smoke pouring from its hood where high-velocity, heavyweight rounds punched through its radiator and engine block. As the driver swerved, attempting to maintain control of his vehicle, a dead militiaman bounced from the side door, strapped in place by a seat belt, his head and left arm bashed to bloody pulps.

A few more short bursts, and the smoldering jeep jerked violently, brakes squealing, before it skidded into a sideways roll, bouncing away from the mechanized patrol.

So far, three enemy vehicles had been taken out. The two left weren't pulling off the chase.

"How much punishment can these idiots take?" Nathan shouted.

"Their egos won't let them back off," Thurpa answered, even though his friend wasn't looking for an answer. "At least not yet!"

Kane's rifle barked and growled, peppering the last two pursuit vehicles. They were slowing down, even though the gunmen in the back still fired their guns. This time, however, they were simply blasting lead into the sky, making noise.

Grant cut a path through the trees, a slender road that forced Kane to duck before he was clobbered in the back of his head by a low-hanging branch. Just as they passed the tree line, Kane pulled one more grenade from his harness and dropped it at the mouth of the skinny dirt road. Grant kept up his speed, and by the time the grenade's fuse burned down, they were out of the blast radius of the explosive. A thick, ugly cloud roared at the end of the trail, and though the barrier formed was nothing more than airborne particulate matter, Kane might have slammed a steel door in the face of the angry militia's survivors. The blast at the mouth of the road through the forest was exactly the kind of face-saving out that the Panthers of Mashona survivors could take.

And they did.

They howled and honked their horns and fired their guns into the sky, standing their ground at the edge of the barren stretch of land. The marauders had driven Kane and his group from the lifeless terrain into "hiding." They were victorious, and when they returned to their base, they would tell tales of the mighty army that they had driven off at great cost to their comrades who were now scattered and smashed, their blood ground into the already rust-colored dirt.

"If they'd 'beaten us' any more, they'd all be dead," Brigid mused, agreeing with Thurpa and all of the others' unspoken thoughts.

"Doesn't matter," Kane grunted. "Anyone hit?"

"Not by bullets," Nathan said. Even through his dark, coffee-colored skin, Thurpa could see the redness and swelling of the bruise where his arm had slammed against the side of the truck bed. Thurpa remembered his own aches, the bumps and bruises he'd received as he was jostled about.

The pickup slowed, and Kane kept watch over the tailgate, staring into the distance. He was never going to let his guard down, not until he was dead certain that the militia was sufficiently discouraged and no longer interested in continuing the chase. It was a half hour and three miles of dirt road before he finally allowed himself a moment to relax.

By then, it was late enough in the afternoon for the

truck to pull off to the side of the dirt road so they could set up camp amid the trees.

Thurpa found himself sitting close to Lyta as they ate. It was a long time before his thoughts returned to existential worry.

Chapter 3

Stopping for the night, the six companions set up a secure camp for themselves. They had things to do aside from resting themselves and keeping their pickup truck from overheating; first among them was finding the location of the tomb that Neekra had sought.

Once the campfire was lit, Brigid sat Kane down across from her.

"I'm going to hypnotize you, Kane," Brigid informed him.

Kane nodded. "You think part of the reason Neekra wanted me so bad was that I might have a clue as to where her body is."

Brigid smiled. "Correct."

"You'd think I'd remember something like that," Kane returned.

"Not necessarily," Brigid explained. "You were affected by the staff in your dreams, intertwining your memories with the memories of a predecessor of yours."

"Solomon Kane, the Puritan," Kane stated.

"His adventures here in Africa had been related but imperfectly. However, his connection to the staff Nehushtan and his encounters with non-terrestrial and pan-terrestrial entities have, so far, given us an inclusive view into the secret history of this continent," Brigid added. "However, locations in those missives are vague at best."

Kane looked to Nathan, who had fallen into the role of

bearer of the artifact. "I thought only weak minds could be hypnotized."

Brigid turned Kane's attention back to her. "Willing minds can be put under, as well. In fact, just the very act of focusing on a subject, distracting the part of the mind that can be distracted, works. Just falling asleep is a form of self-hypnosis."

Kane nodded.

"Get Zen," Brigid ordered, giving him a backhanded slap on the chest.

Though outwardly Kane didn't change his stance or position in the slightest, inside his mind he put his intellect to work, ordering his thoughts so that he could enter the mental state Brigid requested of him. The woman lifted her hand, holding her index finger straight in the air. His eyes locked on that finger, and even as he did so, he heard her voice, soft, soothing, a low, constant beat in his hearing. He didn't know what she was saying, and it could have been gibberish syllables, her way of creating a metronome-like beat to keep his ears focused as his eyes. He allowed himself to mentally drift.

The next thing Kane knew, he was in chains. His clothes had changed. Previously, he had worn a spare shadow suit to replace the one that had been left mostly tattered by the events at the necropolis Neekra had chosen as her base. Now he was clad in folded-over leather boots, belted just below his knees, and, except for the white, simple shirt he wore beneath his vest, he was clad all in black. His hair seemed longer. He felt for his Sin Eater, but it was nowhere to be found, nor was his hydraulic forearm holster. He took inventory of his face, and he became aware of bruises that hadn't been there moments ago. His wrists were bound together by iron manacles, and the weight of chains pulled hard on his shoulders.

He tried to activate his Commtact, but neither the plate nor the implanted pintles were present. All he had was whiskers there.

He glanced to one side and saw several well-dressed Africans and Arabs, some of them possessing familiar arms. He recognized the fine Spanish steel sword, complete with its simple basket handle, and his belt dangling from the shoulder of a tall, burly African. His pistols were stuffed into sash-belts of others.

And an old Arab man held the shaft of Nehushtan. Kane realized that the man was speaking to him.

"…and Suleiman, he who you were named for, Kahani, chased the demons from his lands into Africa," the old man told him.

"Enough, you superstitious old lout!" the finest dressed of the Africans, the one who now owned Kahani's sword, snapped. It didn't take a genius to figure that the black man earned his clothing and sense of authority from one of the foulest sins of mankind: slavery. Kane did not know if the slave master put his own tribesmen into chains, sending them around the world to toil away until death, or whether he profited from war and conquest, sending the surviving warriors of other nations to buckle under to the white man.

Something about the swagger of the African slave master set Kane's teeth on edge. Maybe the bastard didn't give a damn who he imprisoned and condemned to lifelong servitude. As long as the gold that crossed his palm was good, as long as it paid for the rings in his ears and on his fingers and adorned his back and head with the finest silk shirts and turbans, perhaps the slave master would throw anyone in chains.

The Arab who spoke of the legends of Nehushtan, the rod of biblical King Solomon, cringed at the bark in the slave master's voice and could not meet his gaze.

Others were in the caravan, and they appeared all too similar to the procession of Zambian prisoners whom he, Grant and Brigid had rescued from another group of African human predators. Kane could feel his ancestors' ire at his own impatience.

The bruises were the only result of his assault on the slavers. Although his sword and pistols had accounted for some of the security force, it had not been enough, not this time. He could still feel the vibrations rolling up his forearms where he'd brought down the knurled butt of a pistol, breaking a shoulder or crushing a jaw. His other hand had swept and sliced, but an injured African slaver trapped the blade against the side of his body, wrenching it from Solomon Kane's desperate fingers.

The weight of the slavers was too much for even the fanatic's strength that drove the Puritan to protect and liberate his fellow man, no matter the skin color.

The leader of the caravan had demanded Solomon Kane be taken captive, alive. His reputation preceded him, and the African slave master knew that there were many who would pay exorbitant prices, either to slay him, or to take him as a captive. For now, Kane was trapped in the skin of a defeated warrior, about to be sold for a king's ransom as enemies would undoubtedly assemble, seeking his hide, tattered or intact.

"Great place to wake up," Kane muttered to himself.

"Kahani?" the old Arab asked.

Kane narrowed his eyes. Nehushtan had gone through yet another change. Now it was a cat-headed obscenity, almost as if the original face upon the top of the staff had been erased with chisel and sandpaper. No matter the new appearance; the "cat-head" was merely redesigned, but the blasphemy beneath still remained.

It was an unusual aspect, Kane noted, for a many-storied

scepter wielded by prophets who were the chosen emissaries of God. Nehushtan, as far as Brigid related, was a holy relic. But in this form, the "juju stick" had an air of dark magic.

"You are to carry this juju staff with you, brother Kane," came half-remembered words from a witch doctor.

N'Longa, the seer of his tribe, had fought alongside Kane's Puritan ancestor, just as Nathan Longa, his descendant seven hundred years from now, battled shoulder to shoulder with him, against Neekra, against the Panthers of Mashona, against the inhuman Kongamato and vampire-like blobs and reanimated corpses. After their first battle, side by side, N'Longa handed over the cat-headed staff as a walking stick to guide the Puritan on his journeys for the rest of his days.

The staff returned to N'Longa and remained under his family's protection since or at least long enough for Nathan to recall it being in his family's possession for generations.

"Kahani?" the Arab asked, interrupting Kane's thoughts.

"Why are you so concerned for me?" Kane asked him.

The old Arab looked back to Nehushtan. "This is an amazing piece of history. This stick came from the age of Atlantis. It was entrusted to you, Kahani."

Kane was getting tired of being in chains, even though he'd been here for what felt like only minutes. Then he realized that it wasn't boredom but actual physical toil upon the body he was remembering. This empathy swept over him, causing him a transfer of nausea and exhaustion to strike him even harder.

And suddenly, he was fallen back, watching as a helpless observer as the caravan came upon a small stone structure in the jungle. The Puritan watched as the greedy slave master ordered his men to hack at the stone doors, calling for the treasure hidden within the crypt.

He recognized the tomb top, the alien writings carved into the jamb around the slablike doors. Kane could not read the glyphs, but their shape was unmistakable. They were the letters of the Annunaki, and each of them had an eerie glint reflecting in the moonlight. Kane realized that the blue-white tint was not the echo of a full moon, for the sky above was starless.

Something in those runes held their own unholy power.

Solomon Kane's voice, sounding much like his own, barked a warning, telling the slaver to turn back, to flee this dark place.

The old Arab's eyes were wide with horror, also realizing that the cuneiform scrawls portended far greater evil than he could comprehend. He turned toward the captive Puritan, fumbling with keys for his manacles, even as hammers bashed at the slab of granite covering the door.

"What are you doing, you old fool?" the African caravan leader asked. In moments, the Spanish steel sword was out, piercing the old man's back, its point prickling the front of his tunic, turning white cloth dark as the poor bastard was run through.

"Kahani, take…" the old man sputtered before the slave master pulled the blade away, freeing himself to take a lunge at Solomon Kane.

With all-too-familiar reflexes, the Puritan brought up both hands, still holding a length of chain between them. The links blocked the downward sweep of the deadly blade, and with a twist of his arms and a half pivot, he suddenly wrenched the trapped sword out of his opponent's grasp.

He then lunged, grabbing for Nehushtan, bringing up

the staff to counter any other attack that the richly dressed African could launch.

Unfortunately, at that time, the tomb thundered, its stone lid cracking violently. Screams filled the air, horror sweeping all around them as some slave takers took to flight. Others shrieked out throat-tearing wails of agony as they were sucked through the open doors. In the distance, the slaves were trapped, unable to break and run through the forest as their captors could.

The slave trader whirled, pulling one of his own pistols at the cacophony of suffering and terror rising from the opened crypt.

"I warned you to leave it alone!" Kane heard himself growl.

The African fired a single pistol shot at a shimmering arm of pink. Long talons sank into the slaver's chest, and he shrieked, still alive even as bloodred nails poked through the back of his silken shirt. Kane moved forward, the only weapon in his hands being the juju staff.

Was this memory or reality?

It didn't matter because there was Neekra. She resembled an Annunaki, except she was larger, more brutish. Her features were unmistakable, even though they were twisted into a rictus of fury. In one hand, she still held the slaver, red nails hooked around his back. His arms and legs moved less and less of their own volition and only bounced and jostled as she shook him around. She must have been fourteen feet in height, and she was still confined in the mouth of the crypt, only able to reach out with one arm as she bellowed in earth-shaking rage.

The Puritan knew that he was the only thing keeping the pink-skinned horror from escaping, and the closest prey for Neekra would be the slaves, the same helpless humans he had been trying to liberate when he had been captured.

He clutched Nehushtan tighter; long, lean arms filled with corded muscle, strength surging through those limbs as he advanced toward the thing rising from the darkness.

He felt the kinship with his predecessor, be it through their mutual contact with the staff, or perhaps because they were all part of the same entity, an ever-existing time worm, each life and death being brief but forming a single segment that would renew, reincarnate and extend through the centuries of human history. Kane had a brief mental glimpse of that "time worm," a familiar image he had spotted some time ago, when Grant was lost in time and Kane had traveled between dimensions to seek him out.

It was an amazing, yet weird, sight. He could see his spirit's history, the flex and pump extending backward to the dawn of time, and a shadowy rumor of an image stretching forward.

And then he was fading, spiraling back into his body, hearing Brigid's voice summoning him home. His hands were around the haft of the artifact, and it had gone from the two-serpent-adorned healing staff to the cat-headed rod, full of odd and dark omens.

"Neekra…she was there," Kane muttered, still feeling the bruises and the ache of the chains from his dip into history. "She attacked a slave caravan…"

"We know. You related the tale, just as if you were there in person," Brigid replied.

"Oh," Kane said, frowning. He looked down at the ground, trying to get a better mental image of the horrific beast that had stood before him. It was indeed similar to the avatar that Neekra had molded Gamal into, but it was larger. The Annunaki scales were thicker, rougher, cruder, scales that Kane hadn't seen on the goddess's first simulacrum. The glare of anger and hatred in her eyes was soul chilling, something he never wanted to see again.

Grant managed a chuckle, the sound breaking him from whatever lost trance Kane was falling into. "It sounded like you were having a wonderful time."

Kane acknowledged his partner. He noticed that he had Nehushtan in his other hand. "Did it give us anything on the location of that tomb?"

Brigid had out a notebook in which she scribbled furiously. "I had a difficult time since your ancestor's experience was on a cloudy, starless night.

"How long was I under?" Kane asked.

"How long did it feel like?" Grant countered.

"A full evening. After the caravan stopped its march, I was allowed to kneel next to the caravan's leader," Kane answered. "He viewed Solomon as a great prize as well as a potential slave for sale. He took my…his sword."

"She was asking you…him…questions for the past hour and a half," Grant returned. "He was reluctant to give exact locations, and he said that it was no place for a woman."

Kane chuckled. "How did *she* take that?"

"My opinion of his chauvinism was noted and debated for a few seconds, and his chauvinism toward me was defrayed," Brigid stated, continuing to run figures in her mind. "He found me far more formidable than others he had encountered in his era."

Kane glanced toward Grant.

"I recorded it," Grant answered. "It was fun. Especially your British accent."

Kane grimaced. "British accent? And it's already recorded?"

Grant nodded. "Back at Cerberus."

Kane shook his head. "I think I'll be staying with Sky Dog and the Lakota for a few weeks after we get back home."

"You could always be eaten by Neekra," Grant offered.

"Promises, promises," Kane grumbled. He turned back to Brigid. "So, if the stars were behind clouds that night, how will you know where I went, Baptiste?"

"Solomon was a meticulous navigator. He was fairly good at estimating the distances he covered in a day, and he did have a track that he followed," Brigid stated. "The only problem is that he came from coastal Africa, to the northeast, whereas we're coming up from the south. Also, he was utilizing sixteenth-century maps, which were not analogous to current satellite tracking technology."

"In other words, you've got a good start, but you're going to be working courses for a while," Kane returned.

Brigid glanced up from her calculations. "That was implied."

"She's figuring it out," Kane surmised. "Otherwise, she'd devote brainpower to a smart-ass remark."

Brigid waved the two men off, and Grant helped Kane to his feet.

"What's our plan until she comes through with where we need to go?" Grant asked.

Kane shrugged. "Maybe we could hypnotize Thurpa?"

"Brigid's busy on that front," Grant returned. "I mean, I could try, but I don't think I can put him into a trance."

Kane looked down at the staff in his hands. "Maybe the stick could do something."

"Or maybe we could ask Brigid to take a break and do her memory trick on Thurpa?" Grant asked. "Is it like she'll lose her place?"

Kane rolled his eyes, then raised his voice. "Brigid? Can we interrupt you for a moment?"

Brigid looked up from her notes. "Interview Thurpa or, rather, Durga?"

"If the man's inside that head," Grant said, "we'll find out just how much."

"There's one small stumbling block in that," Brigid said. "Durga utilized Thurpa's mind as a means of sharing the psychic load of Neekra's assault on him. What is to prevent Durga from blocking my attempts at hypnosis? Indeed, what if Thurpa were already set up with a preprogrammed response to hypnotic interference?"

"Preprogrammed response," Grant repeated. He looked to Kane. "That sounds like 'go psycho and kill people,' doesn't it?"

"Even unarmed, he has his fangs and his venom," Kane agreed. "Tying him up wouldn't do much because he can spit his venom, as well."

"We do have environmental faceplates, which we've been utilizing for their optic properties," Brigid said. "But we're not certain he'd cause harm to himself, or actually become a time bomb, with a delayed violence response."

"Delayed violence response," Kane echoed. "I'm surprised we're not dead just for talking to the poor guy."

"As am I," Brigid returned. "I'm uncertain of the extent of Durga's mental control over Thurpa, but if we try to find Durga through him, the very least of our problems would be alerting him that we know of their psychic relationship."

Kane's lip curled in disgust.

"I thought about hypnotizing Thurpa and unfortunately came to this conclusion before you did," Brigid explained. "Even so, that was the two of you being proactive and insightful."

"Thanks," Kane said. "Not that it makes anything easier."

Brigid shook her head. "But we're thinking. And when the three of us put our minds to something, we're generally successful."

Kane nodded. "The key word is 'generally.' We can

make all the plans we want, but life is what happens when plans go to shit."

Grant clapped Kane on the shoulder in support. "Don't worry. We're good at surviving when things go to shit, too."

Chapter 4

It didn't take Brigid much longer into the night to determine the location of the tomb—the city known as Negari for the entity imprisoned within. She was asleep after noting its whereabouts on her map and managed to get several hours of good rest until sunrise. Kane and Grant traded watch shifts and were surprised to see Brigid poring over her figures after first light.

"Not sure?" Kane asked.

Brigid looked up from her map work. "I don't want to have us looking and running around in circles while Durga and Neekra get there ahead of us."

"Neekra's still a threat," Kane said. "We destroyed a body she took over, but she's still a free-roaming psychic entity."

Kane lowered his eyes to the ground. She'd spent most of a day inside of his skull, and due to her command over his perceptions, the witch goddess made him feel as if he were wandering the multiverse for months, making his concern over the friends he was separated from even deeper. His struggle to return to his body was made even more desperate by the danger of Grant and Brigid in front of both Gamal's militia and a horde of winged monstrosities without him. That urgency overwhelmed him, and all he could imagine was the horrible tortures and destruction they faced without him to assist them. Being separated from them also meant that he was alone, without someone to act as a beacon to return him to his body.

That anxiety ate at him, concern grown out of love and friendship that was deep and enduring, that had lasted across other universes, across several incarnations throughout the history of humanity. That loyalty had brought earlier incarnations of himself to death for the defense of those others.

It was an emotional layer of scar tissue that Neekra had exacerbated when she had the necropolis "erupt," separating him once more from Brigid and Grant and leaving them at the mercy of the dark goddess and her corpse-stealing, bloblike spawn. Kane's nerves were scraped raw, tender to the slightest thought of either of them in peril.

That threat from Neekra, forever lost from his beloved friends, sat freshly in his mind and threatened to drive him to distraction. And then he'd seen, more and more, like the petals peeling from a flowering bud, what the evil entity could do. The latest nightmare, dredged up from the depths of his genetic memory, was simply the icing on a cake of evil. Neekra, separated from her body, had left her "mortal" form as an insane, terrifying force, a beast armed with natural weaponry that it used to rend healthy, fighting men limb from limb.

That body, combined with her intellect and cruelty, would be menace enough across a heavily depopulated, technologically impaired planet. With the addition of Neekra's ability to produce corpse-reanimating soldiers, the combination was a global scale threat.

Nothing new there, he thought grimly. We've been dealing with that since we got out of Cobaltville that first day.

Sooner or later, he realized, their luck was going to run out. Adding to the sudden jolt of harsh realization was that he knew that Neekra was not simply the goal. No. Her body had been left in that tomb as a sentry, one capable of slaughtering almost anyone, human *or* Annunaki.

Whatever she guarded was something so terrifying that not even Enlil dared leave it unguarded by anything less than a living juggernaut.

"You've got us pinpointed?" Kane asked her.

Brigid nodded. "Within a radius of five hundred yards."

"Pretty good," Grant said with approval. "We'll make an adventurer out of you yet."

Brigid snorted. "The only thing we have to worry about is getting there in time."

Kane and Grant pored over the map, crowding her a little bit, but she didn't mind. The three of them had been shoulder to shoulder for years, in much more confining conditions. She ran her finger across the map. "We have two days of travel ahead of us, barring interference or further attack."

"Two days," Kane murmured. "No shortcuts?"

Brigid pointed toward one sector of the map. "This was part of my recalculations. This area seems fairly empty, but I had Bry run some cameras over the region."

"Radioactive?" Kane asked.

"Seismic wasteland," Brigid replied. "Put on your faceplates and I'll give you two some visual data."

Kane and Grant tugged their hoods over their skulls, then affixed their shadow suits' faceplates. Almost immediately, the same map that had been a mere flat image a moment ago was now a relief sculpture, wrought in first a wire mesh frame following the contours of the broken land, then filling in, showing off rivers of whitish-yellow lava trickling back and forth through the uneven terrain.

"No radioactivity is present, but ever since the earthshakers went off on skydark, they broke the continent,"

Brigid said. "You can see this is an accelerated animation of last night. It's still in dynamic flux."

Kane looked at the undulations, tilting his head as it allowed him to see around the area. "Can we get a real-time feed?"

"For what?" Brigid asked.

"We could cut our trip time down to half a day," Kane answered.

"Driving through the streams of molten rock and constantly opening and closing chasms?" Grant asked. "So we have the equal opportunity to be either burnt to a crisp or flattened like rotten fruit?"

Kane nodded.

Grant smirked. "Sounds like fun."

"We should ask our compatriots if they wish to endanger themselves in that manner," Brigid offered. "We can arrive for certain…"

"Or we can get there in time to stop my father and his bitch," a voice cut into the three people's discussion. They turned and saw Thurpa, standing alongside Nathan and Lyta, forming a strange mirror image to their own group. They were younger, not that Kane, Brigid and Grant were among the elderly by a long shot. However, for the "locals," they didn't quite have the half decade of experience that the Cerberus expedition possessed, though Nathan and Lyta both had grown up in the harsh, often unforgiving frontier of the twin city-states straddling their common border of the Zambezi River, and though likely only a year old chronologically, Thurpa had the memories of Durga as a young officer, fighting alongside his father against an expedition sent by the barons into India.

"The three of you weighed in on this?" Brigid inquired.

Thurpa glanced to Nathan to his left, who clapped the young Nagah clone's shoulder in support. He turned toward Lyta, who laced her fingers with his and squeezed for support. "Yup."

"I could end up wrecking our truck," Grant offered. "And then we'd be running on foot through a volcanic wonderland."

"Better than dying of boredom or getting taken over by a psychotic blob woman," Nathan countered.

"Too many lives are at stake to take the scenic route," Lyta added. "Though, I have to admit, the idea of going through a half-molten desert sounds pretty interesting."

"This isn't a game," Kane warned.

Thurpa frowned. "Oh. Like three-hundred-pound mutants and the Panthers of Mashona were only coming over for a game of chess? We get it. This is serious as cancer. Worse, because every living human remaining on the surface of the planet will end up infected."

"The longer we spend debating the point, the closer Durga gets to his goal," Grant threw in. "Either we plunge through the fire and the flames, or we do nothing."

Brigid nodded in agreement.

"Then it's unanimous," Kane said.

Thurpa and Nathan turned immediately to begin packing. Lyta nodded to the three members of the Cerberus team, then turned to join her friends.

"And this is the one we were worried that could betray us?" Grant asked.

"I hate being suspicious of him," Brigid answered, looking as if she'd sucked a lemon dry. "But we'd all be best on our toes around him."

Kane looked grumpier than usual as he removed his hood and faceplate. She could tell that something was digging at him.

"What's wrong?" Brigid asked.

"I just hope we're not damning them like we did Garuda," Kane said.

"We're making up for that," Grant told him.

Kane thought about the city of the Nagah. Even Durga's attempt to usurp the family tree of the new queen and her consort, Hannah and Manticor, had been a misfire.

The three Cerberus warriors set about loading up the pickup truck. They hadn't done much in terms of unloading for the night, just enough to sleep and to keep comfortable. Within a few minutes, the truck was packed, and the six people returned to their spots in the vehicle.

It was time to dare the volcanic plain.

GRANT AND BRIGID looked out over the hood at the wasteland before them.

"Still think this was a good idea?" Grant murmured.

"You were all up for it," Kane responded through the window at the back of the cab. "And it's not as if we're seeing anything new."

Grant nodded. All three of them had been on a virtual "fly through," but this was an imposing scene before them. The ground heaved and shifted, and whereas the computer-generated imagery was soundless and scentless, here on the smoky plain the stench of sulfur hung thick in the air and the grumble of grinding stone and burbling steam and bubbling lava was a constant companion.

The three adventurers had sent a message back to Cerberus redoubt in the wake of their battle in Neekra's necropolis. Their shadow suits had been damaged greatly, and Kane and Grant both agreed that leaving their allies, Nathan, Lyta and Thurpa, unprotected by the unique uniforms was an unnecessary risk, unlike the journey across this field of lava, crumbling stone and thick, noxious gases.

Fortunately, the shadow suits were environmentally

sealed when all pieces were in place. Usually, they could be hooked to a portable air supply, but they could also filter out environmental toxins for a good amount of time. The suits' polymers would protect from impacts, intense heat or biting cold. But the truth was, even the non-Newtonian reactions of the suits couldn't hold off a point-blank rifle shot and would provide only a few seconds of protection from searing lava. There was a difference between heat that could induce heat stroke and the incredible temperatures of rock that flowed as freely as a mudslide. In fact, Grant even doubted that the shadow suit would do anything to lessen the liquefying heat inside. It had taken them two hours out of their way to get to the replacement garments via interphaser rendezvous, but the thickness of the sulfur and steam made them fully aware of how smart it had been.

Also, all six members of this expedition remembered having to navigate through nearly impossible, darkened necropolis with either flashlights or the advanced optics. The team's equipment was further enhanced by the addition of headset radios for Lyta, Nathan and Thurpa, hands-free communications that put them much more easily in contact with the Commtact-equipped Kane, Grant and Brigid.

Better vision and better "ears" would give the team a distinct advantage in the near future. They had been only limping along in that deadly encounter, and if there was one thing about the Cerberus explorers and those who had proved brave and resourceful enough to side with them, it was that they could all learn from their mistakes.

"We'll be fine in the back here," Kane said, knocking on the roof, even though they could easily hear him over their communications network. "The suits should be able to filter out any noxious fumes. Think that will have any effect on the engine, Baptiste?"

Brigid looked back through the rear window. "Will the

smoke have any effect on a standard Toyota internal combustion engine?"

Kane nodded. "It won't, right?"

"No, the smoke won't harm the engine," Brigid replied. "I'm more concerned about spraying bits of lava. If one lands in or on the truck, it's likely to burn through the chassis, or it'll burn our suits if it lands on us."

Grant scanned the terrain ahead, matching it up to the map, which was quickly becoming more and more obsolete as he observed it. He threw the truck into a lower gear, revved the engine and pushed forward. There was no warning as he advanced, but none of the rest of his group expressed dismay at the sudden lurch of the vehicle. One way or another, they had to make their first move onto the plain.

The truck rocked as a chunk of the "cooled" obsidian glass crumpled under one of the tires, and Grant put everything into the brake. Kane swiftly leaped from the cab and padded cautiously forward.

"It's a hollow tube," Kane announced over their communications network. "It looks about five feet deep, and we cracked through what must have been a thin spot."

"How thin?" Grant asked.

Kane knelt and looked at the tire. "Looks like it was an inch at the edges of the break."

"The tire?" Grant pressed.

"No cuts that I can see," Kane offered.

Grant put the truck in Reverse and backed from the hole he'd inadvertently punched.

"Things aren't going to be easy, are they?" Grant murmured.

"If they were, we wouldn't be paid the big money," Brigid answered.

"You get paid?" Grant remarked.

Brigid elbowed him in the biceps.

Grant tried to remember the "look" of the tunnel on infrared so he could avoid such thin spots in the near future. One thing that the big, cooled flows of obsidian provided was a fairly unbroken, if somewhat slick and uneven, terrain that wasn't through the middle of lava.

"You'll want to head forward by five meters, then hang a left to return to our course," Brigid directed.

Grant nodded, glad to have the woman's eidetic memory to rely upon. He followed her directions, and Kane popped over the top of the cab, firing a single shot into the ground before them. As soon as the bullet struck the obsidian glass, it burst like a bubble, producing a circular gap, dropping down into another lava tube. This was dark and empty, thankfully, but the shattered surface now had a hole three feet in diameter. The pickup could span it, but Grant looked at what each side of the truck would be rolling through. The last thing he needed was to drop and crash through the hole and break an axle, but he also didn't need to put the tires on anything less than sure ground. He hit the optic zoom, switching from infrared to see if there was any sand or other particulate that could compromise their traction.

"Okay, that's going to be bad," Nathan spoke up over the line.

Grant glanced to the bed of the truck. "What?"

"I'm picking up something flying," the young man from Harare said. "Bat-like shapes are the best I can make out through the smoke and from this distance. No way to gauge their size."

"Bat-like," Grant repeated. He tromped the gas and shot toward the small hole before them, gritting his teeth and hoping that the lava tube around the burst bubble could hold them. If it didn't, then he hoped that the sheer speed of the pickup could keep them from getting stuck.

The obsidian beneath the truck's tires held, and the pickup didn't suddenly lurch as its two tons of weight cracked into the lava tube beneath them.

Good—they were back toward a plateau of solid rock, not solidified and cooled lava, and Grant hit the brakes before he got too close to the edge. He glanced back. "Kane, any updates?"

"Kane?" Grant repeated, his concern evident in his tone.

"They're Kongs!" Thurpa shouted. "Kane's gone bye-bye!"

Grant looked back into the bed, seeing his friend sitting ramrod still and staring straight ahead.

"Bad enough we've got those goddamn terror-dactyls, but Neekra's attacking him now," Grant growled.

Brigid whirled and saw Thurpa lunge back toward Kane, who lifted his gun, aiming it toward them at the pickup's cab.

Chaos erupted, just as gouts of steam burst through sections of lava tubes weakened by the truck's passage.

Chapter 5

Thurpa's statement that Kane had gone "bye-bye" was hardly a complete diagnosis of the current mental and physical state of the former Cobaltville Magistrate. However, even as Kane watched his right arm rising, the Sin Eater snapped to extension into his palm, a hydraulically launched weapon that turned a simple pointing motion into a death sentence in most cases, he had to agree someone outside of his skull would get the same impression.

He even could hear Grant's grumbling over the Commtact as Thurpa lunged, pushing Kane's hand up and away from his two friends, the youth pitting his personal strength against the possessed Magistrate.

Kane could feel the struggle but only through a numb, dense filter. His psyche had been partially dislodged from his body, allowing his telepathic opponents to move into his limbs.

Kane had to assume that it was multiple opponents because he could "feel" and "see" two entities, though it could have been just his mind trying to make sense of what was going on. Tendrils wound around him, snakelike tentacles of darkness seizing his limbs, squeezing his chest. Even as he was grasped by the alien thoughts, he was reminded of the quicksilver monstrosity that had been the living navigation chair that he, Brigid and Grant hunted down in the swamps of Louisiana. The horror took that form, and now he could understand the horror that Brigid had been subjected to as he twisted, pulled, fought to escape the sticky, clutching tendrils.

"Get out of my head, you bitch!" Kane growled as he pulled against the forces assailing him. The other "entity"—a shadowy form zooming between Kane's view of the world and his embattled mind—looked over its shoulder at the ongoing struggle.

"Your friends are going to die," came a voice no human on Earth ever had. It was deep, rumbling, all pervasive. It might have been male, but it had an odd, sexless quality. The vibrations of those words burrowed deep into Kane, like termites chewing through the heart of a tree, and threatened to sap his strength.

Kane's immediate reaction was to rage further, writhing and tugging himself from the smothering grasp of his opponent.

"You're going to shoot them," the shadow before him taunted. Kane's right arm tore free from the engulfing mass of darkness, and he reached out, fingertips brushing the icy flesh of the mocking void.

"I'll rip you out of my skull first!" Kane bellowed. "I'll shred you into ribbons!"

Snatching whips of inky blackness slapped around Kane's wrist and forearm, and he continued to stretch forward, wrestling loose from the grabby opposition.

Something slammed him in the chest, hard as a hammer, and Kane felt the breath explode from his lungs. This was not a psychic attack; this was something in real life, and he squirmed his head, trying to see around the void-thing that stood before his vision. The taunting monster cackled, brilliant white teeth visible behind tenebrous lips, rows of gleaming, almost luminous fangs, serrated triangles in layers. Kane kicked, driving himself out of the slithering tentacles grasping at him.

"I will end you!" Kane roared.

And the bubble of his perceptions popped.

He was back in the bed of the pickup truck, Thurpa kneeling astride his chest, fighting to keep Kane's wrists pinned to the metal so that he didn't fire the Sin Eater inadvertently "Kane! Wake up!"

"I'm up now," Kane grumbled. "How long have you been wrestling me?"

"Twenty seconds," Thurpa returned. "We've got a dozen Kongs swooping after us."

Kane glanced around. He could see Lyta and Nathan firing their guns into the sky, the powerful arms of the winged horrors allowing them to swoop, flip and soar, dodging the lead thrown their way, even as the pickup truck twisted and turned on the rocky ground.

Kane rose to one knee, foot braced so that he could pivot against the wall of the pickup bed. He did a quick examination of the Sin Eater, but aside from the magazine needing replacement, it was ready to go. Thurpa had managed to render the gun a single-shot weapon, and Kane could see where the single bullet punched through metal, avoiding Nathan. Kane had to admire the young man's courage and forethought.

"Our one saving grace is that they are reluctant to go through the clouds of smoke. Their sense of smell must be as acute as their hearing," Brigid stated. "Use your forearm display panels to turn on the ultrasonic sensors for your hood."

Kane glanced away from the sky, brushing his shadow suit's sleeve. He grimaced and realized that he was not going to have the time or dexterity to do so, not when the Kongamato were in full-on assault mode. He did, however, keep his eyes peeled, covering the others. He switched to his rifle, scanning the thick smoke, spotting the things as they barely showed up through the hot clouds of volcanic ejecta.

No wonder Brigid said for them to turn on their ultrasonic sensors. The Kongamato had been operating with their bat-like sonar, putting out "pings" of intense noise, inaudible to human ears, which would bounce off of a solid object. In the spouts of steam and hot sulfur, they were actually cooler and harder to see, disappearing behind bright splotches of reds, yellows and oranges.

"Cover me," Kane said to his partners in the back. He turned to Grant. "We're going to need a steadier platform."

"As soon as I find an inch of ground that isn't slick as ice or threatening to come apart," Grant answered. "Tremor!"

The pickup's brakes screeched and Kane grabbed the edge of the truck's railing. Gravity didn't seem to quite work anymore, and he realized that the vehicle was spinning out. Kane held on with all of his strength and he glanced back to see Thurpa hanging on for dear life, Lyta clutching at him to keep him from tumbling loose.

"I said *steadier!*" Kane snapped.

A cone of sonic illumination blazed around them, and Kane grimaced, realizing that the Kongamato were aware of the sudden distress of the truck. It would be on them in a moment, and the only thing that Kane could do was stiff-arm the rifle, holding it straight out. The truck spun, but he did his best to keep the muzzle pointed toward the end of the noise wedge. He pulled the trigger, spraying bullets out of the rifle. The effort to hold the weapon under control was incredible, his biceps and forearm muscles straining, struggling with the bucking and kicking of the gun.

He didn't know if he could hit anything, but he was suddenly rewarded as a thick, powerful form erupted from the cloud, blood spraying from a dozen wounds. The rifle was empty, so Kane twisted it around and tucked it under one leg. He flexed his arm, and the hydraulic holster spit the Sin Eater into his hand.

Kane could aim and fire the sidearm as certainly as he could point his finger, and the slugs it spit were powerful, the gun specially designed around high-energy charges and heavyweight bullets capable of punching through even a Deathbird's cockpit glass.

The machine pistol had proved its worth in blowing big holes in the deadly Kongamato mutants before, and as another of the things swooped down, casting a sonic spotlight ahead of it that easily sliced through the smoke, Kane fired again. Kane hit it in its long snout, the Sin Eater slug shattering a hole in its upper mandible. The impact might not have been damaging, but the equivalent of being struck in the mouth with a sledgehammer sent the Kongamato whirling out of control.

The truck finally found its traction, and Kane could see that Thurpa was back in the bed, Lyta handing over a small submachine gun from their gathered arsenal. The young man's rifle must have toppled overboard.

It didn't matter because the Panthers of Mashona had provided a huge stash of weaponry for the Cerberus expedition to rely on, as well as spare ammunition, magazines and other sundry supplies. If it hadn't been for the necessity of the shadow suits, the rendezvous with Domi at a parallax point wouldn't have happened.

Kane glanced over his shoulder, seeing Grant's huge shoulders heaving as he cranked the steering wheel, navigating the treacherous ground.

"Just how much farther do we have to go?" Kane asked as Thurpa and Nathan cut loose in unison, spraying another of the winged monstrosities.

"We've gone a mile and a half," Brigid stated, interrupting her updates to Grant on their current location. "We've still got three miles to cross."

"Miles to go before we burn," Kane grumbled. He whipped the Sin Eater about and aimed down the throat of another Kongamato swooping through the clouds. Kane pumped a trio of rounds into it, and this one smashed into the rock behind them, wings tangling and ripping as it rolled from momentum. It reached a crack in the stone that Grant had just swerved around, and on striking that bit, immediately burst into flame.

The lava had incinerated the corpse of the cloned monster, the heat so intense that it ignited the fatty tissues within the creature's cartwheeling corpse. Any fluids burst into steam, vaporizing and leaving behind a small landslide of glowing embers and bouncing chunks of ash.

"And that, boys and girls, is why we leave our hands inside the vehicle at all times!" Nathan shouted.

Kane chuckled as he scanned for anything else in the air about them. Three of their own getting shot up, at least two of them down, had forced the aerial marauders to pull back.

"They're retreating," Kane announced.

"Just for now," Brigid returned. "They've been weathering gunfire for at least a minute, but the sight and sound of one of their own bursting into flames has given them enough pause and us a reprieve."

"How long?" Kane asked.

"Until we get to the other side, or we crash through a lava tube that isn't empty," Brigid returned.

"I'm gettin' tired of your endless optimism, Brigid," Grant grumbled. "Keep an eye out. We damn near died twice while we've been in this volcanic playground. I don't want any…"

Kane grunted as he was hurled against the back of the

pickup's cab. Luckily the non-Newtonian polymers of his shadow suit prevented anything more injurious than a bruise from forming on his ribs. Even so, the sudden braking action by Grant had knocked everyone in the bed off balance.

He peered down the hood and saw that there was a quick-flowing river of magma twenty-five feet ahead of them. The heat registered on Kane's faceplate, both the temperature of the running lava and the ambient temperature of the air. If it hadn't been for the environmental seals on the suits, they'd be drenched with sweat, rather than the moisture being wicked away to keep their bodies from overheating.

Kane still felt the tingling as he was perspiring. The shadow suits could keep them from sun and heatstroke under normal conditions, but the air was suddenly blistering this close to such a large flow of lava.

"Where now?" Grant asked Brigid.

The woman was turning her head up and down, as if she were looking over a projected map. Kane only wondered if it were a computer projection on the inside of her suit's faceplate, or if it were simply a construct of her photographic memory. Knowing the efficiency of Brigid's mind, it was more likely she was doing this from her imagination, which was often more concise than most computer reproductions. She'd been able to navigate to an exact location in a nearly featureless desert using the most low-key of landmarks and star positioning.

"Hang right and go 400 yards, and fast. The ground's going to be cracking under the pressure of this lava flow," she ordered Grant.

Like the well-oiled machine that the two people had made themselves into, Grant swerved and hit the gas, changing into a higher gear to get more speed.

Once more, sonic beacon bursts flashed in the sky above them. The Kongamato were still about, but they were keeping their distance. Something was up, and Kane swept the terrain about them. The tremors that shook the ground had their own sound signatures, and the substrate beneath the pickup was pulsing and throbbing.

Seismic activity was visible in the same manner that the sonar bursts showed up on their faceplate displays.

"That's why they gained altitude!" Kane spoke up. "They heard the beginnings of a quake or something."

Brigid looked through the windshield and frowned. "Bry, what can you see?"

"Things aren't looking good," Donald Bry answered from the Cerberus redoubt, where he had access to satellite imagery.

"Earthquake?" Kane heard Brigid ask. He kept his eyes flitting between the Kongamato above the clouds and the heaving ground beneath them.

"Something is acting on the stretch you're crossing," Bry explained. "That's not a natural seismic plain."

"I believe I've noticed," Brigid said. "What had been a simple barrier between us and the final destination of Durga is expanding, turning into a moat."

"Moat?" Kane asked.

"Something's working on the already cracked substrata here and is isolating the tomb," Brigid said. "The pattern is too regular to be random. The bedrock must already have been scored for such a contingency."

"How big a ring?" Grant asked.

"We're looking at a ten-mile inner perimeter," Brigid said. "The caldera itself is twenty miles at its widest."

"We're atop a volcano now?" Kane inquired, an edge of nervousness seeping into the question.

"An artificial one. Yes," Bry answered. "My God, the Annunaki have some incredible capabilities…"

"Of course they'd put the tomb in the middle of a caldera," Brigid mused. "They'd need something utterly inhospitable and something that could assuredly destroy whatever was imprisoned."

"And anyone fool enough to come after it," Grant agreed. "How bad will it be if the volcano erupts while we're in here?"

"We'll survive here in Cerberus," Bry said. "And you won't feel any pain."

That made Kane's skin tingle. "How bad will the destruction be? How far will it reach?"

"It'll cause another skydark," Bry said. "The planet will be thrown into a new ice age. Actual destruction from the pyroclastic clouds will scour the entire continent you're on."

Grant swerved and drove, Brigid continuing to point out where he had to move. The zigs and zags came sharper, swifter. The whole ground beneath them was becoming fluid, if not melted by the incendiary temperatures of the lava, then by the enormous seismic pressures being put on the ground.

"What's our plan now?" Kane asked. "Because things are changing so fast…"

"I'm plotting our course, but it doesn't look good," Brigid returned.

Grant jolted the pickup to a halt, but the rear fishtailed until they were facing a surging slab of stone being lifted up by seismic forces beneath it. It was becoming a perfect ramp. "Brigid…is it good?"

The woman glanced to him, a moment's hesitation, but the answer was on her lips in a heartbeat. "Safe landing beyond. Get to eighty-five miles an hour!"

Grant clutched the wheel, using it as leverage to stand on the gas, shifting up through gears as the motor revved higher and higher. Kane wondered if Grant could get the speed that Brigid suggested in the brief strip of ground before they hit it. The ramplike slab was still teetering, its slope increasing steadily thanks to the swell of forces beneath the surface. At that speed and angle, Kane couldn't imagine how far they'd fly and what they would hit if Brigid were wrong.

He grit his teeth, praying that the rising altitude of the ramp somehow figured into Brigid's mental calculations. If not...

Then the time for worry ended; the truck was airborne. Tons of metal ramped off the slab of shifting stone, and they were rendered, temporarily, weightless.

Kane's tight grip on the side of the truck had his knuckles feeling as if they were about to burst. Kane never enjoyed when a ground vehicle decided to take wing, and he liked the situation even less now that they were soaring over an ever-widening crack of lava. The heat from below was a blast furnace, and under his insulating shadow suit, his skin prickled from the heat that seeped through the environmental seals. Sweat droplets stung his eyes immediately, and he was already swimming inside the skintight uniform.

Then the pickup truck rocked. It couldn't have been because of a pothole because they were sixty feet in the air, according to the sudden flash of altimeter readings popped up in the shadow suit's faceplate display. The closest ground was too far away anyhow, as the flare of heat and light from the lava was still gleaming, illuminating the smoke that their vehicle sliced through. If they actually struck a spurt of lava, the superheated rock would be more like a knife slashing through the undercarriage of the pickup.

And when that happened, it was likely that any fuel in the system would instantly ignite from the proximity of the lava's heat. The deaths of the six people in the pickup truck would be relatively painless as the gasoline vaporized.

A rock, hurled by an explosive release of steam?

Then Kane noticed the motion of a wing on one side of the truck.

His eyes widened even further as he heard what Brigid said next.

"Good…they *did* catch us! Just as I'd hoped!"

The Cerberus expedition was now held in the talons of the Kongamato mutants, and they were rising farther and farther above the volcanic plain below.

One slip, and even their shadow suits wouldn't protect them from the impact with the ground.

Chapter 6

Hours before Brigid Baptiste even contemplated the course across the surging lava field, Neekra opened her eyes for the first time.

Neekra felt drunk, unsteady and the very effort of lifting her own eyelids required consummate concentration and will. Her body felt as if it were only half alive. Then she realized the utter silence, the complete darkness of a world she had been in touch with for two thousand years, was a smothering curtain over her. She fought to part her lips, but they were sticky against each other, the very act of breathing draining strength from what little spark of life she retained within herself.

The "dark" world, that horrible void of silence and nothingness, only seemed to make the small sliver of her senses that still worked seem so much brighter. She could make out the dull vibrations, seemingly gibberish at first, but then she began to associate each grunt and spit with language. And it was not the high tongue of the Annunaki. The sun was just rising in what she presumed was the east, and though the vulgar splash of all colors would seem bright to human eyes, Neekra wept for those frequencies of the electromagnetic spectrum no longer open to her.

"Why are you crying?" came the guttural tongue of humans and other apes. She swiveled her eyes and gazed upon Durga, who crouched beside her.

"What…did…you do?" she managed to croak out in that mutt language. "Why…"

Durga tilted his head. She thought of him as human despite the cobra hood, a sheet of scaled muscle from the sides of his head to his shoulders, and despite the snake scales that armored his fit, trim body. He was one of "Uncle" Enki's silly spawn, the Nagah, long surpassed in favor of the hairless apes from which Enki spawned the cobra men.

Enlil had at least told his children, Neekra among them, that Enki had forsaken the cobra men, leaving them as freaks in a world no longer their own. The Nagah were hidden underground for the very reason that they were inhuman. People outside of India feared cobras, rather than respected them as on the subcontinent. Imprisoned in their own tomb beneath the surface of the Earth, they maintained their exile from humanity, even past the collapse of mankind's civilization.

Although that wasn't quite true.

Durga's people had increased in population as others entered the stability of the underground empire. Many chose to remain human; others opted to evolve themselves in the legendary "cobra baths."

Their corner of India, up until Durga's attempted coup, had become a relative paradise. Unfortunately, a war between the Millennium Consortium, Cerberus redoubt, Enlil and Durga's personal guard had left the city of Garuda heavily damaged and thousands dead. It was still recovering.

Durga was a living bomb, his ambitions as deadly and explosive as any small tactical nuclear weapon. That he now had her, nearly blind and totally deafened in terms of the superhuman senses she'd possessed for two and a half millennia, was a certain enough clue to the kind of "man" that Neekra had been dealing with. He'd approached her as a pawn, as something for her to seduce and use…

And now Neekra, once an immortal goddess, was a cripple.

"Did…you…do?" she rasped.

"Get angry," Durga said. "Raise your strength that way."

Neekra's fingers twitched. A slight movement, but a response to her will. She grit her teeth, trying again to clench her fist.

"Your mind will take some time to get used to the new body," Durga returned. "I know. Anger will help you focus. Or you can wallow, crying like a child."

Neekra glared daggers at him. That he didn't collapse to his knees, his eyes bursting and spraying blood in geysers, meant that he'd completely gelded her psychic ability.

"Bastard," she spat. She now had a fist. She squeezed, and as she clenched, her finely scaled knuckles turning white, she gathered her strength through the limb. "I will tear your mind from your body and use it as a whip to slice the skin from your meager little ape body."

"That's my girl," Durga responded. "Madder. Madder."

Neekra opened her fist, pushing on the ground. Her other hand was moving now, obeying her will, enforcing her accord as she struggled against lethargy and gravity. Even as she did so, her skin shimmered, shifted, moved like quicksilver over her. She grimaced, fighting to get to her feet. She leaned on her arms, folding her legs to gather them beneath her.

The skin tightened. She realized what she was in now. The scaled flesh was a blank template, an inert sack of genetic code, and with each motion, she was altering it. She lifted her head, stretching her neck. The scales began to disappear, flaking off the surface. Instead, she held the semblance of raw, naked muscle and sinew. Striated sheets of muscle pulsed along her forearms, while her hands grew bonier, knuckles and carpals whitening. There was no separation between the bones, however; her skin simply was more and more translucent, sheaths of white fat forming about her joints, as if to signify that she was skinned alive.

Neekra didn't have to look into a mirror to know what face she grew, the white decorative bone of her brows, her cheeks, rising and poking out between the sheets of red muscle fiber stretched between those peaks. She blinked, and she shook her head.

She was bald, though she did not mind. The "hair" she had manifested in other forms had been for the sake of seduction. She was becoming what she had chosen to look like before...

Before Negari took her in his arms, before he promised her power and immortality. Before he and she had been uncovered by the overlords.

"You...gave me my body back," Neekra said. She looked at Durga. "You made me..."

"I made you in the form you originally belonged in," the prince replied.

"Damn you," she growled. She took a step forward.

"Come to me," Durga ordered.

"I will do..." she sputtered, taking another step. Her knees felt rubbery. Her muscle tissue gleamed crimson, and her "bones" showed through white as a bleached skeleton. She felt strong, but compared to what she had once been capable of, she was a kitten, staggering in its first halting steps.

"I will not obey you," she snarled. "I am coming to throttle you."

"Go right ahead, my dear," Durga taunted.

She snatched out, white spear tips of bone, sharp and fanglike in their gleaming menace, swiping at the air where

Durga had stood a moment before. She leaned forward, took another step, reaching, slashing.

"This is quite a beautiful form you possess, Neekra," Durga complimented. "The whole skinless horror is at once naked, sexy and gruesomely unsettling."

"You will…" Neekra began, but Durga sidestepped another swipe.

"Stand still!" she bellowed in frustration. "Stand still!"

"So you can rend me limb from limb?" Durga asked. "I'm not that dumb."

"I will feast on your entrails!"

Durga shifted, avoiding her clawing attacks. He stepped away from a tree trunk, and as she struck it, she gouged into its bark deeply, snapping off a huge chunk of bark and interior wood. Neekra glared at the "bite" she'd taken from the tree.

"Strong," Durga murmured, the corners of his mouth rising in a smile.

"I am not here for your amusement!" Neekra bellowed.

Durga shook his head. "No, you are not. I never said you were."

Neekra paused. "Don't try to play with me…"

Durga shook his head. "If I were playing with you, you'd be in a world of pain, honey."

Neekra stepped forward. "Pain? Even though I am merely Annunaki now, recall that I am your superior."

Durga smiled. "That so?"

Neekra paused. She remembered burning, hateful pain. The venom of the Nagah, as engineered by Enki, had struck her down in her possession of the warlord Gamal. She had animated him, having remolded his body into a more seductive, more human-seeming form, though there were limits to her protean abilities. She could turn a man to a woman, but the finer details were pale imitations of how she had seen herself when she was a "merely mortal" Annunaki.

Now, she was back as she had been in life, before her father clove her in twain, separating mind from body, rendering her intellect as a nomadic virus. It was a heady, uneasy feeling, and that was why she felt so out of touch, out of control of the body she now resided within.

"What happened to me?"

"My clone Thurpa bit you," Durga replied. "You sought escape. But the link between us was strong enough that I could follow you to your old base."

"Link," Neekra replied. She recalled where her mind usually remained. It was the mummified corpse of an ancient wanderer. None would think twice even if they kicked it over and unearthed it, despite its hiding spot in a cave. It was the perfect center for the vat of "brains" she'd nurtured to survive without living organs.

She recalled how she and Negari had been transformed into algorithms, each a living consciousness that could be transferred via a protein string. In essence, the protein strings that formed their consciousness were biological computers, complex genome centers as intricate and versatile as the most advanced supercomputers of the twentieth century, even more so and much more tightly compact. So powerful were the protein masses that Neekra could manipulate cells and matter telekinetically.

It was a simple matter to cause a human body to shape-shift when you could pull apart cells and stick them back together by brute force, like the pieces of a puzzle. The proteins were capable of forming powerful antennae, enabling communication on a scale similar to what the humans called telepathy. Similar artificial means of interface had been designed and replicated by the Annunaki, enabling them to operate the "living starships" and other biology-based technologies that made them seem so god-like. Negari had perfected the complete internalization of the process and in doing so had mobilized Enlil, Enki, Marduk, Lilitu, the whole of the ruling pantheon to the point that Neekra felt cold terror.

Forces mobilized against the two lovers were incredible, assaults coming on physical and mental ranges. Igigi rose and fell against them quickly enough that Enlil decided to simply use semi-mindless drones against them. It was the first time that the overlord utilized them in mass combat, and their success in pestering and distracting Negari and his bride influenced Enlil's decisions in the future.

"Do you realize what you have taken from me?" Neekra asked. "I can no longer see or feel as I used to. I'm trapped in meat that is numb and clumsy."

"It was better than your old situation, a helpless exile as a blob of snot," Durga countered.

"What happened? How did you put me in this?" Neekra asked, looking down at herself.

She'd stopped advancing upon Durga, which didn't elicit one change in him. He didn't look afraid of her and had only made minor motions to sidestep her attempts at assault on him. He still wore a smirk, full of himself. She was no threat to him despite her Annunaki body, despite her knowledge, despite the simple superiority that she possessed as her birthright.

The venom in his fangs was a weapon that he could lord over her. Durga had that advantage, as well as whatever he did to put her in this body.

"What did you do?" Neekra demanded.

"I found the core of you," Durga said. "Once I figured out how you transmitted your intellect, how you communicated, it was easy to trace your 'signal' back to the source."

Neekra's eyes widened.

"My source," she repeated.

"You've been casting yourself far and wide for millennia. You forgot your original 'headquarters,' so to speak," Durga told her. "Come with me."

With that, he turned his back on her and led her down a corridor. Neekra just now realized that they were in an atrium, an artificial park in some form of underground facility.

She'd been concentrating so totally on him and on her rage that she just now noticed that above the atrium was a domed roof with artificial lights burning. She followed him into the hallway as she wondered just what this particular place was.

"This was where we first uncovered the Kongamato," Durga said, as if anticipating her unspoken question. Neekra had to wonder if he were actually reading her mind, but her memories of that first contact with Negari, when he had originally uncovered his psychic ability, confirmed the difference between being knowledgeable and being telepathically prescient.

"And this place is where?" Neekra asked.

"North America, actually," Durga answered. "One of a couple of redoubts that was on the Nagah's radar but not a Cerberus redoubt."

Neekra narrowed her eyes. "Truly?"

"It's not on their radar simply because it has been listed as decommissioned," Durga stated. "The upper levels received damage and were heavily looted. Power cables were interrupted and many of the lighting and door controls were rendered inoperative."

"So how did you determine that this was still a viable alternative?" Neekra asked.

Durga paused and smiled at her. "This is not my first rodeo, my dear."

Neekra raised an eyebrow.

"This was originally deactivated by being the launch point of the barons' assault against Garuda," Durga said. "We followed them back here, and I personally engaged in the assault that left much of the upper levels devastated."

Neekra blinked. "You've had this facility…"

"For approximately twenty years," Durga responded. "This was where we originally tapped into the communications of Cerberus."

Neekra frowned. "So why are we here?"

"Because if we were still in Africa, we'd be behind the curve in our search," Durga responded.

Neekra shook her head. Her wits hadn't recovered since the battle in the necropolis. So much had been shut down, so much taken from her. She was still reeling, and her psychic blindness left her as feeling drunk. Before the battle, before the venom assailed her senses, she could figure her global position of both her current body and her "home" mind.

They entered a laboratory, and Neekra saw the hollow-eyed, mummified form sitting under the bell jar. It was odd seeing that where it sat.

Durga had mentioned Neekra's headquarters before. Only now did she recognize how much jest he'd put into that term.

This was her head, severed from the rest of her body.

The one that Enlil had removed, trapped her consciousness within and then hid away, leaving her as a wandering intellect, roaming the dark continent, seeking out the rest of her body. She stepped closer to the sunken-cheeked, crater-eyed artifact, feeling an uneasy disconnect from reality. Maybe it was the alteration of her perceptions after centuries of being able to feel and to see beyond the senses of mortals, but the shock of looking at her face, her skin shrunken against her skull and faded to the color of parchment, still struck her like a hammer.

"This was well hidden," Neekra responded. "I made certain that none could penetrate the defenses."

"And I told you, I found your frequency," Durga responded. He smirked. "Your defenses were impressive. I simply applied more force."

Neekra looked at her old head in the bell jar.

"What did you do to take away my enhanced perceptions?" Neekra asked.

"Simple," Durga answered. "Your enhanced abilities come from the use of a complex protein structure that acts as a combination of antennae and supercomputer. I filtered that out of the clone body I created and utilized some Annunaki technology to make the personality transfer."

Neekra glanced at her hands. "Why?"

"Because I will not have you lord over me, sweet queen," Durga replied. He stepped closer, brushing his finely scaled knuckles across her cheek. His amber eyes glowed with an eerie inner light, as if a flame was burning behind them. "If you are to rule with me, then you will rule as my equal."

"You push your luck, human," Neekra warned, but her ire didn't have the same weight as it had borne before. She could feel again. Live, in person, the sensation of the nerve endings in her skin registering the tender, loving touch of another body. Negari's telepathic lovemaking had been a heady drug, but even as she stood here before the man who had dragged her down from goddesshood, she felt the warmth, the softness of his caress.

She cupped her hand over his, pressed her lips against his palm.

Durga's smile, no longer cold and cocky, seemed to warm her.

"You remember," he whispered to her, his voice deep, intoxicating. "You remember the joys of the flesh."

Neekra tried to push his hand away, and when she couldn't, she took a step back. "I am the seductress..."

"Yes. You have enchanted me, goddess," Durga told her. "And I apparently return the favor."

Neekra looked around the laboratory. There were others who looked similar to Durga, but they weren't like him. They were the faux Nagah, spawned from test tubes, not true mothers, created in the mass cloning machinery utilized centuries ago in an effort to control the living conditions and the place of occupation of the survivors of the nuclear megacull, which came to be known as skydark.

These beings had a semblance of intellect and discipline. Durga had spoken of how there was a programming code, a fast information dump that would make these things, scarcely weeks old, into trained troops. She had seen their relative effectiveness before, not just in person but through the memories of Kane, during her time holding him psychically imprisoned upon his first arrival in Africa.

They were effective and capable but still not much more than the lobotomized Igigi that her father created, the Nephilim.

Neekra might not have the ability to view the entirety of the electromagnetic spectrum, or peer into the minds of others, but she still had access to the memories she observed. She had knowledge, and she saw, here in Durga, a man much like Enlil would be if he were limited to a human's frailties.

She could now see the intent of Enki in crafting the Nagah; the Annunaki who sought not to become an overlord had created a pleasant shadow, but a shadow nonetheless. Durga was ever the inferior to her father, ever the weakling in comparison to a true god.

Yet she had been within this cobra man's brain, had seen how he'd managed to play, to outwit, to outmaneuver Enlil. Granted, he utilized others as his weapon, but in the collision of his abilities and use other forces—the consortium and, most of all, Kane and his allies—had done much to shake up the status quo of his home city. Had it not been for a lapse of judgment and a moment of greed, he might even have been the unquestioned commander of Garuda.

Even now, in Africa, he'd only been undone by one bit of treachery, and Durga had shut that down, once again utilizing Kane and the others. He'd destroyed the renegade Kongamato clones and their production facility and further punished the man who'd usurped the winged horrors, turning him into a shell, an avatar for Neekra.

And now, here she was. Stripped of her telepathy and of her ability to remold human flesh, to produce drone soldiers.

All by his machinations.

Neekra frowned.

"Kneel before your king, dearest," Durga ordered.

Hating every moment of being returned to a second-class entity, Neekra dropped to one knee as Durga rested his fingers, condescendingly, upon her shoulder.

She could no longer accuse the fallen prince of being cocky. Not when he'd pulled her down so very far. And right now, she had no means of turning the tables on him. Not one single hope.

Chapter 7

"So far, all they're doing is carrying us," Kane announced, looking over the side of the pickup truck, held aloft by six Kongamato. He was impressed by the strength of these creatures, but Kane had seen evidence of that incomparable muscle power in a prior encounter with them. Their chests were deeply keeled, meaning that their chest muscles were huge, firmly anchored and thick enough that they could slow down even rifle bullets.

If they could hammer through heavy steel doors, then carrying a pickup truck through the air shouldn't have been much of a problem. Even so, their wings had more than sufficient surface area to allow them to glide for a good distance between wing beats, so that coordination wouldn't have been necessary.

"We're officially prisoners again," Grant said.

"Which is much better than our previous course," Brigid replied.

Grant and Kane both locked eyes on the woman, then spoke in unintentional unison. "You planned for us to jump into their claws?"

"The way that this terrain is altering, due to forces that had been put into place centuries ago, we would not have lasted much longer," she explained. "While we were making the initial crossing, we had a good chance of crossing without further danger. Unfortunately, the minute that the volcanic moat began filling out…"

"We'd have been incinerated," Grant muttered. He peered out of the cab of the pickup, seeing the swift flowing rock below them between the wings of the cloned monstrosities. "So, you lobbed a softball over the plate."

Brigid nodded.

"Softball over the plate?" Kane asked, not getting the reference.

"Gave them an easy target. I shot us into the air...with your help, Grant," Brigid stated.

Kane nodded. "So what now?"

"Neekra and Durga said they needed us, you especially," Grant followed up. "And Durga knows that you work best in a team. So we'll all be used to break into whatever tomb Neekra needed us to find and open."

Kane nodded. Utilizing memories from an earlier incarnation, Neekra and Brigid had both tapped into and uncovered the aeons-lost resting place of her lover, Negari. The power of that prisoner was so phenomenal that Neekra seemed to have been selecting either Durga or Kane as her champion to breach the defenses holding it in check. Then Durga disappeared, escaping from the goddess.

"It looks as if Durga not only has more cloning facilities, but a command apparatus, too," Kane mentioned. "The things we fought would not have been crafty enough to fly in formation and catch us."

Brigid stretched her neck, leaning out the window. The Kongamato holding on to the frame under the door shot a glance toward her but paid no more mind when it was shown that she didn't intend to attack.

"There are eight," she counted.

Kane double-checked. "I thought only six. How many of these things did he send after us?"

"More than sufficient numbers," Brigid returned. "As befitting someone who utilized both these creatures in a sky-blackening horde, and hundreds of militiamen upon our initial arrival."

Kane nodded. "I thought that he just sent this many in order to grab all of us, considering the sameness of our uniforms. They might not be able to discern much…"

"But Durga could get feedback and target us," Brigid replied. "I noted monitor equipment on Gamal's truck when he was commanding them."

"There weren't images on those monitors, however," Grant said. "I could see that much from our position."

"No, but there were cables for feedback. Input and output as on a video monitor, right down to the various wire color coding," Brigid responded. "The control apparatus can easily be a two-way street."

Grant nodded, getting her meaning.

"And what about Neekra?" Kane asked.

"Regarding your incident from before?" Brigid asked. "Did you get any sense of communication or familiarity?"

Kane shook his head. "Simply a bout of contact. We communicated, but it was an unfamiliar 'voice' in my head."

"Unfamiliar," Thurpa repeated. "So, it wasn't some kind of technology from Durga?"

"No, it doesn't seem like that," Kane said. "It was a similar formlessness to the entity to Neekra when she first appeared, but why would she try to hide her identity?"

"She wouldn't," Thurpa answered.

Kane, here, could see that the similarities between the six people wouldn't be too hard to discern, even for the simplest of organisms. Thurpa's head and the size differences between the men were too great, not to mention the obvious curves of Brigid and Lyta. The environmental seals would have been enough to stymie the sense of smell of the Kongamato, but pure eyeball identification wouldn't be difficult, even for the dimmest of them.

No, Durga had learned his lesson about splitting Kane from the others.

But that didn't make sense to Kane. If Durga wanted an advantage, he should have split the group up, hurling any others aside. Or did Durga actually want the Cerberus team at its peak strength, even with the added assist of their newfound companions? Had he been telling the truth about seeking the destruction of a global menace such as Neekra? They had not spoken since the mention and discovery of Negari…

Kane frowned beneath his faceplate.

Could Negari have been the one to engage in psychic contact? But if Kane were on his way to cut through the ziggurat, breaking whatever defenses were keeping him at bay, why cripple Kane?

It could have been Neekra in his skull, but he knew her feel. He recalled her presence in his brain. And she might have been angry enough to force him to open fire; yet, that didn't seem like her kind of strategy at all.

"Damned telepaths," he muttered.

Nathan gave him a poke. "Think this might help?"

Kane glanced to the shaft, an ancient artifact that had been linked back through the ages. They knew it by the name Nehushtan. A prior temporal incarnation of Kane had merely known it as "the juju stick," a gift from Nathan's ancestor, the witch doctor N'Longa. It had been wielded by King Solomon, by the prophet Moses, by Solomon Kane in his journeys through Africa and Europe. It had been a healing tool and a burning weapon that sent demons cowering into the depths of the dark continent. In Kane's own experience, it had restored men to full strength from complete crippled conditions, and it had shaded Kane and his allies from the probing mind of Queen Neekra, all the way down into her very own necropolis.

Kane started to reach for it, but the doubts he first encountered upon learning of its existence rose once more to mind. The echo of a memory, mixed impulses from his own and Solomon Kane's history, had blended into a prophetic dream that introduced him to the artifact. Back then, he'd wondered if he would lose himself to the staff.

Now, he wasn't so certain what he would encounter the next time he wielded it.

"I don't think so," Kane said.

"It granted you immunity and invisibility before," Nathan stated.

"And it allowed you to fight with sufficient strength to ward off these things when they hunted you," Kane responded. "Keep a hold of it, just in case."

"In case they turn on us?" Nathan asked. He chuckled. "If that happens, they just let go of the truck. If the fall doesn't kill us, the lava will. Or the ruptured fuel tank."

"I shut off the engine," Grant called back. "We won't explode. We'll simply become human pancakes."

"Thanks for that mental image," Lyta muttered.

"The shadow suits' impact-absorption abilities will be a detriment. Although the force of the fall would certainly kill us instantly without them…" Brigid began.

"I don't need to know," Lyta snapped, cutting her off.

"No, you don't need the gory details," Brigid agreed. "Sorry."

Lyta glanced to the cab. "I didn't mean to snap."

"If anything is perfectly understandable," Brigid offered, "it was that response."

Satisfied that they were relatively safe for now, Kane turned his attention to Grant.

"When we land, what are we going to do the moment we see Durga?" Kane asked.

Grant's face was hidden behind the faceplate of his shadow-suit hood, but Kane could feel the waves of frown emanating from him. "We'll be surrounded and outnumbered. But Durga already went this far in bringing us to meet him. I don't think he's going to come at us or even disarm us."

"He wants into that...tomb," Kane trailed off as the clouds of volcanic steam and free-floating ash parted, at least enough in his shadow suit's enhanced vision, to see the ziggurat below and before him.

Grant followed his gaze.

The whole of the pickup truck grew quiet as all six people glanced down at the structure they flew toward. What further astounded them was that they gazed upon the building, and the advanced optics in their suits gave them the range and estimates of its height and width, telling them outright of the blocky, pyramidal object and its awesome size. Kane blinked and tried to refocus, but the numbers remained the same. They were miles distant, but the huge building was a megalith on par with the old villes built by the barons. Indeed, it was as large as three of them combined, easily half a mile in height, two miles wide and two miles deep.

The main block was enormous, and as far as Kane could zoom in, it appeared to be one smooth-faced slab of stone, smaller blocks built in tiers atop it. The smaller blocks themselves were more textured and nuanced than the smooth, almost glassy sides of the main cube of stone that it stood atop. Kane had a brief instance of thinking. If only a half of a mile of this was visible, and he imagined it to be a cube, then that meant there were one and a half miles of stone stuck beneath the surface. Whatever was buried within must have been in that section.

A section that was a mile of stone in all directions.

Stairs had been carved into each of the wall faces, and they appeared to be slender flights, clinging tenaciously to the sides of it, but they were the width of the greatest avenues from pre-apocalyptic cities or multilane highways that had survived since the great cull of humanity.

"Holy shit." Lyta breathed first as she observed the ziggurat. "How the hell did no one ever find this thing?"

Brigid answered almost immediately. "The pyramid of Xian in China was likewise never known or seen. It had been buried under tons of soil when it had been discovered in the twentieth century.

"I'll wager that if we looked at a topographic map of this area, say in the late twentieth century, it would have been much lower in comparison to the rest of the Earth," Brigid continued.

"When Solomon Kane came here, it was forest," Kane added, the memories of another life still vivid thanks to the influence of Brigid's hypnosis and the proximity of Nehushtan. "It was flat land, with no sign of any volcanic fissures or even mountains."

Inky black tendrils crawled across his vision, and the deep, inhuman voice from before resonated within his skull.

"Neekra is not one so easily dismissed, even by one of the largest carnivores you've ever encountered," came the threat.

"Bitch," Kane growled.

He heard his friends, as if on the other side of a heavy door, begin to call his name.

"Who do you think you are addressing, monkey?" Murky pseudopods wound around Kane's throat, squeezing, tightening. The pressure built up inside Kane's skull. He'd been strangled before and had barely survived such force. This was something tactile. This was no mere mental illusion.

He clawed at his throat. Nothing was there but air. He twisted, struggled, trying to pull away from the shadowy figure in his waking nightmare. The strength gripping him was no less powerful for the untouchable nature of the gripping force.

"Neekra," Kane snarled. "You're…Neekra."

Suddenly, the tentacle crushing his windpipe was gone. He heard and felt a deep, booming, echoing roar, rising and falling, crashing on his consciousness like the waves of an angry ocean. The raw power of that sound poured over him, stunning him, drowning out every other thought, every other sensation until it dimmed, weakened.

Only as the "noise" faded did Kane realize that he'd inspired his telepathic assailant to laughter.

"You amuse me, ape," the voice reverberated. "You will make such fine sport."

Kane grimaced. Once more, reality shifted around him. He was now in the bed of the pickup truck.

"Back again?" Thurpa asked.

Kane shook the cobwebs from his mind. "Temporarily, it seems."

"How so?" Brigid asked.

"I said something funny, and he…he let me go," Kane said.

"It wasn't Neekra?" Grant asked.

"No, he laughed at me when I suggested that," Kane responded.

"It's a *he,*" Brigid said. "Which narrows it down. Durga or Negari."

"Or someone else with a telepathic communication ability," Kane offered. "Like Enlil."

"Don't even joke about that," Grant muttered.

"Really? You don't think Durga might get the band back together?" Kane asked. "He did well enough last time."

"We blew him up," Grant said. "Really blew him up."

"And he got better and likely smarter," Kane countered.

Brigid grumbled in assent. "Enlil would undoubtedly be aware of any trespass here. Durga's list of enemies is long, and if he could gather them in one spot…"

"Say, atop a volcano with a living weapon buried in the center?" Nathan offered.

"That does sound like a good idea," Thurpa stated. "But I don't know how close my thoughts are to Durga's. I will tell you one thing, though. I don't 'see' or 'feel' whenever Kane goes bye-bye. And I felt when 'father' was in psychic conflict."

Kane smirked. "But you were the first who noticed."

"In the first case, you were pointing a gun at the head of your best friend," Thurpa countered. "The second time, it was Lyta who noticed. But, you didn't look as if you were shooting anyone."

"No," Kane said. "But it was the same sensation both times. I'm dealing with the identical creature in each of these cases."

"Does it seem like Enlil?" Brigid asked.

"No," Kane replied. "But then, Neekra's appearance inside my head was changing, evolving."

"And her sound?" One thing about Brigid—she was thorough. The force acting on Kane's senses could threaten the whole group. Not could. *Did* threaten the whole group. That mind-controlling force aimed a gun at the back of Grant's head, and only the actions of Thurpa and Nathan had kept him from putting the bullet into his dearest friend.

This didn't occur the second time, but Kane was going to be damned if someone kept compromising his psyche, turning his body into a puppet.

"Her sound was definitely much more feminine," Kane said. "It had the same tone, but it changed. It…It's hard to explain because it's 'heard' without ears, you know?"

Brigid nodded. "The sound of a thought is hard to convey verbally. I understand. But it was definitely male and not akin to Durga, nothing that brought you memories of him, even in his altered state."

Kane closed his eyes, thinking back to the finale of his first conflict with the fallen prince. Durga usurped the body-molding, incredible healing abilities of the "cobra baths" of Garuda. Utilizing nanomachines, he was able to rebuild himself into a juggernaut made half of stone, with incredible strength, and his lower half truly serpentine. Kane and his allies watched helplessly as their bullets and grenades served only to knock chips of rock off his flesh. Only a bomb designed to kill hundreds in one blast, created by the Millennium Consortium, had been able to sever every ounce of "enhanced flesh" in one shot. Still stunned, a knife through the brain was what finished him off.

Even with the knife wound in his skull, Durga survived. So powerful were the nanites in his bloodstream that they gave the last of their repair energies toward resurrecting him and rebuilding his brain. That had left Durga crippled, but that was cured only a week ago, upon the first arrival of the Cerberus explorers in Africa.

Kane pushed himself to recall the sound of Durga's voice when he had maxed out his mass and strength. "You're right, Baptiste. It's not Durga. Even distorted, they don't feel the same."

"That leaves a party we've not encountered yet," Brigid

said. "Otherwise, you would have known Enlil from *his* prior psychic contact with you."

Kane nodded.

"Neekra's lover," Kane announced. "No wonder he laughed at me for mistaking him for her."

"That's not boding well for that happy couple," Lyta mused. "Which is something we should use."

"I agree. If Neekra finds out Negari's opinion dropped so harshly," Brigid began, "there's going to be hell to pay."

Kane looked toward the ziggurat where the Kongamato were flying them. "And it looks like we're ready to make our first deposit."

Chapter 8

The Kongamato released the pickup when it was ten feet from the ground, and if it hadn't been for the protective properties of their shadow suits, Kane, Grant, Brigid and their allies would have ended up more than merely grunting as they were jarred violently by the truck crashing to the ground.

Kane gripped the rail of the pickup truck bed and pulled himself to a position where he could climb out. Instead of the winged monstrosities zooming through the air over them, he saw that there were rows and rows of cobra-hooded soldiers. They were well armed, all with a submachine gun in their hands and side arms in belts around their waists. They were clad in only gray boxer shorts, along with belts and shoulder harnesses with pouches for any other gear that they could conceivably need.

Dozens of pairs of hard, burning amber eyes gleamed in dull hatred toward him.

Thurpa, Nathan and Lyta sat up immediately, catching sight of what stood before them.

"Oh…great," Thurpa murmured. "Well, I've learned two things."

"What's that?" Kane asked, not looking at the young Nagah clone.

"One, I'm definitely not happy to see these guys," Thurpa replied.

"And what's two?" Nathan asked.

"You don't have to be afraid of wetting yourselves in these suits," Thurpa concluded.

"I've learned that lesson long ago," Brigid admitted.

"Yeah," Lyta added. "So, do we throw down our weapons?"

"If he wanted us dead, he'd have left us to burn in the lava," Grant spoke up. "Just don't point anything at them."

"He's going to leave us armed?" Nathan asked.

"Of course I am!" The answer, this time unmistakably Durga's voice, cut over their Commtact frequencies, audible to both groups of explorers, either on the Commtact implants or on the compact headsets used by the non-Cerberus group. "What good would it be to send you down into the tomb if you're unarmed? You'll die without achieving any of my goals."

"Well, he's found our frequency now," Kane muttered.

Brigid cleared her throat. "To tell the truth, our frequency would likely have been known to him. It's just a recent development that he's broken our encryption."

"He broke it, or Fargo did," Kane grumbled.

Durga appeared in the distance, as did a tall, hairless woman. Durga held a threshold, the original Annunaki bio-crystal technology that Lakesh, the man who brought Kane and the others to Cerberus, had reproduced with the interphaser. Like the interphaser, the threshold accessed parallax points on the surface of the planet. Those parallax points were the intersections of magnetic energy fields, places where the dimensions were the thinnest, and thanks to the genius of mathematicians such as Lakesh, they could be exploited as warp holes on the planet.

The threshold was how Durga had escaped the necropolis and likely how he'd gotten to Africa from the Indian subcontinent.

Durga, right now, was dressed in cargo shorts and boots, along with a few royal trinkets, bracelets, a neck chain and a small golden band across his brows. He didn't have a long weapon, but a pistol was holstered on his hip.

The woman was a sight.

On first thought, Kane imagined she'd been skinned alive, her raw muscle glistening, ridges of bone gleaming white as they stretched through the meat and fat. But she had eyelids and lips, even though she had no hint of eye-lashes or brows. The gleaming and seeming wetness of her skin were simply iridescent scales, arranged in lines and rows, looking like raw muscle fiber, and the "bare bone" were ridges akin to the horn structures he'd seen on other predatory dinosaurs on Thunder Isle.

Unlike Durga, she was completely unadorned with a stitch of cloth or jewelry. For someone with such reptil-ian skin, Neekra's mammalian nature was readily appar-ent, with full, lush breasts that were tight and perky on her chest. Her nipples were rosette designs of scales, un-like the chest plates on a Nagah woman, like the queen of Garuda, Hannah.

Kane was unnerved by her appearance, but then, it was not much different from the translucent-fleshed creature he had faced in the necropolis. This was simply balder, and yet bolder. She walked tall and proud, another sign that her "stripped flesh" appearance was an illusion of her scaled flesh. She was strong, unharmed and uninhibited by her nudity. Grim eyes and down-turned lips signified that she was in a rage, and she was not keen about stand-ing too close to Durga.

She hadn't engaged Kane mentally, and that cleared her, at least, of her efforts to control him into shooting his friends in the head. However, it didn't mean that she was any less dangerous or any less worthy of his anger and distrust. With his features hidden behind the shadow-suit faceplate, he felt armored from her, though if she had a hint of her old "doomie" abilities, his brain would be an open book to her.

"I'm not feeling anything," Brigid spoke up softly. Her voice was low and imperceptible to anyone who didn't have an amplified communication system akin to the Commtact or the others' headsets. "Anyone else."

"Feel what?" Thurpa asked.

"Psychic contact," Brigid answered. "Kane?"

Kane looked at her out of the corner of his eye. "Nothing going on between my ears."

"I know that, but what about anyone messing with your head?" Brigid answered, snapping up the bait. Kane smiled at her reaction. The two of them had always had a complicated relationship, to the extent that they were *anam-charas,* or soul mates. As such, they could also push each other's buttons.

Kane's joke had removed some of his anxiety, and he felt looser, more aware and receptive. The unheard chuckle cleared his mind, enabling him to take in more of the surroundings. He scanned back across the forces that Durga had assembled, examining them closer.

He could see that the Kongamato were still present, gliding on the thermals thrown up by the volcanic moat about this island. The creatures seemed to be enjoying themselves, meaning that there were some mental faculties about them, that they had a nature that wasn't one of being a preconstructed drone. However, the Nagah clones were unwavering, not distracted, even by the sound of their master's voice.

Thurpa didn't share any of the emotionless, robotic mannerisms of the ranks of creature before them. Also, Kane could truly feel his nervousness at their presence.

If he shared thoughts with Durga, their presence wouldn't have unsettled him so much. He could also see the tension rise in Thurpa's shoulders upon Durga's appearance, not to mention the same tightening of the young man's muscles when he first spoke over their communication system. Kane had already determined that Thurpa could be trusted, but here especially, he could see that their new ally was ready to throw down against his "father."

The one thing that kept Kane from opening fire on the fallen Nagah prince was that Thurpa and Durga shared at least a minor psychic link, one that had allowed Durga to endure whatever psychic assaults Neekra used against him. Any assault on Durga was shared across the clone's sympathetic nervous system, to the point where Thurpa was writhing in agony at Neekra's wrath against Durga.

Kane returned to studying the circumstances he was in, knowing he'd have to find some other means of defeating Durga that wouldn't involve causing harm to Thurpa if they retained a psychic linkage.

Neekra's walk was clumsy, despite the lean, graceful appearance of her nearly perfect Annunaki limbs. She seemed unused to moving around in that skin and would cast an angry eye toward Durga every time she took a misstep, which was twice across the broad, flat plane of the ziggurat top that they shared. She *was* getting used to it, though, because she made the last hundred yards without a stumble. Even so, she was restless, glancing about as if she were unused to a world with a peripheral vision.

Of course you're not used to peripheral vision, Kane thought. Neekra was, at least up until now, a psychic entity. She likely had sensory input that made being cut down to the five human senses appear to be nothing but peeking through a hole in a blindfold. Each sound made her turn her head, and every movement drew her attention. She was sharp, and she was sensitive, but Kane could feel the frustration seething off her after her crippling at Durga's hands. Her body had been cloned, and that cloning had somehow done without whatever enhancements had made her a free-floating entity.

"With Neekra," Brigid explained, "the proteins surpass, on a microscale, the circuitry and electronics necessary for communications systems. The human brain has no electronics in it, yet it turns electronic impulse into thought and action easily."

"So, Neekra..." Kane was casting about.

"Neekra and her lover, Negari, are organisms with biomolecular devices in them, assembling themselves into strings and large structures," Brigid elaborated. "They look like clusters of molecules bound together with internally and externally motive parts—no different from the selfsame proteins that perform similar tasks within the cells of your body and brain."

Kane squeezed his brow. Whatever Durga had done, he'd removed access to those particular proteins from Neekra. With those mechanisms taken away, she was "only" an Annunaki.

Which meant that she was as tall as Grant, and likely as strong, if not even more durable than him. Kane had hurled Enlil off a balcony on the gigantic living ship *Tiamat,* and despite a fall of hundreds of feet, Enlil crawled away and healed back to the point where he could personally lead an assault on Cerberus only days later.

Grant had fought Enlil's brother, Marduk, in hand-to-hand combat in Greece. Whereas the large Magistrate had proved more than a match for men as tall and broad as he was himself, Marduk was more than a half of a foot taller. Grant's battle against the overlord had relied not only on his enormous strength, but also on his years of training and experience. If Grant had gone at Marduk simply with brute strength, the Annunaki would have plucked his limbs off as if he were a trapped fly speared on a pin.

Utilizing martial arts, surprise and strategy, Grant had distracted Marduk until his enormous "scout ship" was shaken to pieces, blown up by sabotage charges placed by Kane himself.

Kane looked over Neekra, realizing that she didn't have the kind of dexterity and coordination yet to make her more than a match against either himself or Grant, but the Cerberus explorer knew that underestimating her would be a fatal mistake. No, she didn't have the enhanced strength that allowed her to shake the Earth with a stomp of her foot, power Brigid had explained was telekinesis focused and directed by the same protein-based biocomputer that gave her telepathy or the ability to mold a man into a new, feminine body for herself. But just because an Annunaki was without her old weaponry did not mean she was helpless.

She stood taller than Kane, towering half a head over the cloned Nagah soldiers. Neekra was perfectly proportioned, and thanks to the raw, skinless look, her arms were easily as muscular as Grant's, if only slimmer by an inch, and more finely defined against her Annunaki skin.

For a moment, Kane wondered if she wore the same smart-metal armor of Enlil and the Nephilim, and this was the design of that garment. But she was naked. He could see her sexual entrance. This was not body-conforming ringlets that formed a second skin.

Again, Kane found himself torn between revulsion at how she appeared to have been peeled skinless and attraction to her natural femininity, this aspect magnified by her nudity and nonchalance about standing unclothed before her allies and enemies.

Finally, Durga had approached close enough for Neekra to be a part of whatever conversation he wanted her to join. As soon as Durga came to a halt, two of the cloned Nagah stepped forward, prodding her with the muzzles of their guns. Neekra glared at the physical contact but continued walking toward the pickup, where Kane and the others had assembled. Everyone was out of the vehicle now. And, as per Durga's prior interruption, they had been allowed to retain their weapons, especially the staff Nehushtan.

"You…are putting me with *them?*" Neekra asked, glaring at Durga.

The fallen prince nodded. "Get over there."

"Or what? You'll shoot me?" Neekra challenged.

Kane and the others remained quiet, watching this drama play out before them.

"Neekra, I will have you shot, and with your flesh, it'd be no more than a stern whipping," Durga countered, still amused by her defiance.

"You take everything from me, and now you send me into the heart of the ziggurat?" Neekra snapped. She took a step toward him, and a single gunshot cracked.

The Annunaki woman stepped back, clutching her chest and flinching as scales flaked away from the impact of the bullet. Livid flesh pulsed beneath the freshly scaled area. She glared at Durga, grimacing in discomfort.

"One shot. Would you prefer to try for twenty, thirty?" Durga asked.

"I'll dine on your eyes for this," Neekra hissed.

"That's a nice one," Brigid said. "At least she's creative."

"Or hungry," Kane returned.

Neekra turned and regarded the two people.

"Hi there," Grant spoke up. "Remember us?"

Durga cleared his throat, then tossed a small headset

to Neekra. "Put that on. You'll need to keep in touch with them if you get separated."

"You want me to work with them?" Neekra asked.

Durga nodded. "You'll have to be careful with her, Kane. She's my gift to your little ragtag group."

Kane regarded the Annunaki woman. Her flesh, crimson scales gleaming like bright-red droplets of blood, seemed to pulse with barely contained rage.

Nathan took a step between Kane and Neekra. "This is our group. We decide who joins us."

Durga nodded. "Did I ask you if I gave a shit what you thought, mammal?"

Thurpa's fists clenched. "Watch your tongue."

Durga raised an eyebrow. "Such a spirited bunch, aren't you?"

"I don't know what you thought you were doing making me," Thurpa began.

"I was creating a son, an heir to my legacy," Durga said, cutting him off. "It's too bad you fell in with such a rotten crowd."

Thurpa bristled, and Durga's confidence and self-satisfaction seemed to only swell.

"You see the entrance, do you not?" Durga asked.

The Nagah clone troopers had a corridor through their ranks, and at the end, Kane noticed a familiar structure, one he'd seen in his hypnotic regression work with Brigid. It was the tomb, except, instead of being on the ground surrounded by forest, it stood in the center of the huge block at the peak of the ziggurat. The tomb was merely the tip of the iceberg, one that stood a half a mile in height above the ground and still had at least a mile and a half out of sight, embedded in the earth.

"We see it," Brigid spoke up.

Durga regarded the woman. "Then you know what you have to do."

"Humor us," Lyta challenged.

Durga eyed the young African woman. He had not met with her in person. Any knowledge he'd have of her would have had to come from Thurpa. His gaze went from dismissive to leering, the corners of his mouth turning up in a smile the likes of which Kane wouldn't wish any woman to be the subject. Durga had proved himself nothing short of a sexual predator in his time, a proclivity overlooked due to his royal station, his political power and the fact that he'd protected the Nagah people from a violent incursion by a force of Magistrates who'd penetrated the Indian subcontinent, looking for technology.

Even with the last woman to whom he'd been betrothed, Hannah, he'd been a cruel, sadistic lover. There had also been rumors of other dalliances, ones that had ended in violent death.

Thurpa stepped between Lyta and Durga. "I know what you're thinking."

Durga smirked. "Yes. Yes, you do."

Thurpa's fangs sprung down from their folded position against the roof of his mouth. His cobra hood flexed, and he breathed out, ragged, savage, primal.

Kane took Thurpa by the wrist, pulling him back. "We'll take care of him. Durga doesn't look like he's ready to have us killed yet…"

"No. I need you," Durga said. "There is a threat at the core of this structure. A creature who can lay waste to this world. I do not intend to rule any land in the shadow of such a monster. You seven, you unlucky seven, have been chosen to destroy Negari."

"My lover?" Neekra asked. "Why should I throw in with your pathetic little army of mercenaries?"

Durga held up a phial. "The protein that he discovered. The key to your power reborn."

Neekra's eyes narrowed.

"You want that back. You feel as weak as a kitten without it," Durga taunted.

"Remember when I promised to eat your eyes?" Neekra asked.

Durga nodded.

"I was going to do unto you the mercy of being dead before I did so," Neekra said.

Durga grinned, then shrugged his shoulders. "Ohh… scary. Go to your task like good little cattle."

Kane grimaced, but Grant spoke what everyone was thinking. "Thanks, Durga. Just when I thought we would have a nice quiet dungeon crawl, you go and screw us over."

Durga blew the big man a kiss, and his cloned troopers leveled their guns at the Cerberus group, now grown by one. They turned and headed toward the tomb entrance.

Chapter 9

Seven people stood before the small, squat assemblage of blocks. The only entrance apparent to the whole of the ziggurat was this building, no larger than an equipment shed, though its door was a seven-by-seven slab of stone that looked as smoothly polished as a mirror and was made of a mineral that not even Brigid, with her wealth of knowledge and perfect memory, could identify. The stone "door" had a single crack that zigged and zagged in a line across it, and the edges of that crack were the only imperfections in the slab.

Kane touched the surface, but he couldn't make it move with every bit of his strength pushed into it. He looked to Grant, and the two men set their combined strength against the door. Nothing moved.

"We could try the four of…" Nathan started to speak.

Neekra stepped up, brushing Kane and Grant away from the door. Despite the bruise where her scales had been knocked off of her shoulder, her musculature was still grand, finely toned and powerful. She spread her hands against the flat stone and leaned against it. They heard a faint crunch of stone on stone, but her claws, long, white, almost bony talons grown from the ends of her fingers, rather than conventional fingernails, didn't mar the surface of the rock.

She shrugged her shoulders, sheets of side muscle flexing against her glimmering ribs, and the slab moved a millimeter. The noise of that slight shift was as loud as the blast from one of Grant's .50-caliber rifles. Neekra stepped back, then threw herself, shoulder-first against the flat, smooth rock. The slam was even louder, but she staggered away from the stone slab.

"How did Solomon Kane get this open?" Neekra asked, rubbing her shoulder.

"It had been opened by the owner of the slave caravan," Kane answered. He examined the sides of the arch that held the slab in place. "Brigid, can you read anything on this?"

"The markings are a variant on Sumerian Sanskrit, but right now, all it's saying is gibberish," Brigid stated. She turned and addressed Neekra. "Can you read it?"

"No," the surly Annunaki demigod answered. She looked over her shoulder back toward Durga. An army of cobra men stood between them and the fallen prince, but Kane could feel enough anger from her that she'd wade into them, no matter how heavily armed they were.

The only thing keeping her on a leash was that she knew the kind of pain that the Nagah venom could inflict upon her. Kane wasn't certain if the cobra toxins would affect her without the microcomputer matrix that made her into a deadly force of nature, but Neekra didn't seem too keen on testing that out.

"Neekra, focus," Brigid said.

The Annunaki woman looked over the arch. "It…"

Her eyes scanned the markings, and her brow wrinkled the more that she read.

"It's gibberish," Neekra admitted. She glared at Brigid. "Just as you said. How…"

"This isn't the first time I've encountered your people's influence on history," Brigid stated. "Now, how about helping me figure out if this is some form of code."

"If I could not move…" Neekra began.

"If you couldn't move it with brute force, we must use other means," Brigid returned. "An Arab slave trader managed to activate the mechanism of this doorway with only a sixteenth-century level of reading comprehension and code breaking"

Kane frowned. His memories of that adventure, more of a side trip in Africa, left him casting about for rhyme or reason. While the other Kane shared his name and his time stream, all of their thoughts were not in sync. For example, why were the Puritan and the slave master both in the area where there was a tomb, one that could be closed back down with the presence of the juju staff?

Speaking of that artifact, Kane looked at Lyta. She held on to Nehushtan, clutching it tightly, but shifted her feet nervously, on edge, ready to bring that stick around and hit someone hard with it. Her nerves were on edge, which was understandable as they stood atop an ancient structure and were surrounded by an army of pan-terrestrial humanoids, each of them packing firepower that could cut them in half. That wasn't counting the venom they packed into their folding fangs or their inhuman, robotic countenances as they were essentially mass-produced "drones."

That was behind them. Beside them was Neekra, a true-born queen of hell they knew was the mother of gelatinous horrors that could reanimate the dead into her vampiric foot soldiers. Ahead of them was her lover, an abomination so horrendous that Neekra's own father used her mindless body as one of the guards in a structure two and a half miles from top to bottom and stuck in the heart of an artificially carved volcano.

Whatever they were to face, Lyta now seemed to be longing for the days when she only had to deal with maniacal militiamen who chained her up and slaughtered the rest of her village.

Lyta was not a wilting flower. Sure, she was a young woman, about twenty by Kane's estimation, but she'd lived on the frontier of her nation. Africa had been relatively untouched by direct nuclear warhead hits on their cities, despite the seismic upheavals of skydark, but lawlessness and tribalism still threatened the civilization that yet existed on the continent. She was armed, she was trained to protect herself and, from what Kane had seen from her, she'd risen to every challenge with grim, silent courage.

The sight of the dead walking had shocked her, but she reacted to that trauma by fighting back. Neekra's savage telekinesis-enhanced strength, shaking the ground with her very footsteps, still didn't make her run away; Lyta stood her ground and opened fire.

But now, she was waiting, trying to think of what was coming up.

Kane was about to say something when Thurpa walked beside her. His fingers wound with hers. She glanced at him, still a bundle of nerves, but the anxiety in her features no longer built with each passing moment.

Kane turned away from the pair, feeling as if he were intruding on them. Nathan and Grant were both watching Neekra as Brigid conferred with the Annunaki woman. Neekra was looking at writing in her native language, one that Brigid Baptiste had been studying and deciphering for the past five years, and both women, despite their advantages of fluency and photographic memory, were having trouble discerning the strange code on the entrance.

Because the three men had little translation experience, and thus little to offer the pair of women, they simply stood guard. Durga would undoubtedly be more and more impatient with the lack of progress, and Kane didn't want to think of him frustrated. He had little fear for his own health and safety. If the cloned Nagah fell upon them, Kane would take a good many of them to death alongside him. He was concerned about the three young people, as well as for Grant, the man who was his brother, and Brigid, his dearest friend ever.

"Difficulties?" Durga's voice came over their radios.

Neekra's shoulders stiffened and the air grew still, as if the universe were waiting for her to whirl around and launch at the Nagah prince. Instead of doing that, she continued on with aiding Brigid in translating the code of the entrance.

"It's locked," Kane said in terms of an answer. "But don't worry, we've got two smart people working on it."

"I could always bring you some explosives," Durga offered.

Kane grimaced. "You stay on your side of the pyramid."

"Ziggurat."

Kane sighed. "Whatever."

"You're certain I can't get you anything?" Durga pressed.

"I swear, you offer me a beer, I'm coming over there myself and twisting your head off," Kane growled.

"Touched a nerve, hmm," Durga said.

Kane knew that Durga was purposefully being a nuisance and kicked himself for letting him get under his skin. "You said this was our task. If you're in such a hurry to get in there, why didn't you do anything yourself?"

"Because I'm more valuable to myself than you are," Durga responded. "The last time this was opened, many who were present died."

"That's why you have your army, all locked and loaded, between us and you," Kane observed. "And if you *really* need to get out of here, your winged friends are flying about."

"Bring the staff, Lyta," Brigid spoke up, interrupting Kane and Durga's conversation over the radio headsets.

That was something that Kane recalled. His predecessor, the Puritan, had been separated from Nehushtan when the tomb entrance was discovered. Its presence must have been key in unlocking the hard, heavy slab of stone. The artifact had been utilized as a dangerous, deadly weapon against the Kongamato, and its energies were enough to restore Durga from crippling, body-wide agony to walking tall, and it sealed and healed deadly gashes and cuts among the group. Nehushtan also provided a psychic cloaking, hiding them from detection by Neekra when she was at her strongest, a nomadic intelligence going from body to body, able to penetrate Kane's mind and leave him comatose for a day, a mental battle that made Kane feel as if he'd been lost across centuries and had to span the multiverse to return to protect his friends.

And, as had been said on the roof of this very ziggurat, the staff was the weapon of Suleiman, King Solomon of biblical legend, and was the very staff he'd used to battle demons, driving them from Europe and northern Africa, sealing them away in this deadly tomb.

Kane grimaced. The staff had influenced Nathan's journeys, leading him to get into direct communication with Cerberus redoubt. It had transmitted regressive dreams to Kane, influencing him about traveling to Africa. If the juju stick could do that in this day and time, then undoubtedly it had drawn Solomon Kane, and then the slaver caravan, to this very spot.

It had brought these people to it.

Almost as if it were delivering victims to whatever was inside of the ziggurat. Kane tensed and watched as Brigid and Neekra pressed on glyphs built into the stones that made up the arch of the entrance. With each touch, the glyphs flared with an internal glow, cold blue fire that grew brighter and brighter with each activation.

Lyta wielded Nehushtan, standing it so that the tip touched the top of the arch. The black-hued staff itself developed an inner fire, as if it were a key on its own. Even now, Kane could zoom in with the shadow suit's optics, seeing that the head as the artifact was currently configured and fit right into a notch at the top of the doorway.

Just as it may have seven hundred years ago when he was last here, wearing the grim black of a Puritan.

Kane launched the Sin Eater into his fist with its hydraulic arm, the gun slapping against his palm. "Get them away!"

Grant, Thurpa and Nathan were in motion only moments behind Kane as he rushed to the cracked slab. The mighty plate of unknown stone shifted, sank, that blasphemous glow spilling now from behind the door. Kane lunged for the staff of Solomon, fingers wrapping around the stick and pulling away.

Grant tackled Neekra, and both man and Annunaki woman grunted as they collided, but she was dragged away from directly in front of the entrance. Thurpa clutched Lyta from the spill of the pouring, quicksilver glow of the entrance, pulling her into his shadow to protect her from what horrors lay within. Brigid was already retreating, knowing that Kane's instincts were correct when it came to danger, though Nathan was able to catch her and keep her from tripping and stumbling out of control.

Kane held on to Nehushtan as the blaze of the tomb's entrance caught him full in the face. He'd pulled his faceplate down on his shadow-suit hood, hoping that the uniform, designed for space travelers, would grant him protection from whatever eerie radiation burned within. Even so, he felt his cheeks redden and prickle, his eyes squinting in pain from the flare despite the polarization of the faceplate. Electricity tingled up his arm as he pulled the artifact away from the entrance. Something lurched inside, dimming the already eye-burning glow with its silhouette. Kane couldn't make out exact details, but it wrapped its hideous talons around the staff, just above where he grasped it.

It was the same gnarled, twice-normal thickness, twice-normal length fingers he remembered from his hypnotic sojourn. He pulled harder on Nehushtan, knowing that if the staff were lost, they'd have no weapons with which to repel the towering horror within the tomb. At the same time, he raised the Sin Eater, flicked the selector to full auto and fired off a whole magazine into the silhouette before him. Slugs ripped out of the sidearm's barrel, thundering as they did so; bullets struck something beyond because he could feel the splatter of blood along his knuckles. His target was so close he could feel, even through the shadow suit, the "echo" of concussion bouncing off of his opponent.

The machine pistol ran empty and Kane released the grip, flexing his forearm to retract the weapon back into its holster. The creature hadn't released the artifact, but it hadn't moved. Using the staff as leverage, he threw his legs up and out in a double kick. The soles of his boots struck something, and that felt as solid as a cliff wall. There was no give on the other end of Kane's blow, and he could feel his ankles and knees take the punishment of hitting something harder than they were.

Even so, the staff was released and Kane rebounded off of the kick and managed to catch himself before slamming backward onto his head. He dropped to one knee and lowered his head because he knew that the others would be ready to take action now.

Bullets ripped through the air where he'd been moments ago, and a tooth-shaking bellow ripped through the cacophony of guns. Kane twisted and rolled out from under the sheet of fire lashing into the beast at the mouth of the tomb, keeping the staff tucked and parallel to his body as he took the fastest, safest route out through the blazing guns of his allies.

As soon as the cracks and heat of bullets were no longer above him, he rolled quickly to his hands and knees, then kicked to a half-standing position. The others pulled back, and already the cloned Nagah were entering into the fray that had started only moments ago but felt like hours. The snake men cut loose with their assault weapons, the din of their gunfire shaking the atmosphere. Kane and his allies took the momentary reprise to reload their spent magazines.

"Nathan!" Kane called out. The young man from Harare held up his hand to catch the tossed staff and Kane lobbed it to him. Nathan Longa had been the guardian of the artifact for a long time, entrusted to this by his father, his ancestors having been watching over the staff for at least half of a millennium.

Nathan snatched the staff out of the air.

Neekra had borrowed an assault rifle from one of Kane's allies—likely Grant. When the horror emerged from the blazing tomb entrance, she'd been one of the first group firing to cover Kane. She was in midreload, and her gaze fell upon him.

She didn't have the option of polarized lenses or enhanced senses provided by mechanical means, but she stared at the thing that was ignoring sheets of bullets to emerge through the unlocked door. Her features were a mask of disgust and anger.

"Father?" he heard her over the Commtact. "This is what you think of me?"

The woman held the assault rifle in one hand like a pistol and opened fire, the muzzle flash of the rifle a fireball as she advanced toward the huge creature. He could make out its limbs now; they were treelike in thickness and length. Indeed, they had gnarled vines of muscle wrapped about them. The thing's hands were like the barren branches of a dead tree.

Then she stood up. And it *was* a she, the torso, hips and breasts full and feminine despite the corded muscle on her limbs. The head was something just out of sight, obscured by the shoulders and arms of the bestial giantess. It was twice the height of Neekra, but even so, Kane could make out similarities between their two figures. The taller was a perverted, distorted version of the woman before him, and she lunged, sneering at the guardian.

"This is what you think of me?" she shouted, lashing her arced fingers, the bony nails at the tips ripping at her doppelganger's flesh.

"This…abomination?"

The lashings of her claws on the tree-tall horror were akin to a shovel stabbing into gravel, scooping it aside to dig a shallow grave. Finally, the blaze within the heart of the tomb entrance was gone, and the polarized lenses powered down in Kane's vision. He could see the mutated, severed body of Neekra, and its head was a gruesome ball of red, ugly purple and black veins crisscrossing its surface. Any facial features were vestigial, tiny black balls of eyes, slits of nostrils and a mouth, ears mere pinpricks in the side of its head. Stringy hair writhed, and focusing, he zoomed in on them, fat, ugly worms, stretching and pulsating with each breath and movement. The ball of its head was like a pustule, swollen and infected, yellowish fluids sloshing against the interior of the stretched, reddened bubble.

It held Neekra down, pushing her so her raking claws couldn't reach the boil of inflamed flesh that was the head that Enlil had placed on those shoulders.

Lyta fired her rifle, but the bullets bounced and deflected off of the rubbery surface of the balloon-like growth. It swiveled its ebony eyes toward the African girl and took a single step, crossing six feet in one stride, stretching its arm out to clutch at her.

Thurpa threw himself into the fray, jumping onto the giantess's forearm and wrapping his arms around it. The guardian paid little attention to his weight, even though he was 170 pounds of muscle. Kane knew that the young Nagah man had a plan, for he was without his shadow-suit hood, his face bare, mouth free. With a flex of his head, the sheets of scaled muscle framing his head spreading to give him the full effect of his cobra appearance, he brought his mouth down onto the horror's wrist.

The effect was immediate, the giant creature shaking its arm as if it had been thrust into a flame. Lyta scurried away from the jagged nails of the guardian, one hooked talon plucking at her shoulder. The slit mouth opened wide, its pain blowing out of that vent hole, tumorous tongue wagging over the thin lips of the boil. If Kane thought the monstrosity couldn't get any uglier, he realized he was wrong in that assessment as the mouth became a ragged gash as it stretched open. The gash was filled with teeth the shape and color of rotted planks of wood ringed around the bulbous, throbbing appendage, which would have been a tongue had it not been a cancerous mockery of one.

Thurpa yelled in surprise, his body flying off the flapping, injured arm. The shadow suit would take most of the brunt of his fall, but Kane worried that the young Nagah warrior might have injured his head or neck in that tumble. That worry would have to hold for the moment, though. The giantess was hurt, distracted by its venom-burned arm, but it continued to shrug off gunfire from the Nagah soldiers and Kane. Neekra had crawled around to the thing's back, using her doppelganger's body as a living shield.

The Annunaki woman had proved able to shrug off single bullets, but the concentration of fire on the guardian was too much, even for her formidable body. Discretion was the better part of durability in Neekra's case, and she hung on to the creature's back, using her finger and toe claws to cause the monstrosity pain as she clung to its flesh. Blood poured over Neekra's hands and feet from the wounds she tore in the thing that had been made of her old body.

She still shouted, screeching her hatred to her father, Enlil, cursing in the ancient Annunaki language at the top of her lungs.

But that rage did nothing more than serve to anger the fourteen-foot monstrosity. Guns proved useless.

Neekra's doppelganger was a juggernaut, and nothing in their arsenal had dented its hide so far.

Chapter 10

The desperate scene from the top of a ziggurat was surrounded by a rumbling volcano. Even a half of a mile up above the lava, the temperature rose. Clouds of smoke ringed in the gigantic structure, to the point that the winged Kongamatos were orbiting the peak in tighter and tighter circles, thanks to sulfurous clouds that rose from steaming and cooling magma. As the bat-winged giants swirled around the ziggurat, thunderous peals of gunfire were punctuated by eardrum-shattering roars of a fourteen-foot-tall horror. The creature issuing those earth-shaking bellows was a gigantic woman with a ball of tumors for a head.

Around her were seven combatants, those eight walled off by an army of gunmen, none of them stepping forward but firing in unison when there was a clear shot at the giantess. The attacker on the titan's back, fingers clawed into her back like meat hooks, was the new body for the mind that had been separated from the giant's mutant body, Neekra the Annunaki, cast from her flesh as a curse from her father, the overlord Enlil.

Six people, clad in skintight black uniforms, four men, two women, each were armed with a rifle and some form of sidearm. Grant, the largest of the four men, was a menacing, physically imposing man and was prone to packing a lot of firepower when it came to dealing with threats. The shotgun had proved its worth when it came time to do battle with the Kongamato when they were under a previous controller, but now, against the gigantic version of Neekra, all he was doing was distracting her. The pellets didn't have much penetration against her scaly hide, no more than normal bullets.

Still, Grant distracted the huge woman, a defender who'd risen from the small building at the tip of the ziggurat, a building that truly resembled the enclosure of a tomb. In truth, it was more a prison than a tomb, designed to contain a creature even more horrendous than Neekra at her worst. Although the guardian possessed superhuman strength, and Neekra herself had formerly commanded incredible psychic abilities thanks to the addition of a prion-based supercomputer in her brain, the prisoner, another Annunaki named Negari, was a nightmarish force that was buried within a two-mile cube of stone unlike any the world had seen.

Kane was the second-tallest of the men, and he attempted to get around the female titan as Grant hammered at her. He was on his way to grasp Nehushtan, the artifact in the possession of the shortest of the four men.

Nathan Longa's family had been the caretakers of the ancient juju staff for hundreds of years of its multimillennium existence. The staff had guided Nathan miles across the frontier of postapocalyptic Africa, seeking a reunion with the descendant of another of its prior owners, the former Magistrate Kane. So far, conventional firearms had proved incapable of harming Neekra's former body, which was likely the point.

The one person who had been able to inflict injury on her lay unmoving where the fourteen-foot titan had hurled him. Thurpa had risked his life to protect the shorter woman, Lyta. The African girl had joined them more recently than Thurpa and Nathan, but she'd proved herself

courageous in a prior battle. She'd drawn the ire of the giantess by striking the mutant in her tumor-swollen head,
showing at once that the ugly pustule wasn't as fragile as
it seemed and that she could feel pain. Thurpa had hurled
himself onto the thick branch arm of the giantess, sinking
his venomous fangs into her arm. Those fangs, a genetically engineered addition to the Nagah people by a benevolent Annunaki demigod by the name of Enki, had burned
like acid and fire through the giantess's arm.

The last woman, Brigid Baptiste, who was as tall as
the fallen Thurpa and just a little shorter than Kane, had
taken a step back from the fight, watching the current conflict. This was not due to any cowardice; Brigid had faced
larger opponents without flinching. But they faced a foe
whose might was currently beyond most of the weaponry
on hand. With six others already in close quarters combat with the giantess, Brigid decided to apply her greatest
weapon, her intellect, against the tumor-headed horror.

She noted that Nathan and Kane were trying to get together to hand off the Nehushtan artifact to Kane. They
had no doubt that the "juju stick" could cause harm to
the giant thing. She'd heard, almost directly from the lips
of that prior incarnation, that he'd driven it back into the
tomb.

Nathan might have wanted to try it himself, she calculated. After all, he had held off the incredibly powerful
Kongamato with the assistance of the staff, but Nehushtan
had pushed the youth to seek out Kane personally. In his
hands, the staff would likely be at its most potent.

The irate monster woman smashed her foot into the
ground between the two men, driving them away from
each other and preventing the exchange of the artifact.
Brigid could see that the giant was aware of what was going
on about her and had enough intellect to realize the dan-

gers of the staff in the wrong hands. Its one arm now hung limply, numbed by the venom. Unfortunately, Thurpa, the one who inflicted such a disability on the guardian, was now unconscious, hurled aside by the fourteen-foot entity. The kind of strength and the impact from that throw showed itself to be more than the shadow suit could absorb, at least in terms of shock, but Brigid hoped that no bones had been broken on the young cobra man.

She glanced to the cloned soldiers, grimacing. There was plenty more opportunity for venom to be employed, but the drone gunmen weren't that smart. They simply pulled the trigger when they had a free shot, meaning that Durga had programmed them not to harm any of the Cerberus expedition, not even Neekra, whom Durga had bruised himself with a gunshot to the shoulder. The fallen Nagah prince was far back, letting others commit to the battle while he was safe and sound.

Brigid keyed into her Commtact. "Durga, we need some of your troops to spray her."

"Excuse me?" replied Durga. "You're telling me what you need? They're already spraying her with lead."

"Lead doesn't work on that thing," Brigid snapped. "We need Nagah venom against her."

"Venom," Durga mused. He was stalling, and Brigid tossed a glance back toward the scene. Grant had shifted to using his bow and arrow. The shafts, hurled by the incredible tensile strength of his bow and tipped with razor-sharp steel, managed to penetrate the giant guardian's hide, but they seemed to do nothing more than enrage her. Kane moved in quickly, slashing at the thing's knees and thighs with his combat blade.

Again, sharp steel backed by hundreds of pounds of muscle seemed to do the trick in wounding her. Unfortunately, those injuries only served to add fuel to the rage of the enormous warrior. Kane grunted audibly over the Commtact as he barely rolled with a backhanded slap from the giantess. His shadow suit and reflexes combined to protect him from bone-crushing injury as he went into a somersault to bleed off momentum from the glancing blow.

"Grant, get to Thurpa!" Brigid ordered. "And pray he has the strength to spit…"

"Put it on my arrowheads," Grant murmured as he took off in a run.

"You seem to be doing well," Durga said. "I don't see why my soldiers need to risk themselves."

Brigid felt her cheeks redden with rage. "For god's sake, they're just clones!"

"This is how you ask for help, dear?" Durga asked.

Brigid turned and fired a gunshot at the giantess. She'd grown so frustrated that she needed to take it out violently on something. Luckily, a gargantuan humanoid juggernaut provided a perfect vent for that anger.

Grant reached Thurpa and skidded to the young man's side. His eyes seemed unfocused, dazed from his ordeal at the end of a titan's arm, but Lyta was already beside him, cradling his head. She was doing more than fawning over the brave youth who'd come to her rescue on two occasions; she had her pistol in hand, ready to fight off the beast if she took a step closer to him. Kane, Neekra and Nathan were already occupying the big ogress, but Lyta kept her gaze locked on their opponent.

"Lyta, Thurpa, sorry…" Grant began, drawing an arrow from his quiver.

"We heard Brigid," Lyta cut him off. "Get what you can."

Thurpa was at least conscious, and he leaned his mouth to the broad-headed arrow. He flexed one fang, squirting venom onto it. "Don't miss…"

Grant quickly nocked the arrow. "I won't."

He whirled and realized that "not missing" was going to be more of a challenge than he thought. Neekra was high on the creature's back, and it was thrashing around, its single working arm torn between clawing at the Annunaki and swatting at Nathan or Kane. Thurpa's bite was one of the only things that evened the fight between the gigantic guardian and the combatants around her, as she moved so swiftly, she still nearly caught Kane or Nathan with a direct hit. Looking at the ground where she'd stamped her feet, Grant could see stress fractures, circular little craters caused by the creature's enormous strength.

"Brigid? Where to hit her?" Grant asked, nocking the arrow and drawing it to full stretch.

"The head," Brigid offered. She was terse, annoyed, which wasn't much of a surprise. He could hear the taunting and stonewalling she'd encountered asking Durga for assistance.

"Kane, get that bitch to sit still for a minute!" Grant called over the Commtact.

Kane grunted with acknowledgment, then turned and took a step. As he did so, he seemed to catch his foot on the broken stone of the ziggurat roof, already cracked and shattered by the powerful stomps of the angry guardian. Kane threw his hands out in front of him to catch himself, skidding into the fall as he did so, legs splayed out tangled behind him.

The giantess took notice of Kane's sudden disadvantage, staring down at him. The hideous gash of a mouth turned up in a malicious smile and she lifted her foot, ready to bring it down on top of the fallen man.

That moment of stillness was all Grant needed, and he let fly with his cobra-venom-tipped arrow. The shaft whistled through the air at high speed and struck true on one of the black orbs in her pustule-like face. The eyeball exploded in black-stained yellow runoff, and the smile of the hideous warrior turned into a cavernous maw, a volcano of sound as the venom burned where flesh had been sliced by the wide, razor-edged vane of the broadhead. The point continued through until a foot of arrow shaft had sunk into her head.

Grant wasn't certain if he'd struck her brain, but she toppled backward, off balance from raising her foot to crush Kane beneath. She tried to catch herself and twisted, grabbing the ground with one long, gnarled arm. Her bitten arm hung limply as she was on her hand and knees, and Grant could tell that she was still in this fight. She yelled, saliva dripping from her lips, blood trickling off the end of his arrow.

She crawled, seeking to get up enough strength and leverage beneath her to stand, but the agony of the venom burning in her face made her too dizzy to get much up. Grant didn't think he'd have too long, not the way that the blood seeped from her eye injury. Whatever alien vitality the giantess possessed could easily overcome the small amount of poison that had coated Grant's broadheaded arrow.

However, when the titan toppled off of her feet, Kane and Nathan were now unhindered, able to exchange Nehushtan.

Kane snatched up the ancient staff, its head already transforming in some obscene manner, flowing like quicksilver. Kane had harbored a recent thought of the more nefarious nature of this staff, which had ended up in the possession of biblical prophets and legendary heroes. He could feel its surface remolding, new runes appearing in the place of old ones, even as he grasped it. The staff had a core of orichalcum, a powerful, energy-storing alloy that was volatile enough to explode when sunlight struck it. This staff currently had a black coating that itself morphed and molded with the configuration of the staff.

But the one thing in common through all of its forms was the tapered tip, pointy enough to dig into the ground as a walking stick. Even as Kane gripped the weapon, he could sense the pointy end growing sharper, finer, honed to a more deadly point. He rushed toward the giantess as she sat up on her knees, looking around with her remaining eye. Kane had been in her blind spot thanks to the arrow that plucked out the other eye, and by the time she saw the explorer from Cerberus coming, it was too late.

Kane lunged with all of his strength, pushing with each ounce of muscle and momentum he could muster. The point of the ancient artifact clove through the chest and heart of the gigantic she-beast, plunging deep. He sensed no resistance from her flesh, no scrape of bone on the coated metal, but he could feel the staff grow hotter and hotter in his grasp, blazing from within a searing pain that went up both of his arms, throbbing inside of his skull.

The giantess stood up, wrenching Kane from his feet, and both hands were wrapped around the six-foot staff, the pain of Nehushtan through her torso enough to dispel any paralysis of her Thurpa-bitten hand. A single glaring eye locked on to Kane's gaze, pulling him in and freezing him with a primal horror that reached up from the depths of prehistory. He was face-to-face with a demon of legend, and it was more than sufficient to make him flinch, even as his legs kicked helplessly to gain the traction of the ground, but her height was such that there were five empty feet of air to the floor.

Kane released the staff with one arm, hanging on by wrapping his other so that it tucked and supported him under his armpit. His right fist shot forward, and he opened his hand to accept the hydraulic-launched Sin Eater from the reflexive impulse. The machine pistol bellowed, its fresh magazine spitting slugs into the giantess's eye. At a range of mere inches, the onslaught was more than sufficient to shower Kane in tarry black goo and runny yellow pus.

Fingers wound around one of Kane's thighs, squeezing and grasping him tightly. Kane realized that any separation from the staff would be fatal for him, but he also knew he was facing a level of strength that not even his high-tech suit could protect him from. He continued to fire into her face, vowing that if this was to be his last battle, he was bringing down this daughter of the devil with him.

A feminine snarl broke the air instants before he heard the shattering of bones.

They weren't his, thankfully. He even felt the cessation of the crushing grip on his leg. He glanced down and saw Neekra, winding up for another blow like the one that had snapped the guardian's forearm in half. The giant toppled back to her knees, worn down by her conflict, by the cobra venom, by the spear of orichalcum through her chest.

Kane was on the ground now, and Neekra glared at him and then at the thing that had once been part of her body. Anger twisted her blood-splashed features, turning her into a dripping, glistening version of a skinned human being. That the blood was, in a roundabout way, her own only made the sight of her, angry, chest heaving, all the more horrific.

But Kane didn't let go of the staff. He wasn't going to let go; he wasn't going to draw it from the flesh of the giant horror. The energies were still burning between him and the guardian, but slowly, Nehushtan cooled. No more did electrical sparks arc from the giant's chest wound, dancing along Kane's shadow suit and the staff.

Whatever the artifact was doing to the monster's insides, she was finally shriveling. Steam erupted from all manner of minor wounds, her skin and muscle shrinking and sucking against her skeleton. The tumor-like head deflated easily, quickly, collapsing in upon itself.

Finally, skin, dried and brittle as parchment, cracked and fluttered away from bones. Muscle fibers unwound, unraveling and collapsing off bones. The guardian had become instantly mummified, and now cartilage cracked under the weight of bones it formerly had held together.

Kane stood, still gripping Nehushtan, steam rising from the tangle of bones and dried-out flesh, which was all that remained of the guardian of the tomb.

"I think she's done," Brigid said, brushing his shoulder.

Kane broke from the rapid decay of the creature before him. Though it had been trying to kill him, he already realized that the death it suffered had been slow, agonizing and horrible. He pulled the point from the lifeless remains, a gust of hot wind from the surrounding caldera whipping off and blowing away the giant's skin like autumn leaves.

Neekra grimaced at the sight of what was left. She knelt and picked up a bone, looking it over.

The first words out of Kane's mouth were, "Is Thurpa all right?"

"I'll live," Thurpa replied. "What about the rest of you?"

"I am disgusted at what my flesh has been usurped for," Neekra growled.

"Your father thinks highly of you," Brigid noted, icicles seeming to form on each syllable.

"She's not the only one in that boat," Thurpa grumbled. He glared back at the wall of gunmen between the tomb entrance and his father.

"I hope that's all the security that Enlil sprung for," Grant added.

"Does it ever go that easily?" Kane asked him.

Grant shook his head.

They hadn't even opened the door yet and everyone was battered, down on ammunition and thoroughly rattled.

Kane grimaced. The tomb of Negari was going to be the depths of hell.

Chapter 11

Neekra had her Annunaki physiology to fall back on in order to recover from her strains and aches. Even the scales that had been blown free by a bullet to her shoulder were re-forming, newer and shinier than ever. She stood apart from Kane, Brigid, Grant, Nathan, Thurpa and Lyta. The six humans made use of the rejuvenatory energies of the ancient staff, Nehushtan. It was a multifaceted object, but thanks to the orichalcum alloy that formed its core, it produced enough power to engage in whatever activities it was required, be it enhancing strength in hand-to-hand combat or restoring a person to health.

Neekra glared toward Durga. He himself had been the recipient of Nehushtan's healing gift because when she first encountered him, he was a cripple being carried on a cot through the jungle by humans of the Millennium Consortium. She'd probed him, utilizing senses that she couldn't even recall the feel of, discovering that his body had wasted away, muscles degenerated after being exposed to the incredible explosive force of a fuel-air explosion. Whatever power allowed him to survive such a blast had only been able to restore necessary bodily functions. Muscle tissue that had been destroyed remained withered, feeble. Yet Durga possessed within him a drive that attracted her psychically.

Now, thanks to exposure to the staff, Durga stood tall, and had proved to be so sly, so tricky that he had stripped her of the telepathic powers and superior senses her lover Negari had provided for her. It was a nightmare. She felt as if she were living under a pillow, unable to breathe.

When they first met she was a god and he was the cripple.

Now, the roles were reversed, and what was worse, he used her to fight her own body, the original flesh that Enlil had severed from her brain as punishment for becoming Negari's consort. Her brain, actually her whole head, was an irreparable, mummified husk that had been deposited somewhere. And the tomb-prison of Negari was far and away, hidden from even her superior sensory perceptions.

Yet Durga was able to locate not only Negari, but also her head. Once he had that, he somehow managed to separate the prions from her brain, the same complex proteins that could arrange themselves into organic computers and antennae powerful enough to mold flesh and peer into other minds. And now she was in a clone of her old body, nothing like the gigantic guardian Enlil had turned her carcass into. She was mere Annunaki, not fourteen feet of overlord-enhanced juggernaut. Sure, she was stronger than the two strongest men present, and her intellect was still the same after thousands of years filled with broad experience, but she might as well have been a legless stump compared to what she had been.

Shifting through the skeleton of the guardian, Neekra found no skull. The head itself appeared to be merely alligator-thick hide and crude simulacra of normal organs, grown from nerve tissue that branched up from the severed spine. Neekra shuddered at the ghastly inventiveness of her father, how he treated her body as just another wild experiment, the basis for a living weapon that, by its appearance, was nearly as much of an insult to her as its very existence. This abomination was something she was glad to see destroyed, and she had acted in every way possible to stop it cold.

"Are you all right here?" a voice asked her.

Neekra turned, looking over her shoulder. It was Kane, looming over her as she knelt beside the remains of the guardian. "What does it matter to you?"

Kane, his hood off, displayed a flash of irritation at her dismissal of his compassion. Neekra could not care less about the concerns of one of these upstart monkeys, especially when they had spurned her. Kane specifically had turned her down as her lover.

"It matters to me because you're a part of our group now," Kane said. "You showed as much when you fought by our side."

"I fought that…thing," Neekra answered, waving to the dessicated remains. "I sought to remove a stain from my sight. It only happened to coincide with your needs."

Kane nodded. "If you work with us, we'll help you pay Durga back."

Neekra narrowed her eyes. "Tempting? Bribing?"

"Offering." Kane stretched out his hand for her to take. She started to reach for it but stopped, instead rising to her full height of six and a half feet.

She looked down on the man from Cerberus. "I made offers, as well."

Kane still held out his hand for her to take. He neither blinked nor flinched. "You'll forgive me for ignoring them. You'd been stretching me across a psychic torture rack for what felt like aeons."

Neekra looked down at the offered hand.

"I've forgiven you for your tortures," Kane said, his voice grinding as it navigated over the meaning as if it were a jeep scraping jagged rocks with its undercarriage. "You want me to be that much stronger than you?"

Neekra stared at Kane for another moment, then raised her hand, shaking his.

"Did that feel so bad?" he asked.

Neekra shook her head, her mind swimming and off-balance. Though she no longer had the capacity to peer inside of his skull, she could judge a person's emotional states by tone, stance and expression. And even though Kane was still raw about the ordeal, from the telepathic testing she'd inflicted upon him, he genuinely was concerned with her well-being, both physically and emotionally.

He motioned for her to walk beside him, back toward the entrance of the tomb. The small structure had been shattered in the conflict with Neekra's doppelganger, the giantess's fantastic strength making the entrance into the ziggurat larger. Grant paced off the torn open entrance, frowning as he looked down the stairs.

"We can probably get the pickup truck through the new entrance that big beast tore in the top of the ziggurat," Grant said. "The thing is, the ramp as it spirals down doesn't look as if it would allow much maneuverability, if we don't get stuck outright."

Kane nodded.

Grant noticed that Neekra had joined him, and despite a flicker of discomfort, he nodded to her. "Welcome to the party."

"Thank you," Neekra responded. "The inside of the ziggurat is unknown to me, unfortunately. Enlil, in his separation of my mind and my body, was wise in not giving me a view of what lay behind the stone."

"Had you ever come close to this place?" Grant asked. "I'd assume over thousands of years you could have scoured every inch of this continent."

Neekra frowned. "I had some distractions over the mil-

lennia during my search. You know how it goes. Myths to
spawn, legends to give rise to."

Grant smirked. "The snark is strong in this one, young
Kane. She has learned well from you."

"I was trained by the best," Kane retorted.

Neekra smirked. The two of them were tired and nervous about the situation ahead of them, but the humor was
a means for them to recharge. As she went back over her
time spent inside Kane's mind, she examined his behav-
iors and usual thoughts. And she realized the veracity of
his offer of friendship and partnership. He hadn't trusted
her for what she had done to him, but Kane was both prag-
matic—Neekra was a powerful ally in both mind and body,
even without her "queen of the vampires" powers—and
willing to give second chances.

She saw in Kane a man who'd found his second chance
a half dozen years ago and had turned his back on an iron-
fisted dictatorship to fight for freedom and humanity.

The offer of truce and the concern for her was genuine.

"So, are you going to stay on our side?" Grant asked.

"For now," she answered. "Now that I'm going through
Kane's memories and motivations."

Grant and Kane shared a glance. Kane took it upon
himself to ask the major question here. "Are you able to
mentally contact anyone?"

Neekra tilted her head. "I'm blind. I am as an eagle
whose only means of movement is to grind the side of
her face against the ground to inch along, one eye forever
looking at dirt, the other toward empty sky."

She stepped closer to Kane and placed her hands on
either side of his face, staring into his eyes. "I want that
back. I want contact. Blind and limbless isn't half of what
I am feeling at this moment. If I could enter your mind,

that would be the greatest boon of my current, miserable existence."

She concentrated, exerting every ounce of her will, trying to get through to at least Kane. If anything, his mind had been altered, ever so slightly, by numerous psychic encounters over the years. And Neekra had been inside of Kane's head more than enough to realize that he was familiar with other realities, the concept of other planes of existence, other dimensions. He'd *been* to them.

Because of that, they had a common frame of reference. Because as she'd been inside of his mind, he'd seen what horrors she thought would break him. Despite whatever harm she'd wrought unto him, he still showed her a sliver of mercy, preventing Durga from harming her, putting her down for the count even though she was the one who'd constructed that Durga, as a test for him.

"So are we going to have sex? Or are you trying to wake up your telepathy?" Kane asked, looking at her.

Neekra smirked and released his face. "Trying to wake up. This is all a shitty dream, a dream where your eyes are taped almost shut, and cotton is stuffed into your ears."

Kane nodded. "Fair enough. I'd have felt a little uncomfortable stripping naked in front of Grant anyway."

Grant smirked. "I've seen him, and it's nothing really interesting."

Neekra smiled, and Kane feigned a scowl.

"Now that you kids are done making nice, can we get started?" Brigid asked. Neekra glanced at her, sensing a bit of annoyance in her words, but these were true impatience. From Kane's thoughts, he determined that she was anxious to see what secrets lay inside of the ziggurat. She too was a pragmatist, but she was also a seeker of knowledge. As great as the threat of Negari appeared inside of the deadly tomb, the chance to learn more mysteries of the

Annunaki's past and of their technology and culture was also a powerful draw for her.

Neekra knew that Brigid called herself, Grant and Kane the explorers of the alien-altered Earth, archaeologists of the unknown, seeking to solve the problems of the present by delving into the past. The battle against the Annunaki formed only part of their mission. Certainly, Brigid sought to free the world and humanity from the influence of the dangerous alien overlords, but she also wanted to return mankind to a state where it could continue and grow.

Kane and Grant both had much the same hopes and dreams, though Grant was content with the simple lifestyle of New Edo, where modern technology was present but subsumed behind the veneer of samurai culture.

Kane had not yet encountered Lyta when Neekra had been inside of his mind, so anything she knew of the girl was based on merely surface thoughts drawn from the others she'd imprisoned: Brigid, Grant, Nathan and Thurpa. Even so, those four had only just rescued her, meeting the former captive and rescuing her hours before. Her knowledge of Thurpa would have been equally threadbare if she'd only relied upon Kane's memories, but she'd spent time within Durga's psyche, as well.

Yes, the lad was a clone, artificially aged to near adulthood. His memories were constructs drawn from the fallen prince's own experiences, edited to keep the young man from realizing he was merely a copy of Durga. Unlike the other soldiers, who had been programmed with only the basics of discipline and how to fight, thanks to high-speed information dumps, Durga nurtured Thurpa into something akin to a son.

And the young man was smart and brave. It seemed as if Durga were replacing himself by rebuilding himself.

Thurpa was another chance to get himself "right." Almost as if he were apologizing for the past four decades, and change, of his life.

She wondered how much the others knew about the young man and his status as a mere copy. They showed care and concern for him; she'd observed that much during the battle, even as she was holding on for dear life.

She frowned, measuring the worth of offering up knowledge about Thurpa's origins. If she tried it, it could be interpreted as her attempt to shred the team, but if she opened that she knew Durga had removed multiple elements of his personality, that might not seem like sabotage.

But would they believe that information, especially out of her mouth?

Grant was now over by Thurpa, who was glaring hatefully toward Durga.

"What's wrong?" she asked.

"Hoping to glare enough daggers at 'Father' that he feels it," Thurpa replied.

"Oh. So you know…" Neekra began.

"And what do you know about it?" Grant asked.

"I know that Durga created you," Neekra answered. "And I know exactly what he left out of you as he was aging you to adulthood."

Thurpa blinked. "Left…out of me?"

"Out of your mind," Neekra said.

Thurpa glanced back toward Durga in the distance. "How do you know?"

"She was not only in my mind—she was in his, as well," Kane explained. "So, she has access to memories."

Thurpa took a step closer to her. His eyes lost their anger; she could feel the hope wafting off him, though it was nothing like her telepathy. She simply knew what was inside the boy.

"But we're still not going to be certain of that," Kane added quickly.

Neekra and Thurpa turned to him at the same time, confusion on both of their faces.

"Durga is a tricky son of a bitch," Grant added. "And you know all by yourself."

Thurpa turned to Neekra.

"He didn't do this to me on his own," Neekra answered. "You injured me, crippled me to the point where…"

She trailed off. Durga had gone to her side quickly and easily. And even in her last moments with him as he sprayed her in the eyes and gloated how his people were not helpless against the threats against Earth, she never realized.

Durga knew his venom was able to affect either her vampiric form or her Annunaki makeup, a body chemistry she unconsciously altered Gamal's form into to make her feel more at "home." Either way, when she was inside of Durga, she was completely unaware of whatever knowledge Durga had about her body's interaction with cobra or Nagah venom.

And the fallen prince was all too cannily aware of exactly what he could do.

Neekra trembled.

"Any information you got out of Durga's memory, in itself, could have been easily edited," Brigid stated.

"I didn't read that he could harm me with his spit," Neekra told her. "Nor did I realize that it was not just he himself."

"So, if you're operating on the presumption that you've delved into every one of Durga's secrets, just remember that this man had Enlil playing his games," Kane said.

Neekra frowned and turned back to Thurpa. He wasn't looking up at her anymore. His gaze was cast to the ground, and she could see his fingers knot into fists.

She grit her teeth. "Damn it. We're supposed to be enemies. I should be thinking of ways to get out of working alongside you."

"But you're now worrying about us," Grant concluded.

Neekra looked the big man in the eye. He was one of the few humans who could meet her gaze.

"We worked out plenty of anger and frustration onto you," Kane offered. "And you did likewise."

Neekra glared back toward Durga. "You are not the one who did this to me. He threw me at you, and for all my senses, my knowledge and skills, I slammed into you just as he expected me to. And he picked up my pieces, and did whatever he planned."

She frowned, then turned back to Kane and his allies. "He was able to locate me by tuning in on the prion-based transmissions from when I still had my telepathic powers. And using that, he was able to home in on this ziggurat. In a day, he was able to use my powers in a manner that I could not, despite trying for thousands of years."

She clenched her fists. "What is he?"

Kane shrugged. "He's somewhere down the line on our list of people to stop."

Brigid nodded in agreement. "But first on our list is Negari. Are you up for that?"

Neekra looked at the entrance that her former body had torn into the roof of the ancient structure. Negari had wooed her. But she wondered, did that kind of affection cross dozens of centuries?

Or would he see her as a threat now?

Worst, what if he simply disregarded her, as much as she lacked regard for humans over her long quest?

She was the ant now. An insignificant insect, no matter what she had been only a day ago.

Her anger toward Durga boiled.

And her distrust of Negari had planted in her mind, taking root immediately in her thoughts.

"Damn you, Durga," she growled.

"But damn us first," Kane added. "We're going to hell."

Neekra nodded. "Then it's Durga's turn."

Chapter 12

Seven people walked down the zigzag ramp, with Kane in the lead simply because his instincts were the keenest of the group. The man had developed what was called a pointman's instinct, an uncanny sensitivity to danger, which was not necessarily a preternatural acuity, but an observance of all of his senses combined. With his natural abilities amplified by the sensors in his shadow-suit hood, he was the best choice for the group's scout. He'd be able to pick up signs of traps or ambush sooner than the others.

Nathan Longa was right next to Kane, moving along to keep pace. He was holding Nehushtan; the ancient artifact had enhanced Nathan's strength in the past, more than sufficiently to defeat multiple several-hundred-pound winged predators.

Each of the members of this troop, four men and three women, was armed. Neekra, who'd chosen to wear only a loincloth and a load-bearing vest, had been given a spare pistol and automatic weapon from the back of the pickup truck. The pistol was in a holster on her bare hip, and the vest she wore had pouches for spare magazines and other sundries, including a first-aid kit. She gripped the borrowed rifle by the forearm furniture.

Neekra didn't look as if she needed the weapon, especially considering that her height and weight made her equal to Grant in most every way. Her Annunaki physiology was as close to godhood as a human being could conceive of. Even so, Neekra knew her limitations, and there were times when dealing with a threat from a distance was the wiser course of action. Half-handicapped, uncertain of what lay ahead, the group proceeded with caution.

They'd barely managed to survive the first of Negari's defenses through a combination of wits and brute force. Now, they had less room to maneuver, and they no longer had the bonus of dozens of armed drones at their backs.

"You don't think that we could head back to Garuda, pick up a small nuke and just leave it at the entrance, do you?" Thurpa offered as the group walked along.

Nathan turned back to Thurpa. Over the past week, the two young men had become good friends and had fought shoulder to shoulder. "That sounds like a good idea, but we're looking at something hidden inside all of this stone. I don't think that a nuclear blast short of a city-buster, or worse, an earth-shaker, could stop it."

Thurpa frowned. "There's that possibility." Then he turned toward Brigid for confirmation.

Brigid turned to meet Thurpa's gaze as they walked together. "Negari is a threat that Enlil not only sought to keep contained, but also cut off from the planet around him. I'm not certain that the depths of this structure are merely two miles by two miles. We could be looking at a tunnel leading down into a bubble in the basalt layer miles into the crust."

"A bubble...you mean a hidden underground world?" Thurpa asked.

"It would not be the first one we've encountered," Brigid returned.

Thurpa nodded. "Garuda was an entire city underground. But even that was not particularly deep."

"The cousins of the Nagah, the Watatsumi, had found a much larger realm along the Pacific Rim. It was not a natural cavity in the crust but purpose built by the Annun-aki. The light was provided by obsidian glass backlit with rivers of magma and lava. And the deeper you went into this bubble, the denser the concentration of oxygen was, enabling the survival of gigantic insects from the dawn of time. The oxygen levels were so dense that humans, even the Watatsumi, would suffer from blood poisoning, so they had to stay in a plateau."

Thurpa nodded. "What else lived at the bottom of that oxygen well?"

"An offshoot of the Igigi," Brigid answered. "They were psychic, akin to what Neekra had once been, but their powers were nowhere nearly as extensive. They could control minds, groups of animals and men, and thus created the Dragon Riders to keep the Watatsumi at bay."

"Telepaths?" Neekra asked. "The Ramah, correct?"

Brigid nodded. "Yes."

Neekra frowned. "Negari was a Ramah scientist. That was the name of their caste. They were experimenters in the Annunaki mind, always seeking the means of breaking the barriers in our brains to unlock new powers. Father, Enlil, did not like my dalliance with Negari at that time because the Ramah were of a controversial nature."

Thurpa tilted his head. "Romeo and Juliet? You and Enlil were the Capulets. Who were the Montagues?"

"Marduk," Neekra answered.

"Marduk's kid," Grant repeated. "Great."

"What is so good about that?" Neekra asked him.

"Just that he used to be Kane's and my boss," Grant said. "Lord Cobalt, when he was still trapped in the form of a Quad V Hybrid. We then had a knocking of heads later on. In Greece."

Neekra nodded. "He had formerly been known as Zeus in that region. Zeus or Jupiter, depending on the era."

"He looked to pick up where he left off a few thousand years ago," Grant said. "But we dealt with him."

"Permanently?" Neekra asked, hopeful.

"You didn't know that?" Grant asked. "Kane was there."

Neekra paused to think. Thurpa watched her. The Annunaki woman had a clue as to what he really was, what remained in his inner nature. He needed her for the sake of discovering if he was simply a clone, or if he were a bomb, waiting for some countdown between his ears to reach zero so that he could begin slaughtering the people he considered his friends.

"Kane buried many of his thoughts," Neekra stated. "But you mentioned the name Cobalt…"

Grant nodded.

"You fighting hand to hand with Cobalt on the bridge of a ship. It was more imagined. He was elsewhere, doing something else, setting charges," Neekra responded. "If Cobalt evolved into Marduk…"

"Kane's always been a stubborn sort," Brigid said. "He'd be saying Marduk out loud, but in his heart, it's always Cobalt, the man who gave him orders, the one who dropped the iron fist of the Magistrates in situations that Kane hated."

Neekra nodded. "I recall the satisfaction of his imagining Grant pummeling Marduk."

"It wasn't a pummeling. I just kept hitting him with everything I had. The shadow suit helped a little," Grant said. "In fact, the non-Newtonian fibers of the suit act as a good set of brass knuckles. Its hardening against impact protects your body, but it works both ways. I don't think Marduk would have noticed my punches if I'd gone at him barehanded. And worse, I'd have shattered every bone in my hand."

Neekra took a look at him. "I was surprised at your resilience in our conflict. I expected your skull to pop like a zit."

Grant's eyes narrowed. "As it was, I had to rely on the staff. You damn near killed me anyway."

Neekra took a deep breath.

Grant gave her a backhanded slap on the biceps. "We're on the same side for now. Truce."

Neekra looked down where he struck her. It was a good-natured whack, something of camaraderie. It also inferred that Grant thought of her as an equal. Even without the powers of the viral protein computer, which gave her the ability to simulate impossible levels of strength via telekinesis, he felt that she was someone he could gladly accept as an ally.

This was despite her nearly having killed him in one-on-one combat.

"Why?" Neekra asked.

Grant turned to her. "Why am I being so familiar? So accepting?"

Neekra nodded.

"Because I've been up against you. And I've fought beside you. You're brave and powerful. You're not a sniveling weakling who hides behind someone else," Grant said. "Sure, you resurrected corpses…"

"Can't do that anymore," Neekra admitted.

"No. But you leaped at that creature without a second thought," Grant added.

Neekra looked down. "I only did that because it was a living insult. I was furious at my father."

Grant nodded. "For now, you're on our side. And I want you at your best."

"Otherwise we're all dead," Neekra responded.

The group fell silent, Kane stopping their progress with a raised fist. It was the hand signal for them to stop, and they stood still, crouched, searching for the closest cover. There wasn't much; the hallway that they'd been following was smooth walled, no reinforcing buttresses at intervals. If a gunfight ensued, the Cerberus explorers and their allies would have nowhere to hide to avoid incoming fire.

Kane edged forward.

The interior of the ziggurat was lit from within. The lighting seemed to be an inlaid, living, glowing cable built into the spine of the corridor, burning brightly. On first appearance, it looked like a plastic line with regularly spaced small LED lights. However, Neekra was able to correct them. It was an organic carbon filament that burned from an external energy source. No one wanted to mention that the main power core was likely orichalcum, like the artifact that they brought with them. Orichalcum in its pure state was not only a powerful energy source, but in the instances where they had encountered it, it was also highly unstable, exploding on contact with sunlight.

Nehushtan's orichalcum core was protected from that instability by its unique black coating, meaning that Kane and his allies were safe from its detonating among them.

As such, there was no means of sliding through the shadows, not with a prominent, powerful light source above and no wall or ceiling features to intervene.

Kane glanced to Nathan and spoke in low tones, audible only with the presence of the earbud in the young African's headset. "Feel anything?"

Nathan looked to the staff. "I've got nothing. Why?"

"I'm just worried that the stick *wants* us to get to Negari," Kane stated. "Whether it's to help him or to destroy him, that's my major worry."

"We'll burn that bridge once we cross it," Nathan said. There was no need for night vision, so Kane and the others went sans hood. Neekra, without a shadow suit, didn't have to worry, though she too had the communications headset tuned to the Commtact frequencies, as provided by Durga.

On the zigzag ramp, they were still halfway to the next flight. Whatever had keyed Kane's instincts was below them, seventy feet away. They could see most of the flight, but a section of the landing and the ramp leading down from there were still hidden.

For all they knew, they could have had a carpet of writhing, flesh-eating scarabs awaiting their arrival.

"What did you hear?" Nathan murmured.

"It's something like static," Kane said. "A white noise of some sort."

"So how do we handle this?" Nathan asked.

"Grant," Kane called.

The big man moved to Kane's position. As he did so, he brought his bow out, nocking an arrow against the string. "Noisemaker arrow?"

"It'll draw something out," Kane said, reaching into one of his pouches and retrieving a small flat piece of putty. He wrapped it around the arrow just under the broadhead. It wasn't much of an explosive, despite being C-4. However, when it detonated, it would produce a loud enough crash to hopefully spur an enemy into reaction.

With a small-impact cap speared on the tip of the arrow, replacing the razor-sharp, vaned point, Grant drew back on the bow and took aim at the section of ramp just to the right of where the threat Kane had detected would be hidden. Taking a breath, Grant focused and let fly with the arrow. Despite the minor destabilizing weight of the putty wound about the tip, Grant's shot was true, striking the ramp just below where it met the flight.

The crack was loud and violent, cutting through the ominous quiet that had fallen over the explorers.

As soon as the arrow detonated, there was a sudden

rise in sound, and Nathan could hear the rise in the static Kane had detected.

Nathan gripped the staff tighter, his muscles tensing.

"Grens!" Kane bellowed, reaching onto his harness.

That's when Nathan saw the first of the creatures coming around the corner. Clutching Nehushtan, he felt a surge of adrenaline, heat and energy rushing through his arms, coming straight from the juju staff.

The creature he glimpsed, seeming to move in slow motion thanks to the sudden acceleration of his senses by the artifact, was an abomination. It was a collection of charcoal-gray shells, like tin cans assembled into long spindly limbs, each tipped with pairs of claws. The center was more like old paint buckets in diameter. Though it was seemingly insectoid, it had only two arms and two stalks, which it strode upon. It seemed like it was seven feet in height, and each of the segments bounced and jostled against the others.

Nathan tried to reconcile the solidity of the thing, but those canisters were bouncing against each other as if they were linked by a bungee, though there was no sign of the things actually being connected to each other by anything more than their proximity.

The creature's impossibility was matched only by its jerky moments. Whatever motivated those limbs were not of muscle and sinew, nor gears and hydraulics. Nathan could see daylight between the segments as they moved, even between parts that seemed as straight and solid in their formation as the arms on either side of the "elbow balls."

What was most unnerving about the appearance of this creature was not that it was made up of floating pieces that defied gravity, but that its "face" was a cavity cut into one of the paint gallon cans, a black abyss of nothingness in which hovered two burning red eyes. The eyes without a face focused on him, almost as if they were laser emitters, painting him, targeting him.

Indeed, as soon as those baleful eyes caught him in their crimson fury, the insect-like thing sped up and took longer strides. Snapping crab-like pincers at the end of its spindly arms began clicking faster, and Nathan realized, because of his heightened awareness transmitted to him through the ancient artifact, that they must have been cycling as fast as electric-powered grass clippers.

That was the static sound, those pincers opening and closing, razor-honed edges crisscrossing, the flats of those blades grinding against each other. The edges were not smooth, either; they were scalloped, serrated, designed for rapid, devastating perforation and slashing of flesh. Nathan raised the bottom of his staff, the black-coated sharp point aiming at the charging monstrosity. He wasn't certain that there was anything to stab, but he was not going to fall without a fight. He braced, muscles tensing as Kane's arm reached the apex of its throw, elbow snapped straight, wrist bending as he applied spin to the grenade he hurled.

The handheld bomb tumbled through the air, spiraling toward the strange, metallic, insectoid guardian. The creature's right "arm" rose to greet the oncoming munition, the chomping claw returning to a blur in Nathan's awareness. Those scalloped edges caught the grenade in midair, holding it for a moment. Nathan prayed for the thing to detonate, but then it broke in half, its metal shell cracking and coming apart.

The fuse burned down and there was a minor crack as the initial charge detonated the explosive core still adhered to it, but instead of erupting with an earth-shaking roar, the blast served merely to launch the severed half of the grenade off like a rocket. The explosive force no longer utilized all of the accelerant in the core of the grenade, and there was an avenue for the pressure to escape, rather than shattering the metal shell and roll of notched wire outward in waves of concussive energy.

"Damn," Nathan heard Kane growl even as the Sin Eater rose, snapping into his hand.

Two then four more of the creatures came out onto the landing, so the odds were not quite even, but the Cerberus warriors had very little in the way of a numbers advantage. Seven to five was not good odds, especially against these things, which had the power to cut a grenade in half with one claw.

Kane had his hand out, slowing Nathan's advance toward the emerging quintet of guardians, his machine pistol at the end of his long arm barking, blasting, sending bullets down toward the canister monsters. The metal shells of the creatures sang as Kane's fire ricocheted off of their curved surfaces.

Nathan watched as one of the body segments of the first inhuman thing was swatted out of the column of the rest of its body. Now he was certain that there was not a speck of flesh, cartilage or bone connecting the canisters that made up the bodies of these things. The burning eyes of the thing glanced down, twin red beams sizzling along the surface of its metal shells, looking at the empty air where one of its segments once was. It turned the laser-beam gaze toward the fallen part, and the object rose, and though dented with smoke trailing from where Kane's gunshot had struck it with enough force to dislodge it, the monstrosity pulled that canister back into line with the rest of its "torso."

"Fascinating, these appear to be some form of hive entity," Brigid's voice came over the Commtact, her brilliant mind already analyzing, bringing the horrific magic of these abominations into the realm of scientific reality. "They each levitate by means of magnetic propulsion, which is also how they appear to maintain cohesion of their separate elements."

"Great," Grant grumbled over the link. "How do we kill 'em?"

"Keep shooting," Brigid ordered.

And suddenly, all six of Nathan's companions opened up, their automatic weapons snarling and crackling, sheets of bullets scything across the fifty feet of space between humans and Neekra, and the metallic horrors. Bullets pinged on their armored segments, and now even more of the canisters were whipped away from each other.

The five guardians were slowed by the onslaught of copper and lead hammering down onto them, but Nathan could see that each of them was able to make a single step up the ramp. It was a slow, ponderous stride, as if a flood washed down a hillside, threatening to knock them off their feet. Nathan also realized that he'd released Nehushtan with one hand and filled it with his .45 automatic. He cranked the trigger, adding to the combined fire of the raiders of the ziggurat.

"They're not slowing down," Kane grumbled as he reloaded his Sin Eater. "New tactic."

And with that, the former Magistrate pulled his grenade. Rather than throwing it at a level where the insectoid entity could snatch it and disarm it by crushing its detonating fuse, Kane rolled it, an underhanded lob that sent the explosive package bouncing on the ramp, picking up speed from the already powerful toss as gravity tugged it down to the flight where the metal monsters attempted to advance.

This time, Nathan could see the grenade shift its course, drawn in to its target by the magnetic forces that Brigid mentioned. He sent a silent prayer along with the grenade, hoping that it could blow up before the creature neutralized it.

The grenade stopped, clanging against the "shin" of the red-eyed terror, then adhering to the limb as if it had been glued there. The creature reached down for the new attachment, and as it did so, the explosive detonated.

A flash of light, with a roar of thunder hot on its heels, rocked the very air around the Cerberus expedition. When the explosion passed, smoke billowing and thinning from the smashing blast, they saw that three of their new, claw-handed opponents were strewed about the landing, torn asunder into their component canisters.

Lyta let loose a premature shout of "Yes!" as the ziggurat's intruders observed the metallic guardians.

That momentary cheer's energy dissipated as body segments began to quiver, bouncing and rolling toward two piles. Canisters, despite being bent and scarred, took to the air, twisting and locking their magnetic fields to arrange themselves in their former shapes.

The third of the creatures was also reassembled, but all that was left was its torso, one arm and that same empty void of a "face," laser spotlights bathing Nathan in their hellish glow.

Destroying these monsters was not going to be as swift or simple as deploying sufficient explosives.

Chapter 13

After two grenades and nearly two hundred bullets fired at them in a flurry of automatic gunfire, the five metallic, insect-like creatures—in reality, metal components held together by a fantastic magnetic force—had been reduced to four "healthy" but scuffed guardians, and one of the monstrosities left as a torso and a single working arm. Here, on the scissoring ramp that wound its way into the depths of an ancient ziggurat prison, Kane and his allies were fifty feet from a new iteration of the tomb-prison's defense systems. Whether the monsters before them were living creatures or some form of magnetically powered automaton was as yet unknown to the Cerberus expedition, though their lethal intent and relative invulnerability was plain as day.

Kane reloaded his mostly spent magazine from the Sin Eater, watching as the metal hive beings regrouped. The creatures hadn't been made to bleed, but one had been shorn of three of its limbs, and scuffs and scars were visible on the segments of their multiorganism bodies.

So far, he and his allies learned that these things were not invulnerable, but they would need a tremendous amount of explosives against them. And as the creatures climbed, tentatively, up the ramp toward them, the ability to use grenades would diminish with their proximity. The same blasts that were most effective against the slender-limbed robot monsters would do as much harm to themselves.

Kane had been leading the offensive against these creatures, and he realized that their artillery options had gone downhill. He reached for the knife in its leg sheath and then noticed a blur of motion shooting down from their group.

"Think of something," Neekra hissed over their shared communications line. She was one of the hurtling figures bursting into action. The other attacker was Nathan, wielding the ancient juju staff and charging with it as if it were a spear. The two of them moved with a swiftness that stunned even Kane's expectations.

Then again, the Annunaki were an alien species, gifted with physical attributes and technology that had made them seem godlike in comparison to the human race. Those who could last against an Annunaki in single combat required similar technology, superior tactics—which Kane took to mean cheap shots at vulnerable parts—and incredible prowess of their own. Kane and Grant were two humans who had engaged the overlords, Enlil and Marduk to be exact, in single combat. Neekra had that same strength, that same savage endurance that had carried her through single combat with her own hideously mutated doppelganger.

Nathan himself was not one who seemed particularly more gifted in might and stamina than Kane or Grant; indeed, he was a couple of inches shorter and fifty pounds lighter than Kane. However, his clan had been in possession, off and on, of the orichalcum-cored artifact Nehushtan for centuries. With the staff at his side, Nathan had survived against impossible foes who could smash down steel doors with their powerful knuckles. Kane had exhibited great strength when using the staff, as well, so when it came down to it, the two of them were the most likely to survive the longest in close combat with the deadly clawed monstrosities.

"Think of something," Neekra had ordered. And already, Kane pulled his mind away from worrying about the health and safety of the two battlers and applied what he knew about them.

"Brainstorm," Kane grunted. "You said they're magnetic. What can stop magnetism?"

"Something that alters the polarity of the magnet," Brigid spoke up. "Which generally means a lightning strike or a powerful magnet."

"Lightning?" Kane asked. He looked down at his harness. He had a faint memory of being given someone's "lightning in a bottle" as part of his kit. This was one of those times when he wished he possessed the photographic memory of Brigid Baptiste. The woman would have known instantly what she needed, thanks to her ability to recall every detail she'd ever been exposed to.

Kane knew immediately who had given him the "lightning in a bottle"—Sela Sinclair, a "freezie" Air Force officer who'd had extensive military police training. One of the things she'd brought to the Cerberus crew was an appreciation for less-lethal force options, such as the high-intensity LED flashlights, which proved capable of blinding and stopping an opponent without causing them harm. No flashlight, however powerful, was going to do significant enough damage to slow down these insectoid creatures, especially given their own inner fire as represented by their red, blazing eyes.

Because those orbs were most likely not part of anything biological, it was unlikely the second bit of nonlethal kit he'd inherited from Sinclair—capsicum spray—would have an effect on it, either. That left the last of the less lethal options—the Taser. Although both of the prior options would make someone feel as if they were struck in the face by lightning, the Taser actually utilized powerful electric current to stun and incapacitate a hostile opponent.

"Will this produce sufficient voltage to demagnetize one of those creatures?" Kane asked, finally drawing it from his belt.

Behind him, he heard the swish and rush of limbs slicing through the air while Neekra and Nathan engaged in hand-to-hand combat with the horrific guardians. With each second spent seeking answers, they were closer to dying.

NEEKRA KNEW THAT for the assembled explorers to have any kind of a chance, she was going to have to hurtle into the enemy group. She felt a twinge of hope as Nathan seemed to be keeping up with her, but she still was counting on Kane, Brigid and Grant to come up with some manner of equalizer. The numbers were still five to two on this front line, and Neekra had little idea of what kind of strength they possessed. It was one thing to cut a hand grenade in half with a set of claws, but Neekra was instants away from finding out exactly what they could do.

Before she was two strides from the group, she kicked herself into the air, powerful legs lifting her 240 pounds of lean, alien muscle five feet from the ramp, giving her more than sufficient momentum to wheel in a rotation that allowed her to go from curled into a ball to snapping to full height, legs rocketing forward like pistons parallel to the ground. Her weight, strength and momentum struck the first of the insect-like guardians in its upper chest, striking it with enough force to shoot the segment off of its body, allowing its head and arms to topple to the ground helplessly. The canister she kicked clanged off the stone wall of the zigzag ramp way, signifying that it was likely hollow.

Neekra's flight through the air carried her past the other three, an extended arm unintentionally striking one of them across the "face" and knocking its head clear from its shoulders with the deadly efficiency of a guillotine. Even so, Neekra knew that taking the heads and parts of these things was no guarantee of actually stopping the guardians. She'd seen them draw together severed, separated segments of their body and re-form.

However, as she landed in a crouch, legs bending beneath her to absorb the energy of her fall, she knew that at least she was doing something to stop these creatures. Or at least slow them down.

She whirled, remaining crouched, her almost-naked form coiled up with all the potential energy of an iron spring. A third of the horrors swung, its chattering saw-toothed claw slicing through the air over her head, committed to striking her, even though she'd ducked beneath its swing several milliseconds ago. These things had swift reflexes because she could feel the rush of air from that claw's near passage. It'd adjusted its "punch" to trail her, and it was inches from the back of her bowed head.

She waited for the thing's momentum and follow-through to continue past when she surged straight, bringing up both fists in a double-uppercut. Neekra's knuckles split against the iron canister that made up this thing's head, and she felt a brief wave of satisfaction at decapitating another of the oddly animated sentries. The thing in front of her twisted away, chasing after its flying head.

As she relaxed, drawing back down to a standing ready position, she caught movement out of the corner of her eye. She realized that it was one of the spindle-limbed horrors coming after her and despite her swiftness, there was no way she could whirl and respond to its attack in time. Neekra braced, hoping that her alien skin and anatomy had been enough to withstand the initial attack.

The attacker that would have blindsided her, however, burst into pieces with a lunging slash. As she turned to face the blow, she saw Nathan out of the corner of her eye. She'd gone through the sentries in the space of moments and in doing so, had turned their attention away from him. The young man was not spending his time idly. He'd been a few footsteps behind her, and now he was in twirling action. Where Neekra had been a living bullet slicing through the ranks of these alien guardians, Nathan used the reach of Nehushtan to his advantage, acting like a lawn mower. The black-coated orichalcum staff smashed through the still standing remnants of the stunned and disorganized monstrosities.

The speed of the flashing staff was impressive even to the Annunaki woman. Nathan was a tornado of action, and she could see the dents made in the armored segments. His savage slashes and blows scattered the magnetically aligned body parts across the landing, the two people's attack having driven them back down the ramp. Neekra spotted one of the things' heads and lunged for it, hoping to get a better look at it.

Within the space of a heartbeat, Neekra found out that was a grave mistake as those free-floating red balls of fire flared with life anew, blazing and searing her eyes with brilliant, blinding agony. Suddenly, Neekra was even more blinded than she felt. What was worse was that the world she saw was a brilliant crimson explosion, a huge wall of color that floated in her seared corneas. The shock had been more than sufficient for her to release the headpiece. She stumbled, looking to regain her footing, then screamed out in pain as something lashed hot and wet across her calf.

Neekra lost her footing and collapsed to the ground. Things had been moving slower now, her head swimming as she dealt with the slice on her leg and her sudden blindness.

She felt motion near her, the breeze whipped up by Nathan and his staff as he rushed to her side. She heard a clang of metal being punctured, undoubtedly the young man using Nehushtan as a lance to spear through a marauder. Neekra realized that the attack had come from the "wounded" sentry robot, the one that had been dragging itself along with only one claw.

"Are you okay?" Nathan asked.

"Can't see," Neekra replied.

"You're bleeding," Nathan said.

Neekra sneered and struggled back to her feet, even grunting a "thank you" under her breath as she felt Nathan's guiding hand. "It's far from my heart."

"Can you put weight on it?" Nathan asked.

Neekra was about to answer when she heard the clang of metal legs taking long strides toward her. "Duck!"

With a sweep of her arm, she tugged Nathan out of the path of whatever was coming at them, and she raised her other forearm to stave off any slash at her. Neekra wasn't disappointed by her opponents. Fortunately, those buzzing claws aimed closer at her torso and head. Her forearm block broke apart the slender magnetic segments of the creature's arm, sending the whirring chopper sailing past her shoulder.

Nathan swung around her, whipping his staff out in an attack. Neekra realized that her ears and skin picked up Nathan's actions as efficiently as any of her other senses. Her brain, robbed of its extrasensory gifts, latched onto any external stimulus, allowing her a greater acuity to navigate this brutal battleground.

Even as all of this was going on, she was counting the moments since the fight started. She was hoping that the Cerberus warriors could figure some strategy to grant her reprieve, and she realized that it'd only taken seven seconds to reach this point. She and Nathan had been accelerated so that even their speech was cut low.

How Kane would be able to take on creatures with such speed of motion as these was going to border on a miracle. That's when she heard the impact of a body against metal.

BRIGID BAPTISTE'S MIND was blazing in the wake of Kane's question about his Taser, a small handheld air gun that launched two tines from a cartridge and delivered a jolt of electricity designed to disrupt the nervous system of a target with minimal harm. Numbers tumbled through her mind as she recalled the information on the less lethal weapon.

The initial voltage of a Taser charge is 50,000 volts of electricity, but that was simply to establish a current along the target's skin. Afterward, the voltage dropped down to a mere 1,200 volts of charge, which pulsed at 19 pulses per second. Due to the galvanic conductivity of human skin and the linkage of the nervous system to neurons in the epidermis, the initial charge was more than sufficient to render a person paralyzed. The high rate of low-voltage pulses incited neuromuscular spasms that paralyzed the target.

The real measure of paralytic energy came from amperes, which was the rate by which electric charges traveled through a fixed point. Delving deeper into her photographic memory, she recalled that the amperage of Kane's handheld Taser unit was 0.35 amps, more than three times the threshold of the human body's capacity to maintain muscular control. At that point, the spasms incapacitated the subject hit. The reason for the pulses was to break up the current, as 0.1 amperes was sufficient to cause cardiac arrest.

"Here," Brigid said. Kane handed the Taser over, and Brigid attempted to put aside the sounds of conflict on the ramp below.

Sifting through her thoughts as fast as she could, she remembered that there was a mode not utilized for subject paralysis. It was called "Drive Stun," which was a pain compliance mode. The two tines did not launch to create a body circuit, but rather created a circuit from Taser to skin and back, the prongs stabbing flesh like miniature fangs. This would cause a localized shock and had been a reason for some law enforcement watchdog agencies to decry their use. The Drive Stun was a contact use, akin to the so-called "stun guns," which also produced a localized burn.

Again, the Drive Stun was simply lethal against humans over a long term, along the span of minutes or multiple Taser devices. Would that be effective in disrupting the creatures? Brigid scanned down the ramp, pushing aside her awe at the speed and ferocity of the melee. She saw the open "faces" of these entities and made a quick judgment call.

"Jam it in the face hole," Brigid said. "Pull the trigger and don't stop."

Kane looked at her with wide eyes but only for a moment. He whirled and raced down the ramp, kicking out his feet ahead of him and turning the incline into a slide. The creatures circled around Nathan and Neekra, who looked confused. He hoped that they would be able to hold out for the moments it took for them to reach the scene of this battle.

He steered his downward skid toward one of the insect-like assemblies of parts, then dug in his heels and bounded into the air, coming down just behind one of the sentries closing in on the side-by-side Nathan and Neekra. Kane crashed into the thing's back, letting its shoulders support his weight. Interestingly, the whole structure of the creature buckled under Kane's mass. He wrapped an arm around its "neck," holding the head still just long enough to jam the Taser into the open face of the magnetic creature.

Kane squeezed the trigger, holding the head tightly; seemingly instantly, the magnetized segments fell away from him, clanking and clamoring on the ground. Kane looked at the pieces, seeing if they exhibited any sign of recovery, not wanting to give up his advantage over the metallic monster prematurely.

A second of the things turned, noticed the distress of its ally and took a step toward him. Kane grimaced. Though he was holding on to the head of one foe, pumping electrical charge into its face, he could feel the canister twisting against his grasp. There was no possible way that Kane could defend himself from the other entity without releasing the still fighting "skull."

A hiss of air preceded the disappearance of the second sentry's headpiece, and the body whirled about, chasing after the severed segment, now pinioned on the shaft of one of Grant's arrows.

That decapitation and the sound of Kane's struggles caught the attention of the other two, distracting them for the last moment of his opponent's fighting. Then the head felt weightless in his grip.

"They chase after their heads!" Neekra shouted.

"We learned that," Grant stated over the Commtact communication network.

The Annunaki woman reached out and grasped another of the entities' heads and pulled. This time the insect-style automaton spun and wrapped its spindle limbs around the stolen body part.

Grant fired another arrow that punctured the head of the thing on the ground, pinning it to the landing.

The seemingly invulnerable guardians quickly showed how relatively fragile they were. Against conventional firearms, and presumably against ASP blasters, they showed considerable toughness.

Even so, Kane's arms burned with exhaustion from his attempts to keep the animated head canister from escaping its electric torture.

The thing on the ground summoned its head back to its "neck" and pushed up on its lone remaining arm. With a sudden jerk, the stilled parts of the one that Kane put down with the Taser raced off as if summoned to it, returning it to full strength with three arms and two good legs. Its glowing red eyes burned on either side of the arrow shaft that Grant had put there. It reached up with its "spare" arm and snipped the arrow off, removing the fletching from its line of sight.

"That's inconvenient," Kane grumbled.

A shotgun thundered to Kane's left, the crash of its muzzle blast jolting his attention toward Thurpa, who'd borrowed the weapon from Grant. The shotgun at a range of a few yards sent the creature's head flying off its shoulders, once more inconveniencing the guard.

Nathan moved swiftly, stabbing with Nehushtan into the fallen segment's faceplate. As soon as the pointed bottom of the staff struck the creature's "face" the blazing red eyes sprayed out a sheet of red fire. The glow was harsh enough to make Kane flinch from its brilliance. While he thought it was a defense mechanism akin to the one that struck Neekra in the face, this flare was accompanied by a squeal of steel grinding on steel.

It was a death cry, and as far as Kane knew, two of the

insect-like guardians were dead and fallen. The headless body collapsed, crumbling into its component canisters.

Neekra flew through the air and bowled Thurpa over. Kane stooped and grabbed the fallen shotgun, hoping there was enough ammunition in it to take out the head of the third of these things. Kane took a few strides, seeing that only two of the horrors were clambering down the ramp, fleeing as quickly as their spindle limbs could carry them. They displayed uncanny swiftness and Kane had no illusion that he could run them down. Even if he did, he would be alone against creatures who were, for all intents and purposes, unstoppable. He'd drained his Taser killing one.

Grant stepped up beside him gripping an implode grenade in one big mitt. "Now we can blow those two up."

With that, the enormous ex-Mag hurled the hand-bomb with every ounce of strength and skill he could muster. The grenade spiraled through the air, arcing down toward the galloping insectoids before detonation. The flash and thunderclap that ensued sent parts scattering.

"Together, we'll see what's left," Grant offered.

Kane nodded. As usual, he led the way, shotgun in hand.

Chapter 14

Grant and Kane approached the scattered remains of the last two sentries, moving fairly swiftly yet cautiously, weapons drawn and ready to deal with any segments that still remained "conscious."

Grant handed Kane several shells to use to reload the shotgun he'd picked up. "Don't stand too close with these babies."

Kane glanced back. "Explosive?"

Grant nodded. "And in case you're asking why I didn't use it before…"

"Those things were too close to Nathan and Neekra to fire without injuring them," Kane replied.

Grant smirked. "Smart-ass."

"I learned from the best," Kane said.

"Thanks," Grant answered.

Kane chuckled. "I meant Brigid."

"Don't you two ever rest?" Nathan asked, jogging up to them.

"This ass grabbing is our rest," Grant answered. He noted that the young man had his staff in hand. The artifact had more than proved its worth as it impaled and ended the existence of two of the enemy. Grant felt a little more relaxed having it on his side, but he wasn't going to let his guard down. Two wounded guards might be down there, or the fleeing entities might have been leading them into the jaws of a horde of their brethren.

Those guardians might also have been unharmed, especially because it seemed that their heads needed an expenditure of energy to neutralize, as with Kane and the Taser or Nathan with Nehushtan's inner fire. Grant had managed to take off their heads with his bow and arrow, distracting them and forcing them to chase after their lost parts, but if there had been an army waiting around the next turn, it was going to be a close, brutal melee, and one he might not be up to.

Kane slowed, scanning the scene. He'd pulled on his hood, utilizing its advanced optics to study them from afar. Grant and Nathan took that as a good idea, both of them suiting all the way up.

So far, the metallic sentries had attacked with physical means: claws and the occasional brilliant flash of laser light into the eyes. If they had been simply constructs of magnetic energy, there was nothing keeping them from countering humans with things such as nerve gas or other poisonous clouds. Grant had an arrow nocked, ready to pin down a creature's head for either Kane or Nathan to put it completely out of business.

Grant zoomed in on the two skittering creatures. One of them had lost its left arm and leg, those pieces obliterated by the detonation of the implode gren. The other was missing its right arm but was "together" enough to look back over its stump of a shoulder to see the three humans advancing down the ramp. Grant drew the string back to full tension and cut loose with his arrow, the broadhead punching between those burning red orbs.

The canister sailed off its shoulders, the crimson eyes sparkling as the arrow spiraled, then struck the wall. It was just another sign of how durable the stone of this ziggurat truly was as the broadhead merely bounced off it. The thing struck the ground with a clang, and its body chased after its lost noggin. If these things hadn't shown themselves to be bulletproof, murder-minded killers, Grant would have laughed at the ludicrous creature.

Kane shouldered the shotgun and punched a FRAG-12 round into the head of the other thing. The blast was loud, flashing brightly enough to momentarily extinguish the glowing, molten glare of the sentry. As the flash died away, the red eyes flared again, burning their way through the smoke of the explosion's aftermath. Grant noted that the lips of the face had been peeled away even more, though the darkness still formed an ersatz head in the middle of the metallic helmet.

The entity, despite only having one leg, suddenly began to gallop up the ramp, using its arm as another leg. Balanced on the two limbs like some nightmarish bicycle, the sentry rushed forward, its red glare blazing like the hot blood it wished to spill. Kane fired a second of the miniature grenade rounds at the thing, but this time the monstrosity veered, dodging the hasty follow-up shot.

In an instant, Nathan rushed to intercept the attacking creature.

The young man's speed was blinding, but Grant was still able to follow the movement, even as he nocked yet another arrow. The blackened artifact whipped and slashed, but the sentry had regained its standing state, balancing on its single leg and parrying any attack with which Nathan struck out. Grant cleared his throat, the Commtact carrying the sound and getting Nathan's attention quickly enough for the young warrior to step out of the archer's way.

With a loud "thwack" the arrow punched into the head of this particular monstrosity. Unfortunately, this time the sentry was swift enough to reach out and catch its own head as it rocketed away from its shoulders on the shaft.

Nathan swept the staff across the trunk of the insectoid,

but the segments kicked apart, the top half of the thing hopping over the slashing artifact.

Kane cut loose with the shotgun. The other creature had seemingly abandoned its head and was returning to the fray. FRAG-12 rounds detonated against its metal skin, but they didn't have the same explosive force as the implode grenade that had claimed the thing's other arm.

Grant turned back, looking for the other thing's head, then realized that the creature had set it down so that it could look up the ramp, observing the battle while keeping itself distant from those who realized that it could detach body parts. He nocked up another shaft and took aim at the thing, but the one-armed sentry lunged uphill, wading through explosive blasts from Kane's shotgun.

"Kane, stop!" Grant growled, but by the time he uttered those words, Kane was blocking a slash from the thing's saw-toothed claw with the frame of his weapon. Metal rang as the claw slashed at Kane's shotgun. Kane responded by twisting, letting his foe grab the firearm first by pushing it upon him. The shove forced the creature to stumble back a step, and Kane took that instant to drop to the ground and kick at where the knees would have been on an unsegmented set of limbs.

The creature found itself upset at the sudden disruption of its legs, giving Grant more than enough of an opportunity to pull the machete from his belt and bring it down against its cylindrical torso, slicing at an angle. The blade bit into one of the canisters making up the thing's trunk, but the metal of those segments was simply too thick and tough even for Grant and the machete.

Even so, the blow knocked the thing aside, and Grant came away with the equivalent of a lumbar vertebra, an entire section of muscle, a quarter of the entity's torso. The piece stuck to the machete was enough to make the already unsteady magnetic assembly of metal topple. The eyes of the horror in the distance burned brighter, flashing as it tried to sweep Grant's face. The shadow-suit face-plate, however, instantly reacted to the harsh blaze of laser fury, polarizing and shielding Grant from an otherwise blinding burst.

Nathan struck home with Nehushtan, impaling the "skull" of his opponent. The resultant death shriek and flash of dying agony caused the last of the guardians to pull back. Grant suddenly found himself in a tug of war with his machete, grabbing on now with both hands.

Even with all of his weight, strength and leverage, the magnetic force tugging on the errant body part was simply too much for the Cerberus explorer.

"Let it go!" Kane snapped.

Grant opened his hands, freeing the machete from his grasp. The torso piece hurled back toward the sitting head, glaring at them with its blood-red firefly eyes.

As he did so, Grant saw movement from Kane in his peripheral vision. This time his blood brother drew another grenade and hurled it with a near-perfect snap of the wrist and arm. Drilling through the air, it spiraled to its target with lazy grace. The handheld artillery struck the downed head of the metallic sentry and landed right in the slot where those insane eyes blazed.

Grant turned and covered his head, more out of reflex than actual necessity. Even though the shadow suit wasn't the best at resisting cutting attacks, the shrapnel put out by an implode grenade was negligent thanks to the nature of the blast. The bulk of the traumatic damage was the result of a sudden inrush of air, creating the tooth-jarring thunderclap associated with the deadly explosive. The initial burst was actually itself a two-part blast, first being the spreading of a cloud of highly flammable material into the air, then igniting that cloud. The flash of fire was such that it vaporized air and created a vacuum.

No shards of metal escaped a small area; no razor-notched wire or pieces of shell flew at the three members of the expedition.

When Grant looked up, he saw a black smear, the starburst of scorched stone on the wall where the guard's head rested and the bomb detonated.

Grant took a deep breath and held it, peeling his ears.

Kane also listened.

"I didn't hear that thing's death cry," Nathan murmured, low, himself seeking the telltale "chatter" of the insectoid claws scissoring open and shut.

Grant looked up the ramp and saw the others coming down with them. Thurpa and Neekra looked all right for their collision. Brigid and Lyta advanced, weapons ready but aimed at the floor, in case a bump caused them to accidentally trigger a shot.

Kane advanced down farther. The shotgun was a bent, mangled hunk of useless metal now, destroyed by the power of the creatures' claws.

They'd survived a battle with five of these strange entities. However, Grant realized that the struggle had taken nearly every trick in their combined bag. If they met any more, they would be overwhelmed. Staking them one at a time with the legendary biblical staff was not going to be sufficient in the next round of combat.

"Nothing," Kane stated. "No more in sight."

Grant let out his breath. He nodded toward the artifact that had been wielded by Moses and King Solomon. "Thank God."

"I hope that's enough," Nathan stated. He looked at Nehushtan.

He started to look wobbly on his knees, and Grant lunged, catching the young man.

"Too much…" Nathan whispered. "It's a great high when you're all superpowered…"

"But it takes it straight from your tank," Grant concluded. "This is the longest you appear to have utilized it."

Brigid caught up with the group and took off Nathan's hood. "Look into the flashlight for me."

Nathan nodded, acquiescing to her demands.

Brigid realized that this was not a time for any of the seven members of this expedition to collapse from exhaustion. No matter how much the artifact boosted his abilities, the reserves of strength tapped into by the staff still took their toll on his muscles and nervous system. The kind of neurological and biochemical mayhem it wrought in his body could be catastrophic over the long run.

Neekra arrived and picked up one of the metal husks that had made up the odd creatures that they had battled. "I know it's been a long time since I was among Annunaki society, but this kind of thing is right out of left field. If you have questions for me, I'm clueless."

Grant frowned, pulling his hood back, pocketing the faceplate. "How is your leg?"

Neekra glanced at him for a moment, then looked down at her calf. The skin puckered around the wound, and blood no longer seeped down her crimson scales. "I'll live."

Grant grimaced. "We need to make sure she doesn't get an infection."

Neekra glared at him. "The day this world can produce a microbe that can threaten my metabolism is the day I'll gladly lose a limb to gangrene."

"Who is to say this world produces any microbes present inside the ziggurat?" Grant asked. "Enlil didn't want anyone entering this place, and he's not the kind of guy who puts up one or two lines of defense and leaves it at that."

Neekra was about to protest but thought about it. "Good point. But what is to protect you?"

"The fact that these things were obviously meant to overwhelm any of us hairless apes," Kane answered. "He'd spare infectious diseases for Annunaki. Especially ones who were too cocky to come in with a lick of clothing."

Neekra glanced down at herself. She wrinkled her nose, and despite looking like a skinned goddess, Grant could see a level of humanity and beauty in her. "Either way, I do not believe you possess sufficient antiseptics to deal with Enlil's safeguards."

Grant nodded. "Your funeral. I was just trying to help."

"And I appreciate that," Neekra returned.

Grant moved to Kane's side, deactivating his Commtact so that they could speak in quiet. "I think she might be a little too agreeable."

Kane had also turned off his implant the moment he saw Grant do the same. No use in alienating Neekra any further. "Well, Durga told us he gave her a new body."

"So?" Grant asked.

Kane shook his head. "She does feel different to me. Maybe while she was out, he put some posthypnotic suggestions in her brain, especially as he was transferring it."

"With the same equipment that trained his clone troops?" Grant asked.

"And gave Thurpa the illusion of a full life," Kane added, his voice low. As the words came out, each syllable hurt his friend even more.

Grant grimaced. "So, not only do we have one potential time bomb...we have two."

"Why bother with a human, even one with cobra venom?" Kane asked. "He might get one or two of us..."

"And that's all he'd really need. You think you'd be at the top of your game if Brigid and I died?" Grant countered. "I'd be torn up. And furious."

"Anger can make you stupid," Kane agreed. "But Durga doesn't take chances like that."

"He's seeded this group with more than one member," Grant stated. "Neekra. Thurpa. And don't forget Lyta was in a group held by Durga's allies."

"Next you'll say Nathan might be a plant as well," Kane said.

Grant nodded. "We know that he has access to cloning technology. We were all put in cells and separated. It took hours for me to escape using primitive tools."

Kane narrowed his eyes. "What?"

"Durga doesn't do anything without a good reason. He's underestimated us on one occasion, and his plans were arcane enough to leave Enlil blindsided," Grant said.

"Do you remember any blackout periods?" Kane asked.

Grant shook his head. "But that doesn't mean there were none."

"We could be overestimating him," Kane offered.

"We could," Grant replied. "But do you want to take that chance? He impregnated Hannah from a thousand miles away. He assembled an army in Africa. He assembled three of them. Human. Nagah clones. Kongamato. And he stripped Neekra of her powers. And if you don't remember, while we thought we'd exterminated his Kongamato Air Force, there were more than enough to fly and deposit us right into his lap."

Kane nodded. "He's cunning. And the only reason we beat him in our first direct encounter was because he got cocky with the new powers he acquired. So what's the ultimate payoff?"

"He sends us after a threat that he stumbled across, an

enemy too powerful for him to handle on his own," Grant offered. "To put the odds more in his favor, he hooks us up with his personal clone, Thurpa, and Neekra, who makes an Amazon warrior look like a pixie. No matter who wins the matchup, he's then in position to come in fresh and clean up the winner."

Kane nodded. "We've been discussing that for the past few days. What makes you think he did anything to you, Brigid, anyone?"

"Because he's a goddamned snake in the grass. Look at how he treated his son, for one," Grant said. "Damn near killed—twice—by Kongamato. To gain our sympathy."

"And then he recalled his falseness," Kane said. "Which means if Durga has controls set in place, Thurpa can resist."

"Maybe," Grant said.

"Can anyone join this private conversation, or don't you trust me anymore?" Thurpa asked.

"I don't even trust myself, son," Grant returned. "After our stint as prisoners…"

Thurpa frowned. "So I'm not the only one who could have some extra implanted memories or hidden commands."

"No," Grant said.

"And the panic is starting to spread through the group," Kane murmured.

"Are you kidding me?" Nathan asked, moving closer. "I didn't do anything in my cell…not that I could recall…"

"I thought we turned these things off," Grant grumbled.

Brigid nodded. "You did, but Neekra's hearing is acute enough to make up the difference, as is Nathan's as long as he holds the artifact. And I presumed you were catching up to my suspicions."

Lyta frowned. "I cheated and used the hood's audio receptors."

"So the game is out in the open," Grant said.

"Do not concern yourself over a panic among us," Neekra said. "We appear calm enough. We just have to wait until Durga's plan comes to fruition."

"Waiting isn't a strong point for me," Kane answered.

Grant frowned. "But what are we waiting for? What's the other shoe about to drop?"

"Or maybe it has already fallen," Brigid offered. "Durga doesn't strike me as someone who would leave anything to chance."

Grant took a deep breath. "So, what would have been the plan?"

Brigid shook her head. "Something we won't like one bit."

The seven adventurers gathered their things and continued down into the depths of ziggurat. They knew that there was hell ahead of them; they just didn't know what kind.

Chapter 15

"Two forms of security," Brigid spoke up, jolting the procession from its silence.

"Two forms?" Kane asked.

"I've been thinking about how some of these Annunaki 'discoveries' are structured," Brigid said. "The kind of responses that we can anticipate to encounter."

Kane nodded. "And what is your thought on what we've met so far?"

"I'm looking at two very different forms of technology, if those things we just finished off could even be considered technology," Brigid explained. "Generally, the Annunaki are more inclined toward biological-based technology. The lobotomized Nephilim. The psychoreactive gems and technology aboard their spacecraft. Occasionally, we've encountered clockwork-style automatons, in Greece and in China, but nothing with the brand of sophistication displayed by the metal sentries."

"Then whose tech is this?" Kane asked.

Brigid opened a pouch she wore down on her hip. It was one of the shattered heads. "There is no technology inside."

Kane examined the husk. "The other parts?"

"Hollow," Brigid said. "I've been looking various segments over as we've been traveling."

Kane nodded. "So what formed them into bug-looking freaks?"

"I had assumed some form of magnetic field rendering

them as a cohesive whole," Brigid said. "But that wouldn't explain the strange eyes. Also, Grant's arrows are steel broadheads, and they showed absolutely no deviation from their standard path when fired."

"So they weren't magnetic charged. But the Taser still worked," Kane offered.

Brigid took back the flattened remnants of the head. "I don't quite know how to explain this in a way that doesn't sound as if I'm talking nonsense."

"Baptiste, we're in the middle of an unknown pyramid in central Africa, which itself is in the middle of an artificially carved volcano," Kane said. "We're dealing with aliens who have been punished and imprisoned for the better part of five thousand years. Give me a chance here."

"Spirit fragments," Brigid said.

Kane narrowed his eyes. "Ghosts?"

"Take a look at Neekra," Brigid ordered.

Kane did so. "She was able to give birth to semi-intelligent blobs, in her older incarnation, pre-neutering by Durga. They would follow her orders and had their own form of limited intelligence as far as I could tell."

"Due to the complexity of the prion computer structures, she could create autonomous minions," Brigid said.

"Autonomous automatons," Kane said with a chuckle.

Brigid smirked. "Very alliterative."

Kane nodded. "So Negari has his own guards in here?"

Brigid nodded. "But he no longer requires a biological agent to animate bodies, as Neekra required with her reanimated corpses. Nor does he even require a physical component for interaction."

"So what were we fighting?" Kane asked.

"Judging by the smell of the canisters, I want to say some form of corn product, long ago degenerated," Brigid stated.

"We were fighting cans of creamed corn?" Kane asked.

"Yes, meaning that we're dealing with something that has been out and about," Brigid stated.

Kane examined the head. "There were no organs to damage, no muscle to sever. How did our weapons do harm?"

"I'm guessing that these spirit fragments, or ghosts as you call them, are along the lines of energy wave forms. The Taser did disrupt the cohesion that these creatures formed. And Nehushtan showed itself more than capable of dispelling their energies, in far more obvious and spectacular fashion," Brigid explained.

Kane squinted inside. "Ghosts and electromagnetic phenomena are two things we know are closely related. Such as when Grant's 'ghost' visited us at Thunder Isle when we lost him in the time scoop accident. He was able to communicate with one of our science nerds using electronic voice phenomena."

"Correct. Grant himself was caught in an area between dimensional membranes, but he was able to cast his shadows in the lesser dimensions as tesseracts," Brigid returned. "Which brings me to the next problem I've been anticipating—Negari might not actually be pinned down to this universe."

Kane frowned. "These things, the splinters, were just Negari's shadow puppets."

Brigid nodded.

Kane glanced back toward Neekra, who had been listening intently. "Is there anything you might be able to add to this?"

Neekra shook her head. "The greatest of our clan have managed to establish cross-dimensional roots. It's part of what grants us our superior longevity and access to different forms of technology. Living technology, so to speak. But we've never truly done much more than 'spiritually' explore the neighboring dimensions, and that required the assemblage of thresholds and other equipment, nearly as much as could fill *Tiamat*."

"Thunder Isle was a breakthrough," Brigid said. "Mankind managed to locate the minor tears in the time stream and, utilizing the time trawl, was able to attempt a limited form of temporal travel. And we also had gone on our own extradimensional journeys before that. However, we are still trying to guess at the absolute scale of transdimensional space. Grant's incident with the time trawl was one look through that window. Unfortunately, we've only just discovered that window and have peeked through on a foggy night. Negari, potentially, could have been using that as a revolving door for centuries."

Kane glanced back to the canister in his hand, realizing that he'd never seen an aluminum or tin can made of black metal such as this. He scraped his nail on the surface, but the color was nothing sprayed or painted on; it was part of the metal. It also wasn't a polymer. There was only so much give in it as with a standard can, not like the more pliant plastics. The metal he held wasn't from this particular world.

"Oh damn," Kane murmured.

"Now you see my discomfort," Brigid said. "Negari, quite potentially, could be as great a menace as Colonel Thrush."

"Thrush?" Lyta asked. "Who's that?"

"An android," Grant answered. "He's an entity who has somehow assembled multiple dimensional shadows and duplicates of himself and has taken more than a passing interest in this particular reality. The last time we ran into him…was when he copied you, Kane."

Kane turned away from the group as Grant explained to Lyta and the others their history with Thrush. This gave him a moment of silence with which to assemble his thoughts. He noticed that Neekra took a step closer to him, uninterested in those aspects of her father.

"Not another Fand," Kane murmured as she approached.

Neekra tilted her head. "I am nothing like my other siblings."

Kane raised an eyebrow. "So why come join me?"

"You are an appealing human being, Kane," Neekra said. "And you are someone who has successfully opposed my father."

"Exactly like Fand," Kane murmured.

Neekra chuckled. "You flatter yourself too much."

"What do you know about her?" Kane asked.

Neekra fell silent. "I am capable of drawing memories about her. From you."

Kane stared at her. "You have those memories from our time…together."

Neekra nodded.

"From the time you had me all under your control," Kane grumbled. "Torturing me."

Neekra stiffened at Kane's accusation.

"What did you get out of that?" he asked.

"I received your measure, your worth," she told him. She leaned in closer. "I got to see you at your worst. And even then, you stayed your hand when you had the opportunity."

"That was before we got to see what you did to Gamal's men. The militiamen weren't my favorite humans around, but your children went full evil," Kane said. "So don't give me any lies about second chances and seeing who was a worthy lover for you."

Neekra stood silent.

"I trust you, for now," Kane said. "I've forgiven what you put my brain through. But my memory is not short. If

I see even one hint that you're returning to being the queen egg layer and body snatcher..."

"You'll end my existence," Neekra finished for him.

Kane narrowed his eyes. "Getting your telepathy back?"

"No, but it was blatantly obvious what you were going to say next," Neekra responded. "Trust me, I miss the power, but in a way, it was its own prison."

Kane frowned.

"I was trapped in a bodiless existence. Physical interaction was denied to me. Durga understood what could actually filter through the poor maniacs I possessed," Neekra stated. "It was as if I lived my life wrapped in smothering plastic. It took pain to penetrate my numbness."

"Numb, despite all that you could see?" Kane asked. "After all, you spent enough time telling us just how much you could perceive with your all-mighty senses."

"It's one thing to see and hear. But it was half of a universe," Neekra responded. "Slowly, my instincts are balancing back out. I can feel vibrations and body heat so much better."

She took another step closer, until their noses were almost touching. Kane tried to forget that she was naked. To her mind, Kane and the other humans were nothing more than pets, cats watching her step out of a shower.

"I would be so very grateful," she began.

"We'd be grateful if you could concentrate on what our task is," Brigid spoke up, interrupting the Annunaki woman.

Neekra looked back.

"Kane, maybe we should put skunk musk on you before we go traveling," Brigid added.

Kane held up the palms of his hands. "I didn't do anything to encourage her."

Brigid sneered, glancing toward Neekra.

"I thought you were gleefully occupied catching the others up on your Appalachian adventures, as well with Colonel Thrush," Neekra stated.

"You were listening?" Grant asked.

Neekra nodded. "I can multitask, little girl."

Neekra walked off, taking point for the expedition as they continued down the ramp.

Brigid turned to Kane. "What did she seem so interested in?"

"She was looking for some human contact," Kane replied. "Skin-to-skin kind."

Brigid closed her eyes, clucking her tongue at the thought. "We survive a battle, and all she can think about is humping."

Kane shrugged. "Well, when you're in the presence of…"

Brigid opened her eyes, glaring at him.

"I'd quit while you were ahead," Grant said.

Kane nodded in agreement.

"All right, so exactly how much do we have as verification that Negari is out traveling the multiverse?" Grant asked.

Kane pointed to the can. "That metal isn't earthly. I don't think that it's an alloy that turns black, either. So, given simple laws of science…"

"I get it," Grant returned. "It looks a different color because of different universal laws."

Brigid nodded.

"So why are we hunting for Negari if he's sallied off Earth?" Grant asked.

"Durga has some information about him," Kane said. "And that came right from Fargo, who'd tapped into the database Enki left behind. Enki developed the Nagah to be Earth's guardians for a reason, and he gave them venom in order to handle whatever…extra body-chemistry that Neekra and Negari possess."

"Fargo," Grant grumbled. "How he's still walking free…"

"He's smart. He's ducked out when he had the opportunity," Brigid stated. "I'd have killed to get a sample of his knowledge."

Kane and Grant cast a look at her.

"It's not necessarily hyperbole," Brigid added. "Fargo is no saint."

"No, he's not," Kane replied. "I just never figured you for going after such a cheap shortcut."

Brigid shook her head. "Just to know what Negari's true threat is. And why the hell Durga really reunited with Fargo."

"Yeah, they used me as their dead-drop mailbox," Thurpa spoke up. "So they're still thick as thieves."

"We haven't seen him since the necropolis," Lyta added. "But is Fargo done with this? Or is he waiting in the wings?"

"Which wings?" Brigid said. "Austin Fargo might not be on my list for kindest humans of the year, but so far, on this trip, he has not steered us wrong."

"He lied about not being able to touch the staff, remember?" Kane asked.

"We've been getting a ton of information over the past few days, so forgive me for not immediately recalling everything," Nathan said. "He touched it?"

"While you and the others were held prisoner," Kane answered. "He said he lied in order to put us more at ease with his presence. But when things took a turn…"

"He came in and put his hands all over it," Nathan returned. He wrinkled his nose. "What a mess."

"I told you not to trust Fargo farther than you could throw him," Grant spoke up.

Nathan grimaced. "I was thinking that I could throw him pretty damn far."

"No matter what, he lied on that," Kane said. "And I'm not sure that all either of them are interested in relates to Negari and whatever ephemeral 'threat' he possesses. Especially since it appears that Negari doesn't seem hindered by this prison."

"There is something that Negari wants. That he needs," Neekra stated. "He might be able to touch other planes of existence, but he's stuck. Why else would he cobble together guards out of recycled tin cans?"

Brigid looked down at the head. "Recycled cans. Garbage."

Kane frowned. "Are we worrying more about Negari, or Fargo, or Durga?"

"I'm currently ascertaining what the threats are and ordering them by magnitude," Brigid said. "Negari has transdimensional capabilities, but they are so limited that he must utilize castoffs from other vibrational planes of reality in order to organize a perimeter defense."

Kane nodded. "But he can duplicate himself, using that recycling as bodies for his fragments, as you pointed out."

"A similar means that Neekra utilized to act upon our world when she was reduced to a severed head, buried deep in some tomb of its own," Brigid added.

"The necropolis?" Grant asked.

Neekra frowned. "I was so very close to him, physically. Yet it makes sense. I sought out my own remnants of flesh, the anchor of my being. It had been left invisible..."

"That's correct. So how did Durga find it?" Brigid asked.

"He stated that he had radio transmission equipment that was able to triangulate the signal of the telepathic waves," Neekra said. "Why didn't I think of that?"

"Posthypnotic suggestion," Kane said. "After all, your father couldn't have you actually locate where your true brain was."

Neekra nodded.

"But keeping you that close to Negari does pose a bit of a problem," Grant said. "A mile of stone shell and that tumor-headed hulk notwithstanding."

"The place had been breached once before. Seven hundred years ago, within the presence of Nehushtan," Brigid said.

Nathan looked at the artifact he held. "And this thing leads people around. It's a damned good thing that Fargo couldn't mess with...oh wait, you just talked about that."

"We're all off-balance a little here," Brigid consoled him. "Don't worry too much about it. Right now, we're taking a moment to actually think about what we're doing. That's the most important thing."

"Knowledge is one of the most important weapons in our arsenal," Grant added. "We're not the strongest or the fastest. We don't have the best technology on the scene. But we do think things through."

"Most of the time," Kane admitted. "Rushing after the sentries with just the shotgun wasn't my brightest moment."

Nathan turned away from the group and continued walking down the ramp. The seven people had paused in their progress to the depths of this tomb, and now the young man from Harare seemed to have lost interest, striding on toward their final destination.

Kane called after him. "Nathan..."

The African man paid no attention. He simply kept moving.

It was an eerie silence, not even the reflexive jerk of hearing one's name called, and Kane's suspicions grew. He jogged after him, trying the Commtact. The wireless headset wasn't any louder, but it was directly plugged into his ear.

"Nathan, do you read me?"

No response. Kane tensed and reached out, grasping the youth by his shoulder.

Nathan shrugged his way out of the gentle touch with a strength that tugged Kane off-balance. Even as that was going on, he could feel the staff and its hum, the powerful vibration pulsing in the back of his mind. Nehushtan was in control, guiding Nathan, and this time it seemed impatient. It didn't want to bandy about words with the humans; it wanted to achieve its final goal, whatever that might be.

"Nathan!" Kane bellowed. This time he gripped Nathan's upper arms about the biceps, steely fingers closing on both limbs. "Snap out of it!"

The young man kept walking, as if Kane was nothing more than a half-filled backpack, dragging the taller, heavier man along behind him with effortless ease. Kane struggled to dig his heels into the ground, but the smoothness of the ramp provided little traction for him.

Grant and Thurpa rushed to Kane's side. They were confused, but the blank, emotionless state of Nathan and the fact that Kane couldn't slow him down with every ounce of strength and effort proved more than enough of a clue that something was wrong and they needed to help Kane slow down the young African.

Grant decided that the staff was the problem; he wrapped both of his meaty hands around the shaft, clutching it in a white-knuckle grip, and sought to wrest it from Nathan's seemingly casual grasp. At 240 pounds, Grant should have been more than able to lift Nathan and the artifact. Grant even took the precaution of jamming the inside of one boot against the bottom of the stick to give him leverage.

Nathan finally reacted to outside stimulus, turning numbly toward Grant. With one hundred pounds and ten inches on Nathan, the contest should have been one-sided. Unfortunately, the struggle between the two was indeed ridiculously easy. With a twist of his wrist, Nehushtan pivoted at the end of Nathan's arm, and Grant found himself thrown from the ancient stick by centripetal force. Grant landed on his shoulder, sliding down to the next landing with a grunt.

Kane worried for his friend, but the shadow suit's non-Newtonian response to impact force once more proved its worth, redistributing the kinetic force. Kane kept pulling at Nathan's arms, but the strength the staff bestowed upon him was phenomenal. Thurpa lunged, slamming his shoulder against the African's chest, hoping to stun him.

Rather than slow the wielder of the staff down, Thurpa ended up on his ass, bounced off the living equivalent of a brick wall.

Neekra, Brigid and Lyta were on their way down as Nathan paused, reaching the landing. Kane had braced his knees against the young man's shoulder blades, wrenching with all of his might against his upper arms. Nathan barely noticed 180 pounds of lean muscle riding on him like a horseman.

Barely noticed, Kane emphasized to himself as Nathan twisted one arm free with ridiculous ease and reached around to seize Kane's other wrist.

With a shrug, Kane flew across the landing, slamming against the far wall. The breath exploded from Kane's lungs as he slid to the floor, thirty-five feet from where he started his flight.

Nathan was now a juggernaut. One that they had to stop, hopefully without killing him.

Chapter 16

Brigid saw Kane fly, and in an instant she knew that Nathan was no longer on their side. Not when he hurled a full-grown man like a rag doll, smashing him against a wall nearly forty feet distant. Nathan did not pause to evaluate the effectiveness of his throw; he simply turned back to his original path and continued marching downward.

"I'll stop him," Neekra growled.

"You'll do no such thing," Brigid snapped, cutting off the Annunaki woman. "Not if you intend to use lethal force."

Neekra glared at her, red-rimmed eyes flashing with anger. "I did not want to harm him, you simpering, bloodless wench!"

Brigid cursed herself for expecting the worst of the ancient woman. She had become so used to Annunaki being greedy and self-serving. The most blatant exemplar of the cruelty of Annunaki women had been Lilitu, whose greed caused irreparable damage to the living, monolithic craft *Tiamat* and scattered the Annunaki to the four winds, slaying at least four of them. Even in destruction, Lilitu proved to be hard to keep down, reincarnating into three telepathic young women who had nearly threatened Cerberus's very existence.

Neekra, however, was showing a much different dynamic. She was no longer scheming. She'd been stripped of amazing levels of ability, yet she displayed great amity toward the humans she'd tried to destroy only the day before. "I'm the only one strong and fast enough to deal with him without tearing off his arm."

"I'm sorry," Brigid said.

Neekra nodded. "I wouldn't have trusted myself, either. I apologize for denigrating you."

"Enough synchronizing our periods," Lyta snapped. "My cousin's a zombie right now."

Neekra nodded, then leaped with grace and speed toward the young man.

Nathan sensed her approach and, unlike with the humans who attempted an interception, he whirled and sidestepped her initial attack. Neekra's reach was long, but it barely missed him as he ducked her lunge. Brigid knew that she wasn't going to have much of a chance helping the Annunaki woman, and the powers of the staff seemed to have amped up Nathan to surpass her abilities. Brigid idly wondered how Nehushtan seemed so able to dodge and avoid the woman, then recalled that both she and Nathan had thrown themselves into conflict with the odd sentries.

Suspicions flashed through her mind at that moment. In the space of heartbeats, she mentally tallied the events so far.

1. The staff had led Kane, Grant and herself to Africa.
2. Durga had merely happened upon Nathan at the Victoria Falls power plant/redoubt complex.
3. Durga seemed to have wanted access to the staff but then immediately lost interest once he was healed.
4. Durga appeared obsessed with reaching Negari.
5. Negari could only be accessed by the staff opening the entrance at the top of this ziggurat.
6. Durga knew the means by which he could undo the enhancements Negari bestowed upon Neekra.

7. While Nehushtan had been present at the ziggurat once before, it opened up the tomb.
8. This time, when the ziggurat opened, Neekra's intellect was finally present.
9. Negari seemed to have accessed the outside world, even other dimensions.
10. It was highly unlikely Enlil would have left Negari himself whole and unimpeded.

The mental arithmetic flashed quickly through Brigid's mind.

She started to say something when a crackle of energy flashed from the staff, sizzling all too close to the flame-haired archivist. She came to the conclusion quickly, and Nehushtan seemed to have sensed her resolve.

Brigid must have established a contact with the staff, likely while she carried it to Kane's side when Thurpa had originally appeared to the group, gravely wounded from a conflict with Durga's Kongamato. The artifact had boosted her speed and reflexes, allowing her to cross hundreds of yards in the space of a minute, more than sufficient time to stabilize a dying young Nagah.

The staff read her, learned that she suspected its dark secret, that like Neekra's severed head, it was the housing of half of an entity. Negari's intellect dwelled within.

That was the only way the mental equation that brought them to Africa, to this very ziggurat, could make sense. The juju staff had journeyed across the globe, falling into the hands of men of enormous will and ability. King Solomon. Moses. Solomon Kane. N'Longa.

It sought out Durga, it drew one of Neekra's vampiric children to slay Nathan's father, one of the Longa clan who had been off and on watchman for the artifact and now it had fought for control of the young man, urging him downward.

And the goal of Negari was to reunite as one being, a whole that Durga warned them was a world-ending threat, a "one-man" extinction-class event. Nehushtan glowed, crackled once more with its eldritch fire, preparing to fire once more and erase Brigid from existence. She pulled her pistol and fired at Nathan, hoping to distract him.

"I thought you said…" Neekra began.

Nathan whirled, backhanding her across the jaw. The impact of the young man's punch lifted her off of the ground a good two feet. She was twice his weight, and still Nathan felled her as if she were a rotten-trunked tree struck by a bulldozer. Brigid grimaced and realized that the possessed youth had found the measure of the Annunaki during the battle with the animated cans.

The metallic guardians likely had been animated by the staff itself, considering how it was one of the few things capable of ending the existence of the sentries. Brigid's logical mind ran through these explanations even as her body twisted and wove, ducking out of the path of Nathan Longa. No longer did he try hurling bolts of energy but rushed into close combat with her.

Brigid felt the glancing blow of the staff against her shoulder, a jolt that broke her concentration, reinforcing that she was going to need every synapse focused on the enemy before her.

"Why, Nehushtan?" Brigid asked.

Nathan paused, the swinging staff pausing in midair.

"Why attack me?" she pressed.

Brigid didn't know that she'd have caused such a quandary in the artifact, nor the youth it possessed, but she didn't look her reprieve in the mouth. She slowly backed away. "Have we not brought you to where you wish to be?"

"Your assumptions are wrong," the ancient artifact spoke through Nathan's lips.

Out of the corners of her eye, she noted the stirring of Kane and Grant, Thurpa and Neekra gaining their feet already. Lyta was somewhere behind her, and knowing the reaction of the young woman in prior incidents, she was close, a weapon aimed at Nathan, praying she wouldn't have to gun down her cousin from Harare.

"My assumptions?" Brigid asked.

"You are attempting to retard my progress to my ultimate goal," Nehushtan puppeteered through Nathan. He glanced around at the others assembling around him.

Any violence would result in terrible injuries for all involved, and because the artifact had been the one item they had counted on for healing such fatal wounds, the humans and their Annunaki paused, unwilling to initiate an attack.

"What do you mean about my assumptions?" Brigid asked.

"You are thinking that this is Negari within my structure," Nathan stated. "That is wrong."

Neekra visibly paled at that statement.

"I said nothing," Brigid answered.

Nathan rested the point of the staff on the ground, looking around. "You thought it. You followed an erroneous logical path, which I could read and follow."

"Being wrong is a reason for a death sentence?" Brigid inquired.

Nathan's features twisted. She could sense that the young man was struggling against the artifact's control of his mind. Nehushtan's slow loss of command was showing in the face of his puppet, but Brigid didn't dare make an effort to spur the others to action. Not until they could count on the young man's ability to assist them.

Even as the woman thought this, she was multitasking, throwing up a wall of divergent thoughts, putting as much mental chaff between her true intentions and Nehushtan's ability to read her. She'd done this on a few instances before, utilizing her intellect and flawless memory as a means of smoke screening herself against telepaths. She'd even backed up her psyche against the mind control of a god, so she was hopeful about her success.

"Read me again," Brigid ordered the young man with the staff. "It was a side thought, barely a glimmer from my subconscious. One that I utilized provable fact to dispel."

Brigid spoke, and she ordered her thoughts, creating that dismissal of Nehushtan as living threat to the Cerberus expedition in as solid a line of logic as she could. Logic problems such as these were a side exercise for her, something to keep her mind limber and agile for instances such as these.

Nathan's brow wrinkled from concentration, his grip tightening around the haft.

"Was that reason to attempt to murder me with a plasma bolt?" Brigid asked. Talking and blurring her memory took monumental effort, but Brigid Baptiste was up to the task. Her green eyes were alive with thoughts, and she ground her molars. She now knew of the odd sensation of a telepathic probe that Kane described. It was unsettling and powerful, a vulgar display of psychic force.

Muscles tensed and released in the sides of her neck. This was a full-on assault, but it was concentrated between her ears. Her heart rate rose, the artifact's penetration of her ego starting to cause sympathetic stress reactions from her body. Brigid held her ground, keeping the "proof" that Nehushtan was *not* an essence fragment of Negari at the forefront, covering her other thoughts and hopes with a flurry of images.

And still, she pressed the question to Nehushtan. "Why were you blasting me?"

"The object in your hand," Nathan spoke. "You are correct about Negari's psychic fragments. Though the head has been rendered inert, there is still a residual energy, and it is making you susceptible to outside influence."

Brigid frowned. It felt as if she were holding a door shut against a horde with all of her weight against her shoulder, but she had to reach out to grasp other facts. That was the mental image that drew up in her mind's eye as she pushed into her own subconscious, looking for signs of outside interference. Nehushtan's proclamation bore the weight of truth with it, and if that were the case, she had to multitask once more. First she had to seek out evidence of another telepath influencing her, then visualize the angles of Nehushtan's plasma bolts directed at her.

It was possible that the artifact may have fired its weaponry at her in an effort to remove the sentry's head, and its misses were due to the ancient device's own efforts to strike only the infesting, possessed object without harming her.

She split off another part of her mind to re-examine the "proof" that she'd constructed against blaming Nehushtan. Brigid had assembled that excuse easily, almost too easily, meaning that her subconscious actually had evidence proving the artifact's innocence.

"Take the head from her!" Nathan shouted. "Hurry!"

Brigid grimaced. Things were lining up cleanly. She quickly hurled her suspicions up against her mental chalkboard, assembling them side by side, concentrating on holes in one or the other theory.

That's when she realized that she had to continually focus on certain details of Nehushtan's "guilt," elements that were fuzzy in her memory.

With that, Brigid felt the parallel tinges of panic suddenly rush up through her consciousness, terror from some source other than hers spurring her adrenal glands into action. Something else was in her body now, and with its sudden surge, and her own attention split between multiple functions, defending from intrusion from without, she lost control of her arm. She grabbed and ripped the pistol from its holster hung on her curvaceous hip, the slide clearing the nylon before she stopped herself. Suddenly, Brigid turned all of her attention toward the entity sharing her skin, wrestling for command of her limb, the rest of her gone rigid as a statue.

"Not going to shoot my friends," she grunted. The scene in her mind's eye was that she was a phantom outside of her body, and her ephemeral hands were clutched about her wrist, fighting against the force that was tugging the weapon loose. She glanced up to her own face, but nothing was there except for the same black space that had been the visages of the metallic sentries. Blazing red eyes glared hatred at her, struggling to free "its" hand from her grip.

"Get out of me," she growled, throwing all her weight backward, forcing whatever was at the steering wheel inside her skull to battle not only her, but also gravity. It was a symbolic thing and a fluttering tuft of thought, a small flame-haired pixie looking like a miniature version of herself, buzzing past her phantom.

Brigid's ego lifted one long, strong leg and drove it into the armpit of her body, allowing her ghostly form to create a solid, long bar that would prevent further movement. Every ounce of muscle in her captive body was struggling to lift the pistol. In a reflection on the glassy marble wall, she saw herself trembling, fighting with her gun half drawn.

She also noticed that she was alone in the reflection, or

at least her outside body was. Nothing was around them, the landing suddenly turned to an infinite flat plain. This fight was internal, but Brigid realized that she was still fighting the Negari essence's attempt to pull a weapon and shoot.

This was all happening on a purely mental scale, so she wasn't exactly certain at what speed life was occurring outside of her body. She just doubled her efforts.

Because this was a battle of wills, Brigid let loose her imagination. Her arms extended into tentacles, and not just the limbs of an octopus but reflections of the navigation chair's insidious, obscene and snarling tendrils that had engulfed her to the point of smothering. She hooked in tightly with every ounce of strength she could, extending suckers, cilia and spears into her own flesh, penetrating the "shadow suit" of her body. The sentry's burning red glare burned hotter, but the eyes were no longer angry slits; they now were alarmed orbs.

"No!" came an echo of her voice.

"Oh yes!" Brigid growled. She flexed, pulling even more with her amorphous grabbers, and the arm that the sentry took control of stretched. Brigid pulled her gun back into its holster, and the flame-haired archivist struggled even harder to secure it in place. She reached out with a new set of abominable psychic limbs, lashing about the faceless head. The red eyes burned hotly, trying to slice through the inky black of her tentacles, but Brigid was fighting not just for her own body, but also for the lives of her friends. She would not let go, not even as those floating flies of pure fire sizzled the tarry flesh of her pseudopods.

Brigid's ego was not invested in her appearance, and she had no difficulty reconfiguring her thoughts, her willpower for the maximum of strength and efficiency against whatever invasive force that Negari unleashed upon her.

Even so, the empty expanse of the middle of nowhere flashed, lightning crackling against a background of purple clouds. The hot forks of electricity that slashed across the sky now resembled a healing cross with twin serpents. Nehushtan, the very object she'd suspected of treachery, was suddenly on her side, joining her within her psyche. A fierce beam of plasma spit from the sky-encompassing artifact, knifing into the possessed version of herself. Flesh melted and began to flow, sucked up into the tarry biohorror that Brigid utilized to maintain herself.

Now she opened her eyes and saw the others looking at her, aghast. Her hand hovered close to the butt of the handgun in its holster.

"Grant!" she called out. "Get rid of it!"

An instant later, the pouch on her hip was riding her friend's arrow.

The "proof" that Nehushtan was somehow related to Negari now fell apart. The details were induced epiphanies, delusions that seemed so crystal clear and solid but faded in the cold light of logic.

The head bounced on the ground, and Brigid's mind was free of the outside influence, the staff itself withdrawing from her thoughts.

"You took a chance," Nathan said. He was drenched with sweat and looked ashen.

"I had to make certain," Brigid replied. She nodded to the staff. "But when I figured out what was wrong, I had some extra help."

Kane glared at the artifact, then took it from Nathan's hand. "This thing is going to kill you sooner or later."

"I can bear its weight," Nathan offered.

Kane nodded. "Rest up and you'll carry it once more. You need a respite."

Nathan smiled. Thurpa was there, shoulder slid under his, supporting the African man's weight.

Kane stared into the "cat face" of the staff as it had reconfigured itself. "You can talk."

Brigid wondered if the thing would answer out loud, but there was only silence. Kane's concentrated on the artifact, his eyes never leaving those carved into the head.

"Kane?" Brigid asked.

He blinked, then turned to acknowledge her. "I'm fine."

Brigid tilted her head. "What did you get from the stick?"

Kane looked confused. "Get what?"

"You were staring into its eyes," Brigid answered.

The features of the top of the staff changed, flowing like quicksilver drenched in black ink. Now even Brigid couldn't quite place the cat head. It was an old, amorphous symbol that she tried to follow mentally, but the mercurial changes of the artifact were just too hard. The nearest that she could make out was a roiling sea, or a completely blackened version of a torch's flame, wriggling and licking, moving with each breath of breeze.

For a moment, Brigid looked around to make certain that she wasn't in the psychic plane, her mind substituting imagery for incomprehensible abstractions, but the staff really was behaving like that. She blinked, then looked away.

"I don't remember any kind of contact with Nehushtan," Kane admitted. He stepped closer to her, resting his hand on her shoulder. "What's wrong? Are you all right?"

Brigid nodded. "The stick is behaving weird, at least in my vision. It doesn't in yours?"

Kane looked back at it. "I can see it acting weird. Like one of those weird lamps with the flowing jelly in it."

"A lava lamp but without the lamp." Brigid translated Kane's description.

Kane nodded. "Strange."

"Things are getting weirder and weirder the deeper we go," Brigid said. "It's as if the closer we get to Negari, the less we can trust anything our senses tell us."

Kane nodded. He tapped the bottom of the juju staff against the hard, glassy marble. "We'll hold our own, Baptiste. You managed to."

Brigid frowned. "Barely. I had help."

"You'll always have it," Kane answered.

The group turned on the next flight down from where they battled Nathan and saw the internal illumination died out below, an abyssal cloud that made the bottom of the ramp impossible to see.

Even with their shadow-suit hoods, there was nothing for light amplification to work upon.

The inky wall was impenetrable. Imposing.

Steeling their nerves, the humans and their Annunaki companion stepped into the darkness.

Chapter 17

Thurpa held Lyta's hand as they stepped into the pool of oblivion and proceeded down the ramp. Even through the environmental adaptation of the shadow suits, Thurpa could feel the chill of the darkness, like the icy runoff of a stream against his bare legs. With that thought, he paused, feeling the wall of doubt that continued looming in the back of his mind.

Those sensations were not his; they belonged to Durga. Thurpa was his clone, custom built with artificially implanted memories drawn through a cybernetic interface while his body was artificially aged and grown to near full adulthood. He'd never stepped into a cold stream; he'd only existed in Africa, all the memories preceding, the images and words of India and the underground city of Garuda, having been hardwired into his quickly growing brain.

You're nothing but a fraud, he thought to himself, but then he felt the tug of Lyta's hand on his, their fingers entwining.

"Come on, we'll fall behind," she said.

Thurpa took another step, letting her lead him.

You're only a few weeks old, he ruminated. But Lyta still cares about you. So do Kane, Grant and Brigid. Hell, even Neekra shows some kinship.

It was one thing to feel unreal, to have the history you thought was fact turn out to be a construction by a man who almost left you to die under the claws of a winged horror.

Twice, he reminded himself. You might as well have been reborn, fully able to decide your own existence rather than continue to be Durga's attack dog.

The chill rose around Thurpa's face, and for a moment he hoped that it was like a thin skein of oil across the air beneath, but darkness was deep, complete.

He had only the feel of the ramp beneath his booted feet and Lyta's hand in his. He couldn't feel her warmth, but just the pressure of her grasp was a reassurance.

The earphone under his shadow-suit hood crackled, static punctuated by barely intelligible syllables mumbling through. "Can you hear me? Sound off."

Thurpa spoke, and he heard five other responses. He wasn't certain who was speaking, the white noise being so thick and prevalent that timbre and tone were lost. He strained his ears to listen for any more words spoken, but it was obvious, painfully so, that the seven explorers were currently in a blackness that muffled and drowned radio signals.

Thurpa stopped, and Lyta tugged for a moment, then walked back to his side. He peeled his faceplate up just so his lips could move. The cold splashed his face to the point of stinging pain, and as he took a breath, his throat turned raw. He pulled the mask back down, realizing that the chill of the black void they walked in could stop a man's heart if he took too many breaths of it.

"Thurpa?" It was Lyta, and she rested her head against his, the vibrations of her voice resonating through her skull to his. They were forehead to forehead, and Thurpa was glad to have his hands on her hips. The contact helped him to recover his bearings.

For a moment, even just inhaling once in the all-smothering blackness had reduced him to panic. She calmed him, brought him back from the edge of running away in terror.

"There's no heat," he answered. "It's so cold out there."

"I can feel it through this suit, the first tingle of chill," she said. "But you clenched my hand so tight..."

"This is horrible," Thurpa returned. "We're talking over the Commtacts, but there's so much static. Yet we're only a few feet from each other..."

"The void, it's swallowing even sound," Lyta agreed. "We have to just keep going. Walk on through. There's got to be another..."

Suddenly Lyta's voice, the pressure of her forehead on his, was gone, and Thurpa squeezed her hand, feeling her weight dragging against him. He dug in his heels, wishing against all hope that he could get a sight of something. The light-amplification optics on the shadow-suit faceplate didn't operate in a vacuum.

Thurpa held on to Lyta, then felt another hand grasp his wrist. It was large, so the young Nagah man wondered if it were either Neekra or Grant. He hoped it was, reinforced in his belief because Lyta was no longer being pulled away from him. The hand ran up his arm, across the sheet of muscle that created a webbing between his head and neck akin to a cobra hood, which the shadow suit's elastic nature easily encompassed, then rested on the back of his head.

Thurpa felt a tug, then the pressure of another head against his.

"Thurpa," the woman's voice announced; now he knew that it was Neekra. "Kane and Brigid want us to all tie ourselves together so none of us are lost."

"Can you see in this?" Thurpa asked. He felt a rope pressed into his free hand.

"I am as blind and helpless as you," Neekra responded.

Cold shock struck the young man as he realized that Neekra was completely naked save for the headset that allowed her to communicate on their Commtact frequency. Thurpa gripped her upper arm.

"I might have a blanket," Thurpa offered.

"Annunaki are not as fragile as you humans," Neekra responded. With that, she broke contact, and Thurpa groped empty space. Lyta snugged up against him, taking the rope from his hand and winding a loop about his waist. He hooked his arm around her shoulders.

"Lyta?"

"We're tethered," she said. "If one of us steps into a bottomless pit, they have six other people to anchor them."

"I thought something attacked us in the dark," Thurpa murmured.

Lyta nodded. "Me too. You could have pulled my arm out of my socket playing tug of war with Neekra."

"I wouldn't let you go to save my own life," Thurpa responded.

"Now you have other worries," Lyta spoke up.

"She could die in this cold," Thurpa said.

Lyta gave his hand a squeeze. "I don't know Durga much except by reputation, but you are so not a son of his."

Thurpa wished that she could see the smile this put on his lips, but the darkness was impenetrable.

Even though they both had the rope to hold them together, Thurpa and Lyta didn't release each other's hands.

The void was too crushingly empty without that human contact.

KANE KEPT A good grip on Brigid's hand. Even at arm's length range, their Commtacts were useless thanks to the interference that blacked out the world around them. Even so, Kane continued to take the lead, holding the juju staff and tapping the floor ahead of him, making certain that when they walked, they didn't find themselves tripping or, worse, losing themselves down a hole in the floor. Kane didn't like this one bit. He could not hear the tapping of Nehushtan, just the physical feedback of the walking stick striking stone or whatever was solid enough to make up the ramp.

Without vision or sound, Kane was completely disoriented. He was used to having his keen senses about him in almost any instance, but even through the advanced hearing amplifiers and the high-tech optics of the shadow-suit hood, he was moving through this darkness with no feedback. He'd tried to see if he could use his nose, and even that failed. The crushing cold was all encompassing and forced him back into full environmental seal, but after a few minutes, he didn't feel any warmer. It couldn't have been an airless void; they were able to breathe through the air-permeable membranes of the suits, and there was no real border where a vacuum seal could have been created.

No, something was smothering this area.

Kane rested his head against Brigid's, direct skull-to-skull vibrations the only means of communication they had.

"This has to be a security feature," Kane offered.

Brigid grunted an assent. "I'm starting to feel like we've made the wrong choice. That's not right."

"No, you never want to turn back, no matter the discomfort," Kane returned. "This is scary as hell."

"It's rare for you to admit that," Brigid noted.

Kane frowned. "It's rare for me to be in a place that allows my imagination to run absolutely wild. I don't know if it's my mind trying to fill in the darkness, but I'm starting to notice things out of the corner of my eye. That has to be impossible, isn't it?"

"Not necessarily," Brigid answered. "The human mind can cope with lack of input, and does. Studies have shown that more than half of all people, while under sensory deprivation, have experienced visual and auditory hallucinations."

Kane grimaced. "So my mind's filling in the holes. And there's no legitimate way to tell the difference if it's some kind of fragment like we battled, or if it's my mind playing tricks."

"Not unless we take a try at…" Brigid's words trailed off. She lifted her head from his. Kane called her name, but it was lost amid the crackle and pop of the flood of static.

Her fingers started to slip from his and he squeezed tighter, reaching out with his other hand to take her shoulder and bring her back into direct contact with him. He was glad that he'd improvised a small sheath in his equipment harness that he could slip the artifact Nehushtan into, giving him the freedom to hold on to Brigid with both hands. With the staff secured between his shoulder blades, he was able to devote his whole attention to his soul friend.

Was she suffering from a hallucination? Kane doubted that Brigid would prove gullible enough to fall under the spell of the absolute darkness, but she continued to struggle, trying to get free from his grasp.

He clutched the back of her head and turned her toward him. "Brigid! Listen to me! What are you looking at?"

"The red eyes. I see them in the darkness," Brigid answered. "They're surrounding us. I can't tell how many of them there are because they keep weaving among each other. It could be four, it could be a dozen."

"Are you sure?" Kane asked.

"Pos—" she cut herself off. Just as before, when facing off against the possessed Nathan and the staff, she had fallen still, withdrawing from the outside world. Back then, she'd been in a mental struggle with some force, a taint, an infection from the sentry head that had seeped from the inert segment into her thoughts. She was going over her own mind, looking for signs of trickery.

Kane kept his eyes open, looking out the corners of them. He'd seen small writhing serpents of light that looked no larger than gnats, glowing and crisscrossing the edges of his vision. He fought to ignore that. The "floaters" were nothing more than the stars he'd seen on the occasions when he'd experienced head trauma or strained himself too hard. They were phantasms, memories of the stars that would flash in his eyes when he could see clearly and perfectly.

"Brigid?" Kane asked. "We're standing still and being pretty obvious."

"You have to trust me," she said. "Pass it on that everyone should lie down."

"You're going to shoot."

"Right now, I'm the only one who can make out a target," Brigid answered.

"You're going to be shooting at entities that don't have a physical presence," Kane told her. "We shot these things in the face all manner of times. Even grenades didn't seem to cause much harm to them."

"What about your Taser?" Brigid asked.

Kane felt his belt. "I'm glad I remembered to replace the battery."

"Spread the word. I don't need to accidentally shoot any of our allies," she ordered.

Kane looked around. "I hope it's because you can really see something."

"You mentioned that you became more sensitive to telepathic interaction thanks to your time spent with Balam," Brigid told him. "Not actually telepathic, just keener to its presence. Well, presumably this could be the same with me. I've got their scent now."

"You've been inoculated, more or less," Kane said. "So your immune system can lock in on that just like any other infection."

He could feel her smiling on her end of the contact. "Out of the mouths of babes."

"I'll spread the word," Kane said. He pressed the Taser into her hand and then turned away from her.

Kane wondered exactly what kind of harm she could do to something that had shut down nearly every one of their senses or produced an illusion of the cold of the void that was so convincing that his throat burned even now, a minute or so after his first inhalation. He held on to Nehushtan, and unlike before, when he was in the underground abyss of Neekra's necropolis, it didn't illuminate his vision. There was no enhancement of his sight above and beyond the capabilities of his shadow suit. There was just inky nothingness. The darkness did not part, did not burn away in whatever power Nehushtan contained. Indeed, he couldn't even feel the warmth and contact from the handle that normally seemed to seep from its blackened skin.

He yanked on the cord, and almost immediately, Grant was beside him. Two other figures were close by, huddling to him, and Kane was keenly aware that these had to be Nathan and Neekra, given how the group had entered the darkness. He only wished that he'd had the foresight to tether each of them together before taking the first step into this murky void.

After utilizing his LED flashlight at its maximum output, he was convinced that no light could penetrate, neither up from or down from the outside of the cloud. And now he hurriedly made an effort to coordinate his allies so that none of them would be in the way should Brigid fire the twin Taser darts into the darkness.

Kane knew that if anyone would have a chance to dispel the murky entities, it would be Brigid. Her memory would give her more than a sufficient advantage. She had been able to remember the location of a buried object in the middle of a featureless desert, homing them in on the hidden interphaser when no other means of finding it could be utilized. She understood that the others behind her would have to count on the angle of the ramp to gauge where to fire. As long as her feet touched the ramp, she'd know which incline to aim up or down at.

That was if they were facing one such entity as had motivated the unliving metal segments that created the sentries from before.

Deaf and blind, Kane hated feeling so helpless in the face of an enemy. Was it an actual fragment of psychic essence that composed the utter darkness, or was it some other manner of technology, a fail-safe from Enlil's own quiver of brilliance that would ensure that no telepathic force could penetrate past the walls of Negari's cell?

He wouldn't even know if there actually was a success, not until Brigid tugged on the cord that connected the expedition.

Kane sent off a private prayer to aid the woman.

BRIGID BAPTISTE WAS standing alone now, looking at the swirl and lazy drag of the red orbs floating against an otherwise endless void. She had the Taser pistol in hand, holding the grip firmly, her finger resting against the slide of the weapon. In essence, the Taser was an air gun that launched a pair of flesh-biting darts up to thirty feet with fairly certain accuracy. What made the gun so keen at paralyzing targets was the high-frequency pulse of electric charges. Once the darts connected to the same surface, a circuit was completed and the target became a conduit for thousands of volts.

Brigid noted that there was an afterimage trailing behind the firefly-like eyes as they drifted in the void. She took a moment of concentration to mentally photograph the red orbs.

There were actually three sets, but they were moving so that they often crossed trails and had been allowing the gleaming crimson ribbons to touch, making it seem as if there were up to a half dozen more winking into and out of existence. It was a clever ruse, and Brigid felt a semblance of respect for the floaters in the darkness.

She also took a brief moment to compare the double orbs, hoping for an instance of recognition, seeing if they had some resemblance to other things she'd seen in the past. She first thought of the red landing lights, seen from a distance, that were mounted on Cobaltville's helicopter pad where Deathbirds took flight, patrolling and hunting for the Cerberus rebels. She also did a quick check for Domi's own ruby eyes, often seeming lit from within as she stalked the darkness alongside them.

Brigid missed the young woman and missed the comforts of Cerberus redoubt. She steeled her jaw, continuing to follow the paths of the strange hovering lights.

She took a few steps. She'd taken exactly 930 steps since dipping into the darkness, and correlating that against her usual stride of 2.4 feet, she'd gone 2,232 feet, a little less than half of a mile. The ramp no longer was a squared-off spiral, coming down to landings such as on a conventional staircase. They were penetrating deep into the Earth, descending to the crust.

Figuring angles, she and the others were actually 6,085 feet from the top of the ziggurat. They were closing in on a point where, at their original calculations, they should have been at the center of the structure, where the stone would have been the thickest, the sheer mass of the ziggurat forming an impassable barrier for any prisoner within.

Unfortunately, according to the mental map that she'd developed, they were far off from the entrance and below the level of the moat of crusted magma surrounding the building, intersecting it, especially because the visible portion of the structure was a half of a mile above the floor of the volcanic caldera.

This can't be any worse than being on Mars or the moon, she thought. At least we have an atmosphere to come back through.

Of course, she countered, if the ziggurat was compromised, about to collapse, this tunnel they were in would break, and they would likely have to contend with a cascade of lava.

Even in the shadow suits, their lives would be measured in seconds.

"Concentrate on the entities," Brigid whispered to herself.

She focused on the three pairs of burning eyes. Only one Taser charge, and three targets.

Making a choice was going to require her utilizing every bit of her mental acuity. Because if she missed or if she hit the wrong target…

Brigid took aim, following one of the pairs of orbs.

She paused, finger on the trigger, ready to fire.

The pair of orbs crawled closer to her.

Daring her to shoot.

Chapter 18

Brigid stood away from the rest of the procession of Cerberus explorers. They'd walked two thousand feet down a ramp that was plunged into something darker than the void and quieter than any grave. It was a cold, smothering place, and right now, she seemed to be the only one who had a hint that there were other entities inside the darkness. She counted three of them, but through use of smears of afterlight and constant movement, they had done their best to confuse her about their numbers.

That gave Brigid the concept that the orbs were intelligent. She'd chosen her target, hoping that the differences in brightness and size weren't tricks of perception, and the pair she picked started advancing toward her.

Almost as if it wanted to draw her further into the conflict, despite her obvious intent to fire. That caused her to fire, those burning eyes glowing brighter and brighter.

She closed her eyes, and as she did, she realized that there was *no* afterglow.

For all the brightness of the orbs, she should have had some form of afterimage if it were her optic nerve picking up the data.

And if the glows were not registering on her optic nerve, then this void, this blackness, had to have some other source, some other actual effect. She followed the cord back down to Kane. She reached for his hand, then set her head against his.

"Give me your LED light," she said.

"Nothing is penetrating this blackness. I tried," Kane answered.

"Give it to me," she ordered.

Kane reached down to his belt and Brigid felt it. She found the base cap, then the lens and pointed it to her face.

"What are you doing?" Kane asked.

"Playing a hunch," Brigid said. "Keep your eyes closed for this."

"Why? I won't…all right," Kane relented.

Brigid murmured softly. "Disable polarization."

Because nothing was even on the screen of her faceplate to indicate that the natural polarization was in effect, she had to assume it took place. Just to be safe, she rolled up the plate and, eyes wide open, clicked the flashlight, then closed her eyes, tugging it down to reseal the suit.

And as per her suspicion, she now had a blue-white ball temporarily burned into her retinas, something that should not have been possible if light had been smothered and blocked off.

She tugged Kane close. "The blindness, the deafness, even the static. They're all an illusion."

Kane grumbled. "That's why you wanted the flashlight. Something that would have a physical reaction from your body that couldn't be altered. But why do I feel so cold?"

"You remember Antarctica," Brigid said.

"I even thought of the damn trip and how cold the air felt," Kane answered. "What about your orbs?"

"They might be an illusion, as well," Brigid responded. "Especially considering that they have made no actual moves against us in the past several minutes. They've had every opportunity to attack and have not."

"We're otherwise helpless, so yes," Kane said. "That makes sense."

Brigid pulled off her glove. "Where is the staff?"

"I've been holding it this whole time or had it in a sheath between my shoulder blades. It's not going to help," Kane told her.

"It's still back there?" Brigid asked. The illusory cold was painful, and she felt as if her knuckles had copper nails jammed into them. She cast about, finally reaching the head. With a touch, things started to change for her.

"It's still back there," Kane answered. "Brigid, you're touching it?"

"My vision is clearing. The artifact is dispelling the telepathic blindness," Brigid explained. She leaned her head back. "I can even hear your voice normally."

Brigid glanced around, and through the murk, she realized that her mental calculations of their position and the structure of the ramp were correct. She had not imagined the trek down below the ziggurat. She smiled, looking down.

Illuminators built into the ceiling still glowed, eternally powered by whatever Annunaki technology had been installed. The bottom of the ramp was still out of sight.

She drew Nehushtan from its sheath and peeled off Kane's glove.

"Son of a bitch," Kane growled.

"Share the love," Brigid ordered.

Thankfully, as the illusions subsided, Brigid could see that there were no entities about them any longer. She felt a wave of relaxation but still checked the Taser in her hands, flicking on its safety. She also looked about her gear to see if any of it had been otherwise disturbed. No.

Brigid thought about the situation. Nehushtan had a history dating back to Atlantis, according to the transcribed tales of Solomon Kane and N'Longa, meaning that it was likely the product of Annunaki technology. Every bit of evidence that had been uncovered about the lost city over the course of the Cerberus redoubt's rebellion against the overlords and their antecedents, the hybrid barons, pointed toward Enlil and his brethren being behind Atlantis, as well as its disappearance. The weapon found its way to Kane's grasp. That it somehow contained the psyche of Negari was an impossible angle, though she wondered if the Nehushtan also had an ability similar to Annunaki thresholds.

Brigid turned to the staff, waving over the young man who had spent the bulk of their quest bearing the artifact. "Nathan, I remember seeing a similar walking stick to this in the hands of another old man during our first journey to Africa. Yet you say it's been in your family's safekeeping?"

"My family," Nathan returned. "Before I started my quest, the juju stick was returned from being lent to a Waziri wise man. I believe his name was Inkula. It had returned a few months prior."

She nodded. "The mercurial nature of Nehushtan has been such that it has evaded instant recognition of it as the walking staff of Inkula."

"You mean Pakari's old friend?" Grant asked.

"We're sure not talking about that crabby ass elephant," Kane said.

Grant wrinkled his nose and bobbed his head in response to his friend's snark. "Fine. Now we know why you're mentioning this walking stick in relation to one held by someone else long ago. Though I don't blame you. Our main interest was in Prester John's collar, not some crazy staff."

Brigid nodded. "So I was thinking, what if the Nehushtan has a capability similar to Annunaki thresholds?"

Kane said, "Don't forget, we have Durga running around with his own threshold. Any attempt at teleporta-

tion could easily have been rationalized away as the Annunaki item, not the staff."

"Such as Austin Fargo's sudden appearances and dis-
appearances," Brigid said.

Kane narrowed his eyes. Lyta bristled, as well, having
faced the man and been summarily disarmed and humili-
ated by him as he crept upon the two people while Brigid
and the others were Durga and Neekra's captives.

"All right. First Fargo says that he's unable to come
close to the staff, he can't touch it without being mentally attacked," Thurpa said, exasperation weighing on
his words. "Then he tells Kane and Lyta that he was lying
so as not to get us worked up over the fact that he should
want to give his eyeteeth for such an artifact. Now you're
telling us that he's using the staff as his personal rapid
transit system around the world?"

"I wouldn't trust Fargo further than I could drive my
fist through his rib cage," Grant grumbled.

Thurpa wrinkled his nose. "And Fargo's working with
my misbegotten father. Setting things up so that we were
brought to this part of Africa…for what?"

"To penetrate Negari's defenses," Kane answered. "Isn't
that right, Austin?"

"If you ladies and gentlemen wished to draw me out into
the open, I'm afraid that my sense of the dramatic does not
border upon the suicidal." Fargo's voice came over their
headsets and Commtact implants. "I've been with you all
this time, however, observing your progress at various levels of closeness. However, inside of the ziggurat, you are
on your own."

Grant bared his teeth. "Of all the times when I actually wanted the weasel to show up in person, he's hiding
behind a radio microphone."

"So what is your game, Fargo?" Kane challenged.

"My game is trying to protect the world and uncover ancient secrets, not quite in that order," Fargo replied. "As you are by now aware, the venom of the Nagah has shown to be quite effective against Neekra and should also hinder and weaken Negari himself."

"What?" Neekra asked.

"The venom is effective against humans, and it works on Annunaki, but it has also been particularly configured to deal with the metabolism of someone enhanced with Negari's…for lack of a better term…telepathic virus," Fargo stated.

Brigid nodded in agreement with Fargo's choice of terms. Due to the description of producing vast lengths of antennae and a simple binary computer out of proteins, the best way to understand what Negari had created was to identify it as a telepathic virus. Obviously, this particular protein might have developed in nature or coded itself into the chromosomes of certain humans over thousands of years, giving birth to seers, prophets and other psychics across the history of mankind.

"So how does eliminating Negari help you in either case?" Brigid inquired.

"You don't listen to Durga?" Fargo asked. "He's a world-class threat. If he decides to get out, he'll be a one-being extinction-level event. Think of those old Godzilla vids, but multiply it by a thousand. Negari wakes up and enters the world, and it's the end. Of everything. Not even cockroaches would be left afterward!"

"Being the smartest archaeologist alive isn't worth a lot when everything else is dead," Kane summed up. "So you and Durga have the world's best interests at heart, as long as your skins remain safe."

"Durga has his own plans and machinations. He's already achieved his goal of making his own army—he cloned Nagah and the vat-bred Kongamato. And he can walk and talk without assistance," Fargo explained.

"And the threshold that you left in my pocket?" Thurpa asked. "Or what was it?"

"It was a Charged Energy Module," Fargo told him. "Just the thing that Durga required to boost his own equipment and leave Neekra's head unable to defend itself."

Kane's eyes widened. "Why Neekra?"

"Because then Fargo and Durga could test their hypothesis that Nagah venom could render me no more of an organism than you humans," Neekra responded. She sounded sullen, her voice retaining a low rumble that promised to explode into something worse later on. Kane didn't envy Durga. Once they were done within the ziggurat, if Neekra still lived, she'd make a beeline to the surface and achieve her reckoning.

"So you sit up…wherever…"

"Durga said Alaska," Neekra explained. "He has some redoubt facility in Alaska. That's what he said when he awakened me."

Brigid looked at her. She ran over her knowledge of the continuity of government facilities that were registered on the mat-trans network. A couple of redoubts could have proved to be useful as hideouts, but neither of those facilities possessed the kind of cloning equipment to grow Nagah and Kongamato, let alone provide the surgical theater necessary to transplant Neekra's mind into a custom cloned body.

She gave Kane a small wave, marking this inconsistency in Neekra's story, though Brigid was certain that Neekra wouldn't have been able to tell which redoubt was which. Durga lied to her, but just to be certain, *when* they returned to Cerberus, CAT Beta would be sent to investigate.

Brigid continued to figure out potential off-grid units

that might have provided a location for Durga and his conquering army.

"Now that you're out in the open, so to speak," Kane began, "what can you tell us about Negari? We seem to be nearing his tomb at this point."

"I can inform you that Negari himself is not going to be happy to be awakened," Fargo stated. "As to your speculations of transdimensional travel, Negari's skills are quite limited in those regards. Otherwise his fortress would have much better defenses. Steel canisters were the best he could cobble together."

"Ghostly knights," Grant said. "Animated suits of armor but without the actual armor."

"I always knew you were cleverer than you appeared, Grant," Fargo replied.

Grant flipped his middle finger to the air, even though Fargo wouldn't see it. He sneered in a small sense of victory.

"If you are done with your childish actions, Grant, I would remind you that your group will awaken an undying god from his dreamless sleep," Fargo warned. "And all you have is some venom, bullets and, of course, your annoying refusal to die."

Brigid turned to Kane. "You're right. He still sounds like an old-school master villain. 'No, Mistah Kane, I expect you to die!'"

Kane shrugged and smirked. "What else do you have for us, Fargo?"

"My best wishes," Fargo returned. "Because if you lose…I'm truly screwed."

Kane turned to Brigid. "Okay, Brigid, you've been working on the concept that the Nehushtan might have other abilities?"

"Similar to the enhanced knowledge cluster that Fargo

put in his forehead," Brigid said. "He *does* have something more. He's just either going to give it to us at this juncture, or we've been equipped with it all of this time."

Kane gave the staff a squeeze. "All right, Nehushtan. Do you have a course of action?"

Once more, Brigid observed him giving the ancient artifact a long, lingering glance, his eyes locked on the head with laser focus, unblinking. He was utterly rigid, breathing slowly. When he'd first gripped the staff after accepting its burden from a recently possessed Nathan, he'd undergone a similar spell of catatonia. Yet when she asked him what information was exchanged, he admitted to nothing. She wondered if the staff actually was communicating with Kane, or if it were more likely inserting some manner of hypnotic suggestion. Kane's will was strong, and he'd resisted drugs, telepathy and other means of coercion before.

Brigid dismissed the possibility of some form of mind control. If Nehushtan were actually doing something to Kane's mind, it might have been steeling Kane's already considerable will, armoring him for their confrontation with the imprisoned Negari. She didn't want to press him, not until he broke contact, for fear of somehow distracting him and disarming him of some gift that would mean the difference between victory or subjugation and extinction for mankind.

Kane glanced back to her. "The stick says that your assessment is correct, Brigid."

Brigid nodded. "Anything else?"

"Nothing at the front of my mind," Kane answered. "I'm going into this battle alone and blind."

"Alone and blind?" Brigid asked him.

"Nehushtan states that it is time for you to stop and hold your ground," Kane ordered, sounding numbed, stricken.

"Others will be coming from the surface, and you are to keep them out of Negari's clutches. Meanwhile, I go to greet Negari with Neekra."

"Greet," Brigid repeated.

Kane nodded. He drew her close, embracing her tightly with his free arm. Over his shoulder, Brigid could see that his knuckles were white about the haft of the staff.

"Come on, Neekra," Kane said aloud. "Time for the two of you to have a reunion."

The tall, naked Annunaki woman stepped forward, joining Kane shoulder to shoulder.

"Durga is coming. Don't let him into Negari's chamber, no matter what," Kane warned.

Neekra remained quiet.

The two walked down the ramp, even as the floor beneath Brigid's feet shifted, flattening out into a landing. Buttresses and waist-high walls rose behind them, providing places of cover for what looked as if it would be a battle for the ages.

"Come on," Grant said to Brigid. "The stick hasn't led us wrong yet. And despite…the recent changes in the architecture, we've got some prep work ahead of us."

Brigid silently agreed. The war in Africa, against what forces of darkness existed, was not going to be won on only one front.

Grant put down his war bag. "Grab some ammo and grens. We've got bloody work ahead."

DURGA LISTENED IN on his own headset. Neekra's inclusion in the group was not just a means of bolstering the forces he'd pitted against Negari; it was also his means of eavesdropping on them, learning what information they shared, ascertaining the possibilities of the forces they were up against and gathering intelligence about their estimates of him.

And when Neekra mentioned the "Alaska" base, Durga smiled with satisfaction. It was one thing to have access to a laboratory complex with its own mat-trans unit, but with the gift of a threshold from Enlil, Durga honestly had little need for an actual redoubt. All he needed was room to build and a place to bring in technology as necessary. The other surprise that he had in store for Kane also had to do with Neekra, though that truth would develop in its own good time.

Now, however, was the time for Durga to tie up several loose ends from his plots. Neekra, because she had been crippled, would be deleted shortly. Thurpa, however, having proved the viability of crafting a self-aware being from electronic input and stored memories, was simply going to be an annoyance if he survived and returned to Garuda. Certainly the young man would be looked upon with suspicion, but his nature had all of Durga's charm with none of his sinister nature.

Thurpa would simply prove to be an asset to Manticor and Hannah, the current and "rightful" rulers of the Nagah, one more soldier on their side when it came time for Durga to reinstall himself and claim his regal blood right.

Because Kane was the one necessary to Durga's plan to eliminate Negari, neither Brigid nor Grant would be suffered to live. Durga intended to sweep in and pick up the crumbs with his army. Both Grant and Brigid were going to be difficult crumbs, but with his crack force of Kongamato and Nagah clone troops, they would be in for the fight of their lives without the assistance of Kane. The others, the two Africans and Thurpa, would not add much to their resistance.

Durga chuckled. All this time, Kane and the others,

even Thurpa himself, had seemed to be worried about the potential for the young clone to be a time bomb in their midst.

The Nagah prince would not have been so blatant and vulgar as to have Thurpa, even subconsciously, be ordered to attack his allies. For all of the Nagah clone's fighting ability, such a betrayal might result only in the wounding of one of his Cerberus enemies, and that would be at Thurpa's luckiest.

No. When it came time for the expedition to expire, it would be in a straight-up battle, and all of the odds were on Durga's side.

Chapter 19

The wall slid, almost noiselessly, down to the stone floor of the ramp, inserting itself into an ever-deepening rut on the incline. It descended behind Neekra and Kane as they continued toward their showdown with Negari. Neekra turned and looked over the slab that now sealed them in.

"This is the point of no return," Neekra said. "Actually, we're two feet beyond that point."

"It caught me off guard," Kane stated. "Did you want to turn back?"

Neekra narrowed her eyes. "The way the stone is moving, changing. Is it the staff? Is it Enlil's security protocols for the ziggurat? Or is it Negari?"

"If I knew that, it really wouldn't matter. Can you punch through two feet of granite?" Kane asked.

"This looks more like polished basalt," Neekra said.

"Don't avoid the question…"

"No. I cannot. Annunaki are strong, but this was designed to defeat one with far more physical power," Neekra snapped.

"All right," Kane said. He gave the stone a tap with the bottom of Nehushtan. There was no response, not like when the top of the ziggurat opened up when he planted the staff in place. Though Kane had some plastic explosives in a pouch on his load-bearing vest, he doubted the small amount would do more than create a black scorch mark on the surface.

Exiting this tunnel would likely only occur if they defeated the prisoner of the ziggurat. Whether this was a fail-safe against escape, or a last line of defense for the prisoner who made the structure his fortress of solitude, that was the question that left Kane's nerves on edge.

Explosives. Grenades. Bullets. He had enough of these to take on any conventional opposition, but Negari had shown too regularly that his ziggurat was filled with unconventional threats. Kane did, however, have one small advantage hidden in his knife sheath.

Thurpa had shown his ability to coat arrowheads with his venom, so Kane and Thurpa made certain that his combat knife and machete were tainted with the cobra poison. Whether it would last on the steel was another bit of discomfort for Kane. He hoped it would prove more than sufficient to deal with the monstrosity, but then, considering the way Negari had battled them with the animated canisters, Kane also had to wonder if his opponent would have any physical features that he could use that venom on.

Kane smothered those thoughts. He wasn't certain if Negari had been watching them all the time, as Fargo and Durga had been. Whereas Fargo and Durga had the ability to spy on their radio communications, Negari would be able to do his spying telepathically.

"Too late to worry now," Kane said aloud.

Neekra nodded in agreement. "If Negari wanted to, he'd have seen it coming from miles away. We're going into this behind the curve."

"How so?" Kane asked.

"You haven't felt his telepathic presence in your mind, have you?" Neekra asked.

Kane shook his head. "You're saying he's either too powerful and subtle to be guarded against..."

"Or he simply peers through wormholes with his expanded consciousness," Neekra returned.

Kane wrinkled his nose. "That is bad."

"I know," Neekra answered. "This fight might already be done before we even take the first step in his direct presence."

"You're still going," Kane said.

Neekra nodded. "He promised me the universe. Instead, I'm a ghost wandering Africa, occasionally farther. If he's been able to slither out to other dimensions, why didn't he come back to me? Why didn't he try to find me to help me return to being whole?"

"Especially if he had your body in his prison. That thing was strong and tough, but you'd think that it'd have been susceptible to his control," Kane said.

"My stomach is turning," she said. "I don't know what the truth is. Especially given Brigid's explanation of her possession by that fragment, forcing her to doubt the artifact you're holding."

Kane gripped the shaft of Nehushtan tightly. He realized that with the glove on, he might not be able to tap into the ancient artifact's abilities. However, if there was some form of environmental attack…

Kane dismissed it. Negari had come at them physically and mentally. He peeled off his gloves, then flexed his fingers. As he wrapped his hand around the staff, warmth and tingles pulsed through his palm, syncing with his nervous system. Brigid stated that when he looked at the artifact, he'd zoned out twice, mentally disappearing as if in intense, silent conversation with it. Kane remembered nothing from those lost moments, though he'd returned with a message just before breaking off from the main group.

"All right, what has you nauseated?" Kane asked.

"I don't believe that Enlil was the one who set this whole

thing up," Neekra replied. "I think that maybe, Negari intentionally set this up. That he implanted the wrong memories in me, making it impossible for me to even locate my own head or this tomb."

Kane nodded. "Either way, you've been out in the cold."

Neekra seemed to ignore the statement. She checked the magazine in her rifle. She cinched her web belt tighter around her high waist. The belt and harness she had on were concessions to the need for pockets, but she was still naked. She moved with fluid grace, and her voice was husky, almost musical in her alien reverberations.

For some reason, Kane couldn't think of her as the same creature who had tortured him in a telepathic assault. She was different, which made him wonder exactly what her true motives had been, past and present. This *was* the woman who gave birth to gelatinous horrors that killed men, took over their corpses and then went forth to slay more.

Just remember what she'd been, Kane ordered herself. She's been helpful for now, but that could have just been from self-interest.

Neekra was seething, though. He could see it in her eyes, in how rigid her shoulders were, how tightly her fists were clenched.

Neekra might not care much for us, but she's royally pissed at Negari, Kane thought. She's going straight for his throat.

Kane and Neekra moved side by side, weapons held low and at the ready. Kane looked the Annunaki woman over and wondered at her familiarity with human automatic weapons. Granted, she had the strength and coordination to ignore recoil and to keep the gun firing straight, but the knowledge to aim, to reload, to make safe, all of that must have come from another source. Kane began to think that it might have been programmed into her by Durga when he realized that, in her prior existence, she had been a telepath. As these kinds of rifles had been around for more than 250 years, the pan-terrestrial alien would have picked up the basics of an AK-47 as easily as someone picked up a conversational knowledge of a language in its local environment.

Even if she hadn't had that knowledge before she'd met Kane, she'd spent more than sufficient time inside of his head to glean all manner of fighting skills and perhaps even the ability to fly a Manta craft while she was at it.

The doors at the bottom of the ramp were enormous in stature. Even the monstrous aspect of Neekra would not have needed to stoop to get through the doorway, and Kane wondered how the two of them would even move them.

The doors were made of wood, which seemed incongruous, given the "living" stone that they had trod through for the past several hours. Kane glanced back up over his shoulder. Brigid and the others were out of sight, fifteen hundred feet above them, digging in for a fight against Durga's forces. He couldn't help but think that things were falling neatly into line for the Nagah prince. He was separated from his friends, two people with whom he'd challenged gods and monsters without fail for the past five years.

Now he was alongside another who Durga considered an enemy, getting ready to face off with yet another impediment to Durga's plans of conquest. Nehushtan warned them that the Nagah prince was about to sweep in and eliminate the group, so forewarned was forearmed for Kane's allies. Though Brigid and Grant were up against nearly impossible odds, the two people had three proven, courageous allies at their back.

The doors ahead of them were easily twenty feet tall.

And if the timbers were as thick as they were wide across, then they were likely between two and three feet thick.

"No, Kane, I don't think that I could punch through this, either," Neekra said, a sneer crawling across her lips.

"I wasn't thinking of that. But it is rather unusual that there's no bar across these doors…on this side," Kane said. "Totally impractical for keeping someone prisoner when the doors can't be secured from the outside."

Neekra's brow wrinkled for a moment.

"This is getting worse and worse," Neekra said softly.

Kane tilted his head. "What do you mean?"

"It feels as if more and more of my life is disappearing into lies," Neekra answered. "Negari isn't a prisoner but emplaced in a fortress? A false set of memories implanted in Brigid that the stick we've had with us across all these centuries and miles was Negari, as well?"

Kane narrowed his eyes. "You think that you are Negari."

Neekra nodded. "An aspect, a clone, something like that."

"Did you see anything like that in Thurpa's mind?" Kane asked.

Neekra frowned. "What…you mean…when he first met me, saw me talking with Durga and the others?"

Kane nodded. "Could you tell the difference?"

Neekra closed her eyes, thinking back. She was delving into the depths of her own mind.

"No. I remember nothing," she said. "And I probed him deeply. I do that to all the men I meet. I was looking for hosts and minions at the time, ones who wouldn't be reanimated corpses run by my blobs of pseudo flesh"

"Yet Thurpa was a clone," Kane said. He thought about it for a moment and then looked back to Neekra, who stood looking at the doors. Her features were in the same mode as before, tense, angry, studying the doors to look for a way in. Maybe the woman had put aside the mystery for now, but something didn't feel right for Kane.

"Neekra?" he asked.

"What?" she returned.

"Did you say something?" he pressed.

"I said 'No, Kane, I don't think that I could punch through this either,'" she said, repeating herself from earlier.

"I meant after that," Kane told her.

Neekra looked at him. "Maybe talking to ancient artifacts is screwing with your memory. That is all that I said...though, it's strange that there's no locks on the outside...just the inside. As if Negari weren't a prisoner."

Kane kept his mouth shut. The last thing he needed was a confused *and* angry Annunaki woman at his side. Any restraint she possessed toward Kane would end up evaporated. But he could tell that the past few seconds of conversation, determining her origins and whether she was a part of Negari or not, had been reset, suspicions erased from her mind even as she thought them. Kane grimaced.

This likely was Durga's doing. Or was it?

He was already tense enough from the proximity to the end of this maniacal quest. Now he was back to second-guessing his ally and which enemy was the more dangerous.

A loud boom shook the timbers that made up the barrier, and Kane and Neekra leaped away from the heavy, giant doors. Kane's Sin Eater was instantly in hand, and Neekra brought up the assault rifle. Whatever shook the doors was enormous. Then the two structures swung outward, slowly, ominously. Light trickled out once the doors parted. Kane could see a two-foot shelf on the inside of the doorway's arch, though there was an "eye" pivot that served as the hinges, thick arms keeping them under control. Anyone who tried to bust in would have to break not only the stout timbers of the doors' makeup, but also somehow try to dislodge them while several feet of stone thickness buttressed them. Kane could also see stone pilings sinking into the floor, placed for reinforcement. He wasn't certain how tall they were, but this kind of security was not half-assed. Looking up into the four-foot-thick jamb, he saw indentations for the columns to lock into.

Anyone who could get through these doors would have needed far more strength and energy than a dozen men. Kane had felt the wooden doors, and they had been calcified. His shadow suit's optics showed that they had once been trees but had now been impregnated with a strong carbon material, a compound he couldn't understand because he was not a chemist or an architect. Still, he'd chipped the tip of his backup knife against the wood, meaning that the material was harder than 440-grade steel.

These were gates meant to hold back a siege of enormous force.

And they were locked from the inside. Kane retracted the Sin Eater, holding the staff tightly. They were looking down into the bowl of an arena that would have made the Colosseum seem tiny by comparison. Steps were all around, half steps connecting them at various intervals, allowing hundreds of thousands to sit and gaze down upon whatever was in the center.

The place was eerily clean and silent. As always, the lighting powered by the Charged Energy Module continued to burn. At the bottom of the enormous amphitheater was a flat disc of a floor, seemingly at least one hundred feet across. In the center was a single object sitting on a low, fat pedestal. It looked like a throne, but there was no front or back. Spires poked up from it on all sides, perhaps as legs supporting the object in the center. He zoomed in with the advanced optics of the shadow suit's hood and saw that a strange shag carpet or pillow was between the tines. He also received exact measurements. They were two hundred feet up, and the thing below was ten feet tall—minus a four-foot pedestal—and eight feet in diameter.

Kane frowned. "Does that look like a crown?"

Neekra turned quiet. Her eyes were dish-like in their shock, lips drawn into a taut, bloodless line. Terror struck into the chest of the Annunaki woman as his audio receptors picked up a hammering heartbeat. "Neekra."

"She cannot hear you," a woman's voice spoke.

No. It was not speech that reached Kane's ears. These were the whispers of alien thoughts ferried to Kane's mind. The tone of voice was joltingly familiar to him, and now Kane sympathized with the lightning-struck fear that had seized Neekra. Unbidden by his will, Kane began to descend the steps, Neekra keeping pace with him.

The man dug deep down, struggling to put up interference against the forces that manipulated him, but his ego was not being affected. An external force moved his legs, his body; he was a marionette dangling from telekinetic strings, guided with a deft hand. He flexed his muscles against the invisible bonds holding him captive to Negari's will, but he might as well have been trying to clap one-handed. There was no resistance; he simply moved.

Neekra remained blank, walking astride him with not a hint of life behind her crimson eyes. Kane grit his teeth and struggled harder. He could not even flex his forearm with the minute, trained action that activated the Sin Eater. Nehushtan remained clutched in his hand, but no warmth, no pulse of life and stored energy tingled within the ancient artifact.

Kane was not a man who could be called a coward. Yes,

he felt fear, even abject terror in the face of the awesome things he'd encountered over the years. Now, completely without control of even the most minuscule of muscle twitches, Kane felt sheer panic at the inevitability of his demise. What made Kane the hero he'd become, though, was how he used that fear.

Kane grabbed hold of that formless, bottomless fear, feeding on it. He had to focus his panic, and he wrestled his instincts, harnessing the adrenaline rush of terror into greater and greater strength. Neekra was held by a similar force, but Kane desperately hoped that Negari gripped her with more strength than he was imprisoned. Negari, according to legend once an Igigi himself, was more knowledgeable of the limits of an Annunaki than of the mere humans involved.

He twisted, feeling his hips move against the phantasmal threads by which Negari dangled him. Kane shrugged his powerful shoulders, trying to wrench free, and the staff he gripped started to throb with energy.

Nehushtan plied Kane with more than enough strength to break free, and in an instant, he leaped to one side, landing on the flat area between the half steps. There was plenty of room for sitters to lie back and recline or for those above them to rest their feet. He leaned against the staff to get to his feet more quickly but saw Neekra turn and move toward him.

Kane might have severed his own marionette strings, but the enemy retained another puppet. Neekra didn't move with the swiftness and grace she normally would have, giving Kane enough room to jump down further toward the center of this amphitheater. Whoever was sitting inside of that strange gazebo would undoubtedly become more distracted, freeing Neekra and giving the two of them the opportunity to strike back.

Behind and above him, Neekra took her own bounding leap, crossing more steps and landing far more surefootedly than Kane had. As Neekra came down, she pivoted to challenge him. Kane hurled himself, thinking a silent apology to the Annunaki woman as he crashed across her chest shoulder first. Neekra toppled onto her back, and the pair slid down more of the steps.

Kane hoped that his ally's skin would be more than enough to endure this kind of punishment, but as Neekra struck one landing and stopped cold, he slithered past her. With a shoulder roll, Kane was back to his feet, taking the steps two at a time, Nehushtan granting him the balance and prowess to make such a dash, his strides taking him ten feet per two stairs until he jolted under another impact.

Neekra had him about the shoulders, but Kane writhed in her grasp, using her momentum to throw her underneath his bulk again, letting her act as a cushion. Finally the two of them struck the flat disk that was the arena. Kane glanced about, and in truth, the shadow suit's optics had been correct about the dimensions of the colosseum floor.

Unfortunately, as he focused on the thing in the center of the arena, the shadow suit had no answers.

What sat in the center of the floor, atop its pedestal, was a misshapen oval, flat on the bottom. Through the middle of its height were two red eyes, each the size of a watermelon, blinking under reptilian lids. The rug was a mat of hair that dipped down the tall, scaled forehead to make a widow's peak. Beneath the eyes was a flat nose with slit nostrils that flared as the entity breathed. Feminine lips, scaled much like Neekra's, remained closed, even as Kane "heard" the thoughts cast into his mind.

"Welcome, human. Look upon the truth of Negari, deposed queen of the multiverse."

Despite the horrific distortions of its face caused by

size, despite its withered form with dangling arms and legs sitting on a throne that supported the bulk of a head, which must have weighed a ton, Kane recognized her.

Neekra had not been Negari's lover. She had been Negari's drone. A duplicate, a splinter just like the animated sentries formed from canisters.

Kane grunted as the mind-controlled Neekra crashed into him once again.

Chapter 20

The first wave of Durga's "clean up" was just as Grant expected. Aerial bombardment before the arrival of the ground troops was necessary to the renegade prince's efforts to overwhelm the five defenders. Grant glanced toward Thurpa, who braced himself at the block providing the younger Nagah with cover. If Durga hadn't activated the clone by now, then Grant felt he had little to worry about.

The aerial bombardment came in the form of a trio of screeching Kongamato. Grant was glad for the sound dampeners on his shadow suit's hood because the bat-winged horrors had more than apelike muscle at their disposal. Even so, the sonic pulses the hideous beasts emitted made Grant's teeth buzz. The winged horrors' sonar cries served also as sonic stun bursts, and Grant had seen militiamen flattened yards before a Kongamato even slammed into them. Those bellowing pulses crossed multiple frequencies of audibility, and what was worse was that it was causing feedback among the defenders' Commtact units. The group had lost contact with Kane as a wall closed him off at the bottom of the ramp, but Grant wanted to keep the line open to improve the tactical coordination of the expedition.

Unfortunately, the feature that made the Commtact units so particularly useful to Kane, Grant and Brigid was that they required very little volume to transmit sound; the "microphone" that picked up their speech was actually their jawbones, which carried vibrations from their vocal cords to the communications plates. Those same pickups didn't have the dampening effects of the shadow suit's earplug units, which provided both auditory amplification and auditory dampening as necessary.

The sonic screams jarred Grant and Brigid in their hiding spots before the two Cerberus explorers could deactivate them. Grant tried to grin and bear the vibrational assault on his jaw, but his coordination dropped off as the pulses reached his inner ear. It was all he could do to hang on to the ledge he had taken cover behind. Brigid was out of sight and too far on the other side of the sheet of mind-numbing pulses for him to seek her out.

Not having Commtacts, merely headsets with conventional microphones and earbuds tucked under their hoods, Thurpa, Nathan and Lyta sprung into action. Thurpa rushed to Grant's side as Nathan triggered his FN FAL rifle, big heavy bullets chopping into one of the attacking Kongamato as it swooped down the ramp over the group. Lyta pulled her .45-caliber pistol and followed suit, hammering the biggest slugs she had on hand into the flying targets. The Kongamato alighted for a second on the ramp beneath them, allowing themselves ground to make a faster turn than their winged flight would allow in the relatively close quarters of the corridor.

Thurpa had Grant's shotgun ready and aimed at the trio's landing area, aiming slightly above. The first one of the Kongamato off the ramp leaped into the air, right into the path of one of Grant's shotgun-launched grenades. The blast struck the gorilla-like barrel chest of the bat-winged monster with a crash of thunder. It toppled backward, a fist-sized, smoldering hole sizzling and smoking from its clavicle, savage eyes gone glassy in death.

The violent demise of their mate drew the attention

of the other two flying monsters as they glided over its tumbling body. That moment of distraction allowed Nathan to take careful aim at another of the Kongamato and pump six .30-caliber slugs into it, 180-grain packages of lead and copper tearing through thick muscle and heavy keel bone with brutal effectiveness. Nathan's target lost its flying agility and tumbled face-first into the ramp with an ugly crunch.

The third whipped its attention toward the young African man and opened its fanged mouth to loose a sonic burst.

The Kongamato's plan had one small problem. No longer jarred and off-balance from the flying things' sonic cries, Grant was able to focus. The Sin Eater snapped into his hand with a thought, and Grant smashed a burst of high-powered bullets down the thing's throat, cutting off its high-pitched pulses forever.

The wounded beast watched another of its kin crash to the ground, riddled with gunfire. It snarled and leaped forward. Grant thought that the creature believed that retreat would only end in death. The opposite was true, as Grant would have allowed the animal to run for its life, but in full rage mode, it was a sitting target for a salvo of bullets from Nathan and a FRAG-12 grenade round in the face.

Lyta had her attention back to the ramp leading down from the entrance. She'd transitioned back to her rifle and gave a shout as she spotted movement above. Grant slapped Thurpa on the shoulder. "Keep the shotgun. Hit them with what you have left."

Thurpa nodded and shouldered the shotgun, firing upward in an arc. The grenades launched from the big blaster wouldn't fly straight, not with their great weight; that was good for now because it allowed Thurpa to drop explosive rounds on them like artillery. The indirect fire resulted in airbursts that elicited dozens of cries of pain and discomfort from those splashed with explosive pressure waves and shrapnel. One of the attackers, a Nagah rifleman, stood up and fell back, Brigid sawing him open with an extended burst from her Copperhead submachine gun. Lyta also threw in, bouncing rifle bullets off the edge of the landing and making another of the Nagah clones cry out and topple down the slope, his face wrecked by a deformed slug that bounced up into him.

Grant fired his Copperhead at the wounded Nagah; he was not enjoying the ruthlessness, but he continued to hope that the cloned army would learn of their eventual fate and rebel against the commands of Durga. That all disappeared when he noticed that the cobra-hooded troopers each wore a headband. They were programmed and under the will of Durga. A quick glance back at the fallen bodies of the Kongamato, zooming in with the hood's optics, revealed that the poor animals were also similarly bound to the Nagah prince's will. He grit his teeth.

"These poor bastards aren't going to stop," Grant said over their communication network. "Durga's pushing them on to the end."

"Just like Gamal back during our first party," Nathan said. He pulled the pin on a grenade and threw it with all of his might. It was an uphill throw, and his bomb fell twenty feet short of the landing, but on detonation, it sprayed a sheet of force and shrapnel that caught the Nagah gunmen lying prone at the top of the ramp at eye level. Eyes wrecked and faces slashed by razor-sharp bits of wire and casing fragments, the attackers let out agonized screams.

The tactic was brutal but effective, smothering incoming fire toward the Cerberus expedition. The cobra clones were no longer shooting at them, giving the defenders a reprieve.

"This was supposed to sweep us away?" Lyta asked.

"Do not tempt fate, kid," Grant said. "Durga has a plan for us, and it's going to be a son of a bitch to stop."

The roof of the corridor suddenly shuddered under the force of a massive explosion.

Grant threw his forearm up to shield himself despite being wrapped head to toe in the shadow suit, the faceplate protecting his eyes from the torrent of dust created when shoulder-fired rockets pulverized the stone.

"They're trying to open up the roof of the tunnel!" Lyta announced.

"Their weaponry will be insufficient to the task," Brigid replied. "Look!"

Grant had been watching the ceiling of the corridor in any case, and what he saw were only small dishes, shallow craters that the optics already measured as six feet across and only half of an inch deep.

"It will require a steady stream of forty thousand missiles striking the same area to 'burrow' upward to the magma surrounding the ziggurat," Brigid announced. Grant was glad she did the math. Durga might have had an army of cloned soldiers, but that amount of firepower was not available at the drop of a hat. Unfortunately, Durga was smarter than attempting to drill through to magma with shoulder-fired rockets. Even as the dust cleared, the sonic bleats of flying Kongamato slammed into Grant.

The clouds of detritus thrown up by rocket detonations had served both as a distraction and a smoke screen for the real assault. The first three of the Kongamato had been a feint, as had the Nagah gunmen. Durga had sacrificed sufficient forces to allow the defenders an illusion of preparedness and security. Now, this masterstroke made it so that Grant and his allies were forced into close-quarters combat.

Grant whirled and took cover below a waist-high wall;

at the same time a limb snapped as a Kongamato swooped
too low and struck stone, not him. Grant saw the fanged
face of the winged horror just above him and reached up
with both hands, hooking it by the back of its neck. With
a mighty yank, he slammed the creature's throat into the
corner of the barrier, and a fetid cough thick with phlegm
and blood sprayed over Grant's hood. He pushed up on the
stunned thing's head, then wrenched downward forcefully
a second time before the Kongamato could recover its wits.

This time, the cough was accompanied by a sickening,
wet crack, and the beast's eyes turned glassy, tongue loll-
ing between lifeless lips. Grant rolled from under the dead
thing and was on his feet as two more whipped through the
thick clouds of dust. Another rocket burst against the ceiling, but Durga had underestimated the shock absorption
qualities of the Cerberus shadow suits. The clone gunmen
were only providing smoky cover both ways for the fighting forces among the barriers on the landing.

Grant swung around and looked to see if any of his allies required assistance, and from the sound of gunfire, he
could tell that this was a close-quarters slugfest. Grant
didn't care for that because in such situations, sharp talons
and sheer muscle were favored over firearms. Even so, he
noted that Nathan had his machete out and was lashing
violently, chopping at the wing finger of one of the Kongamato attacking him. Steel severed the digit and tore into
the leather web that made the mammalian monster's wing.

The thing shrieked, withdrawing instinctively in
agony. Nathan wasn't about to let his advantage fade, so
he charged in closer, blade lashing and striking wetly into
solid muscle before Grant turned to leap at the creature
assaulting Lyta.

The beast had wrapped its jaws around her forearm, the
shadow suit the only thing preventing Lyta's arm bones

from shattering. She'd jammed the muzzle of her pistol against the thing's belly and had gotten off one shot before the pistol was left out of battery, unable to cycle and feed a fresh bullet into the chamber. Still, the bullet had weakened the thing, and the burning agony in its gut kept it from hearing Grant as he whipped his own machete down and between the shoulder blades of the Kongamato. Bone cracked under the assault, blood gushing from either side of the mighty chop.

The thing toppled off of Lyta, who scurried to her feet, getting a hand up from Grant.

The two of them saw Thurpa in a savage melee with two more of the cloned abominations, swinging his empty rifle like a club. The folding steel stock was bent off its hinges, evidence of the savagery the young Nagah displayed in this battle.

Lyta cycled her pistol, bringing it back into action, and fired into the back of one of the Kongamato's heads at a range of only a few inches. Her .45-caliber slug smashed the creature's skull and whipped its brains into a froth, instantly killing it. Grant had taken a heartbeat to nock and fire an arrow into the ribs of the other monstrosity. The broadhead hunting-arrow struck with such force that it sliced clean through the thoracic cavity of the cloned horror, exiting the other side of its ribs and shattering against the far wall.

The Kongamato winced, coughing up blood, but its eyes still burned bright with rage and the urge to battle. It identified Grant as the reason for its sudden pain and lurched a single step toward the man before Thurpa plunged his pistol up under the thing's jaw. With a pull of the trigger, the Kongamato's sloped forehead burst, erupting like a volcano—blood, bone and brain tissue vomiting out like a cloud of devastation.

From behind, Grant heard the crashing detonation of grenades set up as booby traps. The Cerberus warriors were not counting on just their weapons and strength to deal with Durga's extermination force. They had made certain that any force attempting to flank them and approach through the risen array of barriers would face doom. Hand grenades and trip wires made mincemeat out of whoever tried sneaking up on the defenders as they slugged it out with the Kongamato.

Grant turned to check on Brigid; the woman coolly was feeding her Copperhead machine pistol a fresh magazine, stepping around the bullet-riddled corpse of a lifeless winged assailant. Grant turned his attention to see if any of the other gorilla-sized monstrosities took a higher road without risking improvised mines. He knew that the Kongamato were adept at running on all fours like horses, leaping like frogs, or flapping and gliding in the air. However, the things had stopped screeching their sonar cries, meaning that they were not flying and relying on echolocation to navigate with speed faster than normal sight. That didn't mean that the beasts weren't clamoring like apes or pouncing with the strength and agility of leopards.

Grant spotted two bulky forms in the clouds of smoke still billowing about them and lashed out with a backhanded slice across the one on his left, machete meeting the skull of one of the stalkers in the mist. He punched out with his right hand, Sin Eater leaping into his grasp. His hooked finger struck the trigger, and the other silhouette shuddered under a 3-round burst from the mighty machine pistol. One of the assailants was a Nagah clone, the top of his skull shorn off by Grant's machete, whereas the other was a Kongamato who loomed on all fours, its open jaws allowing it to swallow Grant's salvo of bullets, which smashed the base of its skull and crushed its spinal column.

The dead creatures toppled to the ground, and the snarl of Brigid's Copperhead was unmistakable at Grant's right.

He turned to see more of the assaulting Nagah clones drop. Durga's disposable soldiers writhed as they died under a withering burst from Brigid. He glanced to her, and through her faceplate, he could see her disgust at this bloody work, but the poor clones were already doomed.

If not here, then their lives would be thrown away in Durga's future campaigns of conquest and cruelty. The crackle of gunfire filled the air as Lyta moved up to Grant's left. She'd traded her pistol for a rifle, though she favored her battered forearm by resting the forearm of the long gun in the crook of her elbow. Bursts of automatic fire lanced into shadowy forms that moved in, trying to overwhelm the expedition.

"It's just not Africa without a Zulu charge," Brigid said aloud. She plucked the pin from a grenade and sailed it into the midst of an oncoming throng. The bomb ripped the group of soldiers apart, cloned cobra men flattened to the ground, more than a few limbs scattered by the severing force of the grenade's pressure wave and shrapnel.

"This time, the explorers win, not the savages!" Grant bellowed. To punctuate his point, he cut loose with both his Sin Eater and Copperhead SMG. The advancing line of Durga's killers was thick enough that even without aiming, he was able to hit the wall of enemy bodies.

"That's what the white man called us, Grant!" Nathan countered. The young African threw yet another of the swiftly dwindling supply of hand grenades, but its shattering burst broke the ranks of the advancing force.

"Durga's the one whose shown his savagery. You've shown your humanity," Thurpa amended. His borrowed shotgun bellowed four times before he let it hang on its sling, grabbing his AK-47. The automatic rifle's report was not as deep and air-shaking as the shotgun, but the results were much the same, Nagah clone and Kongamato abomination alike twisting under an onslaught of flesh-shredding slugs.

"You guys sure talk a lot," Lyta grumbled. She continued to mow down targets as they appeared in her vision, her lines of fire sometimes intersecting with the flaming lead attention of one of her fellow defenders. Where twin streams of bullets struck, bodies burst apart brutally, blood spraying like a fine mist in the air.

Grant reloaded his guns, scanning up the ramp for another wave of attackers. Bodies were smeared all along the length of the downward slope leading to the edge of their defenses. Blood trickled down the incline in thick rivulets like the runoff of a summer thaw. "All right, cease fire."

Thurpa looked at the magazine in his rifle. "This is the last of my ammunition. Half a mag for the rifle, and my pistol is full."

"We're all running low," Grant said. "The kind of firepower we used to turn back this attack exhausted most of our supply. It was meant to."

"So, if Durga has another assault in reserve, we're screwed," Lyta said.

Grant nodded. "I'll cover you guys while you grab rifles off the dead. Hopefully we can resupply from them."

Thurpa grimaced, and Grant could see that his shadow suit had a streak of slick red running down its side. "I was grazed."

"Anyone else hurt?"

"I took a couple of shallow scratches dealing with the Kongs," Nathan said. "Long, but they look worse than they feel."

"Brigid, cover me," Grant said. He didn't move out with a spring in his step, winded by the exertion of close combat with the winged monsters. He felt the bruises under his shadow suit, glancing bullets, falling chunks of stone and Kongamato fists leaving their toll despite the protective qualities of the high-tech polymer second skin.

As he stepped out into the open, he saw Durga himself standing on the landing above. Grant nocked an arrow and aimed at the cobra prince. Unlike the clones, who'd worn only cargo shorts thanks to the warmth of Africa and the toughness of their hides, Durga had on a loose shirt. As if on cue, the renegade Nagah's shirt fell open, revealing several rectangular cakes of putty strapped together around his chest and waist.

The prince held an object in his hand. It looked like a dead man's switch, but Grant didn't believe this.

"You're not that stupid, Durga," Grant grumbled, knowing that the serpent king listened in on their Commtact frequency.

"Of course not, Grant," Durga said. Grant noted that the mouth of the man he faced did not move as those words were spoken. "But it's a good image to freeze you out in the open."

Grant released the string, the arrow flying at Durga's duplicate. He turned as the bow snapped back to its normal flex, the bowstring vibrating against his forearm. He lunged in long, loping strides down the ramp, heading back to the barrier, hoping to reach cover. The dense pack of explosives on the doppelganger's chest would mean a blast radius of at least fifty feet, maybe farther given Durga's flair for the dramatic.

Grant's arrow sliced through the throat of the clone, and in a heartbeat, the suicide bomber and its vest tumbled, sliding down the ramp, skidding closer to the explorers' defensive position.

"If I can't destroy you, I can at least trap you," Durga

taunted over the radio waves. "Let's see how well this An-nunaki construction holds…"

The rest was drowned out by an explosion that slammed into Grant like a freight train, hurtling him against a wall and causing him to black out.

Chapter 21

The distant rumble of thunder resounded in Kane's ears even as he blocked and parried the swift chops and strikes of Neekra. Though the Annunaki woman now occupied a cloned body created by Durga, she was an exact duplicate of Negari. And if the tumor-headed abomination at the entrance was somehow the former body of this thing, it was no surprise to Kane that it wasn't even supported by that fourteen-foot horror, which was easily two-thirds the height of even that hulking, rampaging beast.

Sunken, soulless eyes stared out of the mockery of Neekra's face, pupils only shifting to follow the swift violence playing out between man and Annunaki. Kane was grateful for the strength and speed bestowed upon him by Nehushtan, allowing him to block and parry punches that would have crushed stone if they'd landed on a wall. The orichalcum core of the staff and its black, alien carbon shell proved invulnerable enough to withstand frustrated chops as he intercepted them.

Neekra's own face was filled with dismay and terror. This was not her doing, but she'd suffered such an enormous shock that she had no will, no strength to resist Negari's manipulations. Then again, these were not the acts of someone actually manipulating her will; this was someone who had seized the atoms and cells of her body. Those same threads of psychic force had gripped Kane before he drew upon the energies in the semiautonomous artifact Nehushtan.

"Neekra, you can fight this!" Kane said, grunting with effort as the alien woman struck again, this time a glancing blow deflected off his right shoulder. The impact whirled him to the ground and Nehushtan's shaft bounced loose, but landed only inches from his outstretched fingers. Kane looked over his shoulder as he stretched to reach the artifact, but Neekra moved past Kane, kicking it away and across the arena floor.

"I am trying, but how?" Neekra asked. Negari made her bend down and grab Kane by each shoulder. She effortlessly lifted him from the ground as if he were a rag doll. Kane kicked in empty air, hoping to find some kind of leverage as Neekra's fingers closed tighter on him. His bruised shoulder was ablaze with pain, the slow squeeze of Annunaki fingers circumventing the non-Newtonian nature of the shadow suit's properties. With gradual force applied, the polymers didn't stiffen and harden in reaction to sudden, sharp force.

Pain also flared in Kane's other shoulder, but all he could do was dangle in front of Neekra, who turned him so that he was face to face with Negari.

So, you are Kane, Negari's voice echoed in his mind. *My father thinks of you often, and Thrush has spread tales of your exploits to other universes.*

"What can I say? I make friends in all the wrong places," Kane rasped through the pain of Neekra's steely grip on him.

He saw no emotion in the slack face of the gigantic head, but a psychic chuckle reverberated between his ears. *Thank you for bringing my errant fragment home.*

"Next time, make sure she has her tags on her collar. Finding this joint was…" Kane gurgled as the crushing grip tightened even more. Something popped in his shoulder.

A little of your snark goes a long distance, Kane.

Sweat burst on his brow, and he scanned about, looking for where the staff had fallen. Almost as if on cue, the artifact rose to full height, its base inches from the flat disc of the amphitheater floor as it hovered just beyond an arm's reach to Kane.

You mean this fascinating little device?

Kane nodded. His teeth were grit against the untenable pain that speared through his shoulders. His skin felt wet beneath the shadow suit, and rivulets of blood trickled down his biceps. He still managed to keep his head up.

You think that if Neekra could grab Nehushtan, she might grow in the might necessary to wrest free from my control.

"It's as if you can read my mind," Kane rasped.

The emotionless facade of the overgrown skull showed a slight flicker, the corner of those massive lips rising in a smile. *You are defiant 'til your last breath.*

Kane narrowed his eyes. "I might be, but I'm sure that it's not going to be today."

Your courage does you a disservice. You are precisely the sort of man that I programmed Neekra to locate and bring back to my fortress.

Kane sneered. "Looking to settle down, raise some baby giant heads and spend the rest of eternity sitting in theater in the round?"

"No, Kane, please," Neekra whispered.

"No. I know what she wants. She wants a vessel," Kane answered her. "A mate for her most successful minion. Then there can be two vampire lords, heading out onto Earth and doing what…draining psychic energy?"

You think too small, Kane. I envision you spreading my power across the universe.

"I see one little problem with that scenario," Kane said. He coughed. His hands hung limply at his side now. They tingled, possibly from the circulation cut off by Neekra's iron grip. "Durga knows what you are. Who you are. He and a guy named Austin Fargo had access to the truth about you."

Yes, I've read that in your mind, the suspicions you had that Durga reprogrammed my vessel.

"Wh…what?" Neekra asked.

"You are Durga's weapon against Negari. So you *can* break this ugly bitch's hold on you," Kane growled. "You were meant to."

It is an amusing story, Kane, which is why I have been careful not to access her mind, rather her body. Whatever trap that Durga might have placed in her psyche to use against me, it would be useless thanks to my psychokinetic manipulation of her flesh, rather than direct access to her brain.

"You made me think that I had love…" Neekra growled.

Negari's jet-black pupils swiveled toward Neekra's face. *You had my love, Neekra. The love of a creator for her creation. But you have returned to me damaged, poisoned. Useless.*

Kane could sense the struggle going on in the woman's mind as the blasphemous mass on its throne attempted to keep control of her. The crushing grasp slowly slackened, and Kane shrugged himself loose from one of Neekra's claws. Immediately he saw the spurts of blood pop as the nails withdrew from his skin. Unfortunately for Kane, he still hung from the shoulder where Neekra had punched him. Kane's own weight on that shoulder combined for a whole new level of pain, forcing the man to bite his tongue.

He had one hope for Neekra.

"Keep your claws in me," Kane growled under his breath.

Neekra might have heard, or she might not have, but Kane twisted himself, getting a single point of contact with the ground with the toe of his foot and he stretched forward. He had to get it on the first swing; otherwise Negari would drop Nehushtan, or the abomination would force Neekra to release him. Kane needed that skin-to-skin contact to form a continuous circuit between himself and Neekra.

Fingers touched the artifact, and in a heartbeat, the contact between the three of them, Neekra to Kane to Nehushtan, lit all of them up. A surge of strength flowed through Kane's limbs, and all the pain, all the remnants of punishment through his body, disappeared. Even his free shoulder stopped bleeding, and in another instant, Kane clutched the ancient staff tightly.

For a moment, Kane felt as if his arm were now complete, his mind flashing back to his hypnotic dream of his earlier incarnation, Solomon Kane, who also wielded this juju staff, discovering that this was not an item of deadly black magic, but a holy symbol that was as effective a sword against the forces of hell as anything else. The charge showed in Neekra's eyes, her own confidence and power seeming to return to her. She released Kane, and he dropped to both feet with the balance of a cat. His other shoulder throbbed as Nehushtan's energies flowed through him, reinforcing torn tendons and sealing ravaged blood vessels.

The former queen of the vampires, Neekra, had regained her strength, ironically, through the blood of the man who had fought tooth and nail against her vampiric horror. The Annunaki woman burst from the telekinetic bonds restraining her, and she hurled herself toward the ugly, stagnant head on its throne. A sheet of will, made solid and visible by Negari, blocked Neekra, but only barely, the force wall buckling for an instant before bouncing her back onto her ass.

Kane lunged, bringing the spear end of Nehushtan up to bear as a weapon, plunging it at that field of telekinetic energy. Negari's black, dull pupils rolled in Kane's direction, and with an act akin to a shrug, the man and the artifact were brushed back and aside. Kane tumbled, feeling as if he were resisting an avalanche before he dug his feet into the floor and stopped his out of control tumble.

Neekra lashed out with the rifle she still carried, hurling a whole magazine of automatic fire at the enormous Negari. Kane watched as the bullets stuck in empty air as if caught in translucent gelatin. Thirty projectiles hung in front of Negari before they slowly turned in unison, like a school of fish. Half of them pointed their conical noses toward Neekra; half of them turned toward Kane.

"Damn," Kane growled, leaping to his feet and throwing himself out of the wave of projectiles before they smashed against the ground and wall where Negari had casually tossed him. The bullets made deep gouges as they struck the ground. If the material of the arena were similar to the rest of the marble making up the ziggurat's walls, then she'd hurled those bullets far harder and faster than the original rifle could fire them; those slugs had barely left scuff marks against the glassy marble.

Kane didn't think too hard about the power of Negari's mind. As far as the Cerberus exile was concerned, Durga was correct about Negari's treachery and lethality. If her mind could throw a bullet faster than the rifle designed around it...

Enough with your worries. Act! Kane ordered himself.

He launched the Sin Eater into his hand and triggered the weapon. A spray of lead ripped through the air toward Negari, an immobile quadriplegic entity who only existed as an oversized head. This should have been the easiest shot of Kane's life, yet his machine pistol's slugs stopped in midair, captured by her telekinetic powers.

Kane threw himself to the ground in a shoulder roll. The air popped from the passage of slugs breaking the sound barrier. Those miniature sonic booms told Kane all he needed to know about what would happen to him. His shadow suit provided minor small-arms protection, but against those kinds of physics, he might as well have worn a chocolate shell for all the power of her mind.

Your resourcefulness and defiance grant you credit, Kane. But you are merely human.

Kane grimaced and crouched deeply, bracing himself for her attack. He gripped Nehushtan and said a quick, silent prayer.

"I've been leaning on you a lot, stick. But bullets are not cutting it against her," he whispered.

The head of the artifact changed shape once more, the twin serpent heads coiling together, this time possessing more than a passing resemblance to the ASP forearm blasters of Enlil's Nephilim drones. They glowed brightly, crackling with sparks of plasma energy. Kane allowed his Sin Eater to retract into its forearm holster and gripped the ancient Annunaki weapon with both hands. He aimed both serpents at Negari's throne and, in a brilliant flash, unleashed a stream of sizzling energy toward her.

The lance of flaming force stopped inches from Negari's cheek, the air around its "impact" rippling like the surface of a pond, except for the pinkish hue of those psychic ripples. Although the energy shouldn't have had a weight to it, Kane found his feet skidding on the ground beneath him.

Negari turned her attention on fighting against the burst, and suddenly it was an inside-out tug of war, Negari pitting her willpower against the orichalcum energies. Kane threw every ounce of strength and leverage into preventing this push back, and it seemed to be working.

The force of this lance is as much your will as the energies within, came a thought from the Puritan Kane, a bit of information transmitted across nearly a thousand years. Kane concentrated, flexing his muscles, trying to translate the force of his personal physique into the focus necessary to increase the power of the artifact. Negari's features slowly began to change. She too was making an effort to deflect the deadly plasma burst. Expanded on a scale of her distorted head, the scowl was at once huge and horrifying, thousands of wrinkles squirming against each other, as if her face were composed of a carpet of worms wriggling. Sloughing flesh, long neglected in the arid environment of this arena, made her deformity even more stomach-churning.

"If you're trying to get me to be *your* lover, that ship's sailed, lardface," Kane growled.

There was a flash, a flicker of movement behind Kane, the soft song of steel on the collar of his machete's sheath. The same machete that…

"Did you hear me?" Kane interrupted his own thoughts, hoping that while he and Negari were engaged in this battle of willpower, she wouldn't try to read his mind or that like before, in the necropolis, Nehushtan somehow shielded his thoughts.

No need to bellow. I already sense your duplicity, the truth of the blade my minion plucked from your sheath.

"You know that this blade is dangerous," Neekra said, racing around to Negari's "blind spot." Kane was doubtful that a powerful telepath like Negari could truly possess an area she could not sense.

The resistance of the huge head declined, and Kane found himself take a large stride toward the mutated Annunaki woman. Kane didn't know what kind of power she truly had, but apparently the force of the artifact was taking enough energy that she didn't grab Neekra.

Why do you insist on thinking of that drone as a separate entity from me?

"Because, Negari, she's proven herself different than you," Kane grumbled.

With a flicker of incredible speed, Neekra lunged, racing in toward the bloated head and swinging the machete, the blade coated with Thurpa's cobra venom. Negari's shield parried the initial slash, an impact that caused the edge of the machete to chip and spark. Again, her defense against Kane's onslaught with Nehushtan's ASP-style blaster component buckled but only slightly.

A second thunderous strike resounded against Negari's shields on the other side. That drew Kane a little off-balance, losing his step as the Annunaki freak's telekinetic forces buckled.

Are the two of you insane? You keep trying, but my will is more than up to the task of repelling your puny attacks!

"The definition of insanity is doing the same thing over and over again with hope of a different outcome," Kane said from rote, drawing on every ounce of his concentration. He spotted a glimmer of Neekra's movement. With a nod of his head, he beckoned the Annunaki woman.

With a surge, Neekra vaulted, somersaulting with ease as Negari picked up on her movement. Lashing tendrils of phantasmal force smashed stone, creating fountains of dust and rocky pebbles where Negari struck. Neekra, however, had the speed and agility of a full-grown Annunaki woman, and her adrenaline was likely through the roof thanks to the stresses of combat.

A tentacle of telekinetic ectoplasm shot out toward Kane, but Neekra's reflexes were swifter. She slashed at the manifestation of Negari's power, the machete blade chopping through the ethereal energy and causing a grimace on the features of her huge, distorted face.

"The old lady feels feedback when you whack at her," Kane said.

"That's because that energy is an extension of her. Her entire body is rotten with the viral proteins that form the biocomputer that allows her to focus and manipulate the universe about her," Neekra said. "If I'd been lazy enough or distracted enough to use TK tentacles against you, I'd have felt the same as her."

Silence! Don't go to him!

Neekra did not pay attention to her sire. Her red scaled fingers wrapped around Nehushtan, and suddenly, the plasma lance increased in strength and brightness. The flare of energy made Kane's cheeks tingle through the hood of his shadow suit. That same suit was meant to withstand naked sunlight on the airless surface of the moon, which only served to remind Kane of the sheer power inherent in Nehushtan and the will of even a "clone" Annunaki.

Negari's lips parted, and deep from within a withered throat emerged a weak, keening voice. "You cannot. I made you!"

"You didn't give me shit to be grateful for!" Neekra bellowed in response.

Even with the power of Nehushtan doubled, Negari continued to fight against the powerful energies pouring against her. Tentacles of ectoplasm rammed themselves into the ground, rooting her in place as the throne where her head rested groaned under the unrelenting pressure placed upon her.

"You have this?" Kane asked.

Neekra nodded.

And with that, Kane broke contact with the ancient artifact. In one swift movement, he pulled the foot-long combat knife from its sheath.

Kane had thought ahead, not only to have the machete coated with Nagah venom, but also to have a backup knife ready with a similar patina. The equation for preparing for a battle was that two was one and one was none. Already the machete had received enormous damage, its surface burnt and pitted by its contact with Negari's telekinetic fields.

Neekra screamed with a rage that shook the amphitheater to its highest point. The plasma lance she laid out from Nehushtan hammered away at Negari's defenses.

In the distance, at other entrances to this colosseum, Kane noticed insectile figures gathering. It was the alien metal sentries they had encountered earlier, and this time, there were more than five. They leaped and scurried down the seemingly endless steps to the arena floor. Kane was in a full run, dodging and weaving as ectoplasmic whips smashed at the ground, trying to catch him and kill him before he could get close to her.

The rustling was in the hind parts of Kane's brain. Another brain was transmitting telepathically, and he realized that while Neekra had possession of the artifact, she was tapping into its energies to rebuild the protein strings inside of her. She drew upon the ancient Annunaki technology to bolster her own might, to increase the incredible force of the artifact even as she "healed" back to the creature she had assumed herself to be.

Kane lunged out of the path of a telekinetic hammer blow, which punched a two-foot-deep hole in the basalt before him. No shadow suit or polycarbonate armor could protect Kane if he stumbled or allowed Negari to touch him.

But he had to touch her. He leaped, lashing out with the tip of his combat knife.

Her mummified, wormy hide parted, black ichor seeping from the slit cut through it.

"No, no, gods curse you," Negari's all too human, too feeble voice croaked as she felt the nick.

Nagah venom entered her wound, entered the putrid black ooze that itself was the liquid protein suspension forming the basis of Negari's psychic abilities. It was such a small amount of chemical transfer, but Enki had crafted the Nagah for the purpose of protecting mankind from a threat he had foreseen. Where Enlil had toyed with duplicating his daughter's experiments with the prions that formed the building blocks of enhanced perception and power, Enki had developed Nagah venom. It was more than a simple cobra toxin.

Somewhere along the way, Kane recalled his journeys with Durga across the psychic sphere where Neekra had imprisoned them. Durga spoke of Enki's manipulation of the cobra people and how the "cobra baths" were a rite for every Nagah, even the true born.

Those baths were nanomachine suspensions that not only rebuilt a human being as a semi-reptilian humanoid, but also produced the venom glands. Those glands themselves had been designed for a single purpose—to produce a breed of microscopic bot, themselves only protein molecules capable of viral self-ambulation, which would attack Negari's telepathic virus.

Upon contact with that prion, the nanomachines would replicate as long as there was a "food supply." Against humans, the cobra venom was simply snakebite poison.

But against one whose power flowed from a living, biological structure that was at once antenna, lens and computer for manipulating psychic powers, the venom would spread like a fire. As long as a "telepath" protein existed in the target's bloodstream...

Negari wailed in agony, and Kane grunted.

An invisible tidal wave crashed against his body, hurling him against the steps of the amphitheater. Non-Newtonian polymers absorbed the cruel impacts as well as they could, but Kane knew that his back and arms would be masses of black-and-blue flesh for days after this. Yet even striking the steps did not stop that psychic tsunami's push against him. Kane was lifted and thrust up the slope of those steps.

The arriving insect sentries attempting to reach the bottom struck that invisible wave and blew apart, metal deforming, segments shooting off like shrapnel. Kane gripped a ledge and tried to hang on.

And then, as soon as the flood of telekinetic energy had begun, it abated.

All that was left on the floor of the colosseum was a tall, triumphant Annunaki woman, blazing with power. Negari's head collapsed in on itself like a deflating hot-air balloon, except as it withered, flesh dried out, cracked and then disintegrated into dust.

The aura of power pouring off Neekra whipped up the residue that used to be Negari, forming a swirling, bright, glowing cloud about her.

Kane's assessment of the scene below was concise and eloquent, if vulgar.

"The bitch is back."

Chapter 22

Neekra seethed, brimming with the might bestowed on her by the ancient artifact Nehushtan. At this moment, Kane realized that he was facing a living bomb. She was easily more powerful than she had been when he, Grant, Brigid and the others battled him in her necropolis. Rage flared, seething around her in a halo of visible energy, her telepathy turning emotion into palpable force. She brimmed with unmatched power, and suddenly the guns and venom-coated knife he was armed with might as well have been feathers with which to tickle her.

Her body transformed, and the white streaks resembling sinew and connective tissue between the red scales that formed outlines of muscle on a skinned body were no longer lifeless elastic tissue. They burned from within with a blue-tinged fire. Her eyes, once red-irised, now glowed like spotlights.

"Neekra?" Kane asked.

"Kane," she answered, voice rumbling in that all too familiar multitoned alien echo. The very utterance of a syllable packed the force and pressure of an exploding shell, Kane's own name slapping him harshly.

"Are we…" Kane searched for the words, fighting his panic. He'd been at ground zero with these kinds of gods before, and he did not want to spark her to rage. One flex, one flinch, and she'd splatter him against the wall, protective shadow suit or not. "Are we all right?"

He edged closer to her, hands down, palms empty as his Sin Eater retracted into its hydraulic holster, knife in its sheath. He prayed internally, silently, that whatever good-will he and his allies had established with the goddess still echoed in her memories.

"Yes, dear Kane. I recall your kindness, the good will that you and your friends established with me," Neekra voiced, echoing the phrasing of his thoughts exactly.

Kane froze, his heart rate skyrocketing with that state-ment. He felt the tickle of another mind, that familiar rustle of his thoughts actively scanned by another. His sensitivity to that presence in his thoughts had been honed by Balam's mental conversations with him. "You're telepathic again."

Neekra smiled, blood-red lips parting and her pointed teeth gleaming anew. Even the polarization of his shadow suit's faceplate did little to diminish the fury of that glare. Her stance turned from battle-ready to relaxed with shoulders squared, and she gave him a wink. Confi-dence filled her as she calmly stepped closer to him, work-ing her hips seductively.

Kane took a deep breath, realizing that she did not see him as a threat. "Of course, you're not worried about me attacking you. I'm only human."

"You said that, not me," Neekra responded. Her words boomed, battering his ears despite the dampeners of his hood.

As she walked, she released the artifact that had led them all to this spot, five miles below the surface of the Earth. This was where the staff that once belonged to King Solomon now hung in the air, as if supported by phantom hands. She ignored it now, walking away from it, and ap-proached Kane, who was frozen in place. He willed his limbs to move, but an outside force was acting upon him, seizing him as surely and tightly as the hovering Nehushtan. It was the same telekinetic bonds Negari had used on him earlier.

Neekra pressed her body against Kane's, brushing her fingers across his cheek in a manner that she would have thought was seductive. For Kane, it was as if she were raking his face with a bed of nails, his faceplate popping off from his hood and the hood itself snagging and sliding back over his hair. The heat of Negari's throne room, raised by the unleashing of Nehushtan's limitless energies, throbbed heavily against him, and his pores opened immediately, sweat pouring through them.

"Do not fear, lover."

With the heat, the power of her caress of his cheek and the rumble of her five syllables slamming into his eardrums like hammers on either side of his head, Kane found himself clinging to consciousness, fighting against the weakness of his flesh. Kane had endured extremes of environment, both with and without his Magistrate armor or the shadow suit's environmental systems, but the air was so hot that his sweat evaporated immediately. As Neekra's arm slithered around his waist, his spine bent under the crushing force that made an anaconda seem puny. She didn't speak now, knowing that her words were simply too much for his mortal ears.

Neekra ascended to full godhood. Where once she had merely been an avatar, a fragment of Negari herself, Neekra's blazing glow seared at his eyes. The sheer energy washing off of this woman was far beyond anything he could comprehend.

And still, Neekra leisurely strolled among the contours of his psyche as if she were visiting an art museum, but one that allowed the touching of sculptures. These sculptures were Kane's body, and she was taking an all-fingers-on-deck tour of each of his sexual encounters, both real and wistfully imagined. As if on the heels of her afterthought, waves of erotic pleasure from those memories, those imaginings, even the ones he'd experienced in "jump dreams" and in alternate casements, crashed against Kane, threatening to drown him. He gasped for breath, her telekinetic bonds on him released as an arm as sturdy as solid iron pinned his body against hers. The heat of her cut through the environmental regulators of the shadow suit. Underneath the skintight uniform, he was drenched.

Kane's mouth was dry, his tongue cracking. Every movement of his features made it seem as if his skin were parchment, ready to crack.

Despite the pains and discomfort, every inch of his skin surged to electric life, replaying thousands of kisses and loving caresses, the lap of a woman's tongue, the pressure of her sex engulfing him, no matter how tight. The drugged weeks of his imprisonment as a breeding stud for the Quad V Hybrids were no longer lost behind a chemical haze, and the tiny, child-sized women's anatomies smothered him. Neekra was feeding now. She was gorging herself, catching up with thousands of years of enforced, bodiless celibacy.

The weight of all of this beneath his skull was nearly as bad as when Neekra flogged him across seeming centuries of telepathic torture, seemingly months ago when he first became aware of the deadly goddess's presence. Kane willed himself to fight against her intrusion into his mind and body, going for a desperate maneuver. He dredged up their personal encounters when she had psychically imprisoned him.

Those memories flooded to the front of his mind's eye, and suddenly Kane was no longer pinioned by her arm. He crashed to his knees, his torso threatening to explode a flood of vomit onto the floor at the naked Annunaki's feet. Out of the corner of his eye, Kane noticed that the fiery glow no longer burned in the seams of her skin, nor from the cores of the suns that made up her eyes. Her lips parted in horror and realization. Kane's mind rustled as that emotion flashed across their psychic link, bone-chilling terror that washed him clean of all of her sudden influence.

Neekra stumbled backward, tripping over her own feet, dimming eyes trailing light as she toppled to the glass-smooth floor beneath the two of them.

"No!" she yelled. Despite being belted out at full volume, her shout didn't carry the explosive impact of inhuman lungs expelling words with the force of sledgehammer blows. She rolled to crawl on all fours, staggering with all of her strength to even be able to support herself with rubbery limbs that once were hard as steel. "No!"

Kane wanted to move, and he fought the urge to hurl his last meal onto the ground. Something was wrong with the woman, and his urgency grew greater as he realized that he no longer had any contact with her mind.

"What's wrong?" he croaked from a dried throat. He pulled his hood back into place, attaching the faceplate once more. The sweat beneath his shadow suit had been whisked from his skin and was already being transferred to his dry-roasted face. He blinked, tears soothing the soreness of his eyes. Maybe the Annunaki woman's body couldn't handle the sudden rush of power slamming into her.

He pushed to his feet and staggered to her side, resting his hand on her shoulder.

Touching her was a mistake; the brief moment of contact broke her meltdown. With a shrug of her shoulder and the impact of her elbow into his gut, he was lifted from the ground and hurled twelve feet. Fortunately, this time his shadow suit was up to the task of cushioning those hammering collisions. Kane easily got back to his feet.

"Durga! Damn you, where are you Durga?" Neekra howled. She tried to rise as high as she could on her knees, but a spasm folded her over. She clutched her stomach as thick, clotting fluid bubbled over her lips like tar. Kane wondered if the woman vomited blood, but he swiftly realized that her illness was Neekra's body. The cloned body Durga had given her was rejecting the prion proteins Negari utilized to give himself and her extrasensory powers. The ichor represented the biological mechanisms that assembled to form antennae and processors for mental energies. Nehushtan had held the healing factor at bay, but now body chemistry expunged that which Durga denied her.

The Nagah prince no longer had to worry about a telepathic, telekinetic ex-lover hunting him down and exacting revenge on her.

"Neekra? What's wrong?" Kane asked.

She was still heaving, but these weren't spasms of vomiting or nausea cramps. They had taken on a new emotion, one of bottomless sorrow and terror. No longer did she feel physically ill; she was suffering on a whole other level.

"I thought I'd been Negari's lover, Enlil's daughter, but I was…that abomination's creation," she sobbed over lips still gummy with the gooey remains of her prion antenna and biocomputer structures.

"But you destroyed her," Kane said. "You are yourself…"

"No, you don't understand," she interrupted. "For all this time, since Durga had awakened me, I thought I was still, at least, the original avatar inserted into a new body."

She looked up to Kane, her red eyes gone dark now, no longer burning from within. "I'm not."

Neekra let her head hang. Kane kneeled closer, resting his hand on her shoulder again. This time she did not fight him off. "Neekra?"

"I saw the truth when I entered your mind, when you pulled up...pulled up the true Neekra's assault upon you," she sobbed. "I was not the creature in your thoughts. I could never have been the creature in your thoughts. I saw what that bitch did, and it made me ill."

Kane tilted his head. "But isn't that a good thing?"

She rested her hand atop his. "It is good that I'm not a monster. It's good for the world. But I am merely an echo of an echo. Negari created Neekra to seek out a man like you to enslave you. Then Durga made me, a copy of the Neekra he captured and destroyed."

"Not many people have a third chance at life," Kane said.

Neekra shook her head. She looked toward the few wisps of dust left over from her eruption into goddesshood. "Negari needed someone like you, the mightiest steed in the stables, so she could take great pleasure in breaking you. I read those leftover thoughts from her in your mind. I *saw her.* I stared into the abyss she represented and saw nothing of myself. It repelled me."

Kane blinked. "We've been wondering why Durga had made Thurpa. For a moment, we thought it was so that he could have a new son. We've worried that he might have been a planted weapon in our ranks."

Neekra nodded. "I thought so as well. Durga made Thurpa from whole cloth as an experiment. He believed with all of his heart that he was twenty years old, an individual who had grown in Garuda. He still retains those memories. It was an experiment, and using what he learned when he had woven the young Nagah's mind through implanted memories, he constructed me. And he used Neekra's own echoes in his psyche as the model for...me."

Kane was confused as to how Neekra could have known the difference between herself and the Neekra who had trapped him in a coma for almost a whole day. Then, as if in a fevered dream freshly recalled upon awakening while wracked with coughs and pain, the she-devil's presence in his memories bubbled to the surface, shaking the very foundations of his coordination. The totality of that entity, the original temptress and scourge who'd lashed and bedeviled him for hours that felt like aeons, crashed to the forefront of Kane's consciousness. He struggled and realized that his subconscious had constructed its own detailed, horrific simulacrum of the original.

"But…that could just be how my subconscious remembered you," Kane offered. "Distorted by dream and imagination."

As he spoke to the crumpled, sobbing Neekra, vibrant images from the Annunaki woman's memories blurred past his mind's eye. The events they represented were real enough, and Kane could tell that they were the aftermath of the psychic goddess's presence inside of his skull. She'd left an imprint that wound more and more around his subconscious, barbed wire tines spearing into his soul.

Kane was torn between wishing for Brigid Baptiste's keen photographic memory and revulsion that these echoes, these shadows of a horrific history nestled somewhere within him. Although the knowledge he might have tapped would prove beneficial on some scale, the grisly facts weighed on him like cold lumps of poison in his gut.

Neekra must have left similar impressions in Durga when she seduced him. Even if Durga had not shared Kane's comatose state and helplessness at the same time, he *saw* Neekra and Durga as lovers, entwined mentally in a tangle of limbs and brutal passion. He'd placed his imprint upon her, and she had poisoned, darkened him with her essence.

Kane grimaced, his legs starting to feel rubbery as

the "aftertaste" of the deadly goddess tainted the world around him.

Once more, Kane was reminded of how devious Durga had to be. When Neekra invaded the prince's mind, choosing him as one of her pawns in the search for Negari, Durga took her and made her his own pawn. Durga used that imprint of her to create a weapon that could be utilized against a threat that could have opposed him. With Annunaki's biological interfaces and mankind's cloning and rapid-indoctrination technology, Durga honed his own personal sword and gave her to Kane.

It was easier to destroy the original abominable goddess and build a clone from the ground up, free of the viral protein enhancements yet believing herself to be the original. There was far less likelihood that she'd break free of his control and turn back to slay him.

Granted, the Neekra before him could try that, but she wouldn't be the almighty queen, creating a brood of body-snatching blob soldiers, nor did she possess inhuman sight beyond sight or the telekinetic energy to shatter stone as if it were dried mud.

Kane turned from her. He grabbed up the artifact as it hung in the air. As he touched it, it felt different. It no longer had vibrant power; it didn't have the warmth, the pulse that it used to have.

Had they truly spent all of its power in battling Negari?

Kane prayed that they hadn't. With the staff in one hand, he reached down and helped Neekra back to her feet.

"What are you doing?" she asked.

"Helping an innocent," Kane said. "You're not the monster you thought you were."

Neekra rose. She was unsteady at first.

"While we were fighting, while Negari controlled you,

I heard an explosion in the distance," Kane said. "It was hard to miss."

"Someone set off a bomb up the ramp," Neekra answered. "The others might have been caught in its blast radius."

Kane nodded.

As much as she was the image of a creature who had mentally tortured him, she was innocent of that. Though right now she felt as if the rug of her entire history was pulled out from under her, she was a new person, a clean slate. She was actually concerned about the people that they had left behind, and with each step, she picked up speed.

Worry covered her face. She looked around at the mangled remnants of the insectile sentries, a new pang of angst gleaming in her eyes. "These things…swarmed out when Negari summoned them…"

"Our friends are on the other side of a barrier," Kane stated. "And they are our friends."

Neekra nodded. "Yes."

"The only friends you've truly known," Kane pressed.

Neekra's eyes narrowed. "I'm not a simpleton, Kane."

Kane stopped climbing the steps as she glared down at him. He wondered if he'd pushed too far. They had developed some goodwill, but the anger on her face showed a level of offense that might undo that. He only had two words that might help, and they didn't always work. "I'm sorry."

Neekra's lip curled, then her mouth turned up in a smile. "That's all right. You're used to speaking with humans. They are not swift on the uptake."

Kane rolled his eyes. "Don't scare me like that."

"I'll keep it in mind," Neekra said. "You look a little more energetic."

"It's either adrenaline from concern about my friends, or this damned stick is returning me to full health slowly," Kane returned. "I hope it'll have enough juice for our friends."

"It should," Neekra offered. "It works to amplify your own natural emotions and thoughts. And if your worries are spurring you on…"

"Then I can move heaven and earth to save them," Kane grumbled. He gave a canister component of the defunct sentries a kick, the metal clanking hollowly off the steps as it bounced to the arena floor.

It was time to get out of here. As much as this had been where Neekra enjoyed her rebirth, it was also a place of death.

Chapter 23

Grant realized why the clone had been used as his arrow dropped the poor, "disposable" being, sending the corpse into a dead slide down the ramp, bringing the center of the explosion closer to him. Especially because the target had the face of Durga, an opponent who had been responsible for cruelty and death. If Grant, Brigid or Thurpa could not put some kind of projectile through the face of this devil, it would because the prior assault had killed them.

Even Nathan and Lyta had learned to despise the Nagah prince for his deadly actions. A chance at taking out the leader was nothing to turn their backs on, and for that reason, Durga had delivered death almost into Grant's lap.

He peeled off his shadow-suit hood and looked around. The corridor was dimmer now, the CEM lighting units having received considerable damage in the wake of the explosive blast. Whatever the charge that Durga had used, it had carved a ten-foot-deep crater in stone that had shrugged off shoulder-fired anti-tank missiles.

Grant shook his head and looked around for his allies. One by one, they rose from behind cover, looking stunned and bewildered by the horrendous blast.

"Is everyone all right?" Grant asked.

"We're still as banged up as we were before," Lyta said. "What about you?"

Grant grimaced. "I've got a killer headache."

"Understandable," Brigid said. "You've got a bruise where a rock cracked you on the noggin."

Grant squinted. "I'm going to get the flashlight in the eyes…"

Brigid nodded. "It's a precaution, checking your autonomic reflexes. We can't have you stumbling around with a concussion."

Grant winced as the blare of the LED torch burned in his eyes. "No. But now my night vision is ruined…and it's gotten dark in here."

"There doesn't seem to be a way to climb up," Nathan announced. "Thurpa gave me a boost, but the ramp has been trashed."

Grant started to stagger to his feet, but Brigid held him back. "What's wrong?"

"Your pupils are different sizes," Brigid stated. "That's not good."

Grant frowned. His stomach hadn't quite quit churning, and the headache made him want to lie down and not move for the rest of the year. He'd gone beyond a concussion, according to his Magistrate medical training. The symptoms running through his body matched up with a brain injury, but because he could concentrate and still sit up, it wasn't as terrible as it could be…

"Any blood in my ears?" Grant asked.

"No, but you do have a small laceration," Brigid told him.

Lyta looked at the hood. "It cracked. The miracle plastic cracked under the impact. So you could have been a lot worse off."

Grant creased his lips tightly. A veil of moisture was building around the corners of his eyes. He felt Thurpa and Nathan hook him under his arms and help him to a sitting position. Brigid continued to test his neck and the base of his head.

"Where did Kane get to?" Grant asked.

That made Brigid's demeanor grimmer, alarm widening her eyes. "Please say you're joking."

Grant took a deep breath, wishing that he could tame the Kongamato doing aerial somersaults in his gut. "I don't have shit in me to joke."

"Did you lose consciousness?" Brigid asked.

"If I can't tell where Kane went..." Grant began to complain.

"We'll assume yes," Brigid answered for herself. "No neck injury, but keep him braced, boys."

"You know we will," Thurpa said.

Nathan frowned. "Just how bad can it be? Would the staff be able to help?"

"It proved capable of closing Thurpa's wounds from his first Kongamato attack," Brigid began.

There was a rumble, the sounds of a thunderstorm, but they came from deeper in the earth. Down where Kane had gone, shoulder to shoulder with Neekra.

Grant finally remembered that little fact. "Either things are going well, or they suck."

"Let's prepare for the worst, then hope for the best," Brigid said.

"Prepare what?" Grant asked. "I don't think I could aim to hit the broad side of a barn."

"Lyta, stay with Grant," Brigid ordered. "Nathan, Thurpa, we'll see if we can get to Kane and Neekra."

"If they survived," Thurpa murmured.

Brigid's features grew stern, emerald eyes flashing angrily. "Do not even begin. No one is dead until we see the body. And even then..."

"I get it," Thurpa said.

The three people headed down the ramp. The incline was littered with rubble, all blown out from Durga's detonation. The Nagah prince's bomb was powerful indeed to crumble the stone of the ziggurat's walls and floors.

Brigid's visual assessment told her that the stone was easily as durable as basalt, one of the hardest and least brittle of all stone. She had not seen the Durga clone, so she could not ascertain the amount of explosive packets he wore, but given the depth of the crater and the width of the debris dispersal, it certainly was not an amount of plastic explosives a single humanoid could carry. Which meant that Durga had used some other form of weaponry to turn the ramp and corridor into an impassable hurdle to return to the surface. Even from down here, scanning upward with her shadow suit's optical enhancements, she could see that the landing itself was strewn with slabs of broken surface stone, fallen so that they were an impenetrable barrier.

"He likely used either a Charged Energy Module or he got a hold of some orichalcum," she mused aloud.

"You said that orichalcum explodes on contact with sunlight. That's why the staff is coated in that black shell," Nathan said. "Oh…the C-4 on Durga's, or the clone's, vest set off the metal."

"Yes," Brigid answered. "Chances are, there have been other detonations further up, as well, covered by the sound of our battle. If we manage to vault the hurdle of Durga's suicide bomber, we'll find other impediments."

Thurpa frowned. "The bastard knows full well that he can't count on just one means of stopping you three. Of course he's going to use redundant measures."

Brigid turned to him. "You are a clone. But you've gained something other than the nurture he received. You are a completely different being."

"Yeah. So different that I couldn't see that coming," Thurpa said, gesturing back toward the blast crater. "We're just lucky that the roof held. Otherwise we'd be swimming in lava."

Thurpa's shoulders sagged. "What's the use of being Durga's copy if I can't anticipate…"

"None of us could, and we've battled him before," Brigid cut him off. "Don't beat yourself up about it."

Thurpa looked at the basalt wall that had slid down behind Kane and Neekra. He ran his scaled fingertips across the smooth surface. Brigid could see the turmoil in the young man, and she could sympathize. She knew full well what it meant to have the entirety of your history be proven a lie. She had been an archivist at Cobaltville, rebuilding the knowledge and history of the world after the horrible megacull known as skydark before she met Kane and Grant.

Whereas Brigid had Kane and Grant were her spiritual support, Thurpa had the budding friendship of Lyta and Nathan.

"Don't think about your yesterdays," Brigid told him. "You are Thurpa. Your life is your own now. You've discovered your compassion and your courage."

Thurpa rested his forehead against the basalt. "Do you really know how I feel?"

Brigid rested her hand on his shoulder. "I used to be a city girl, living as nothing more than a glorified librarian. Five years ago, I would have laughed at you if you'd told me that I'd encounter clones, telepaths, phantom knights, gods…*Nagah*."

The corner of Thurpa's mouth rose at her emphasis. "Yeah. I'm proof that anything can happen. I'm a cloned cobra-man whose venom was specifically configured to bring down a telepathic god."

They heard a tap on the other side. Brigid activated her Commtact, realizing she had neglected to turn it back on once the menace of the Kongamato and their sonic cries had passed.

Static assaulted her, despite the nearness of Kane merely on the other side of the corridor blocking slab. "Brigid… read…me?"

"The signal's barely getting through to me," Brigid enunciated loudly, slowly. "Grant needs help. He's hurt."

"Trying to get the door open," Kane returned. "The staff is responding slower. We used up a lot of its energy."

Brigid looked around the door, glancing to Nathan to see if he had seen any hints. The archway and walls were devoid of symbols or adornments that could have been keypads or controls. She even made a concerted effort to look closely with the advanced optics on her hood. Everything was stymied.

"Is anything on your side?" Brigid asked.

"Blank," Kane said loudly, his bellow clearing the static for a moment.

Brigid frowned, her emerald eyes scanning every inch. She even touched the surfaces of the barrier, of the floor and walls around them, hoping for that one small imperfection, that one tiny bit of a pressure plate or a switch or a plug where she could interact with the ziggurat with the power of her mind.

Nothing. Nothing whatsoever. Frustration mounted as she explored.

"Logic," Brigid mused. "Nehushtan warned us, correct?"

"Yeah," Kane answered over the radio.

"And then produced a landing and several blockades from which we could easily defend ourselves," Brigid added.

"I guess," Kane said.

"Can you perhaps entreaty Nehushtan?"

"Treat the stick? Okay, but I think the bartender went home!" Kane shouted.

Brigid shook her head. "Ask the stick to open the barrier!"

"Oh, entreaty," Kane returned.

There was a sudden shift. It was only a quarter of an inch by her reckoning, simply by following the smudge of a Nagah bullet strike on the door.

"That's it!" Brigid called.

She waited. Listened. There was no subsequent movement.

"Kane?" Brigid asked.

"Trying!" Kane called back. She knew that tone of voice, even through the static. He was frustrated. Stymied, as she had been.

"It stopped?" Brigid asked.

"I thought I'd wait and let Grant suffer," Kane growled.

Brigid wrinkled her nose. "At least the signal is clearer."

Kane grunted on the other end. "What's Grant's injury?"

Brigid looked back. "Head trauma. I don't know how severe, but he lost bits of memory. He was unconscious for less than a minute."

Brigid knew that Kane had similar emergency medical training to Grant, so he was aware of the potential for tragedy. Almost immediately, she heard him grunt over the Commtact. She couldn't hear through the door, though. That only confirmed the thickness of the hatch.

"All right, don't hurt yourself," Neekra said, also audible over the Commtact's frequency.

"She's right," Brigid added. "If you break something…"

"It still won't be as bad as Grant suffering a stroke, or worse," Kane grunted, rasping. "Open this bloody door."

Nathan and Thurpa had their machetes out, digging at

the crease between door and floor, but the tiny crack that allowed radio signals through still was too small for them to use the long blades as pry bars against these doors. Brigid could feel her soul friend's concern on the other side of the basalt barrier, the anxiety and desperation to get the healing power of Nehushtan to Grant. Brigid tried her machete, as well, but all she got for her trouble was chipped steel.

"Guys, I have movement up here," Lyta interrupted. "Something is moving in the rubble on the landing."

Brigid turned and looked back, zooming in with her faceplate.

The grunt and thud of Kane was audible on the other side of the barely opened blast door. He must have tried to drive the artifact into that slender crack, using whatever strength he could muster.

The thought of something still alive up there, especially with Grant injured, spurred Kane on. Of course, Brigid jogged a couple steps back toward where Grant and Lyta waited.

"We're coming down to you," Grant said. He didn't sound well, but she saw him walking, if relying on Lyta for stabilization.

Grant never ceased to amaze Brigid with his feats of strength and endurance. To walk, even with head trauma…

"Coming," Brigid said, running back up the slope, watching her step around strewed stone and debris.

Thurpa and Nathan remained behind, still hoping to worry their machetes into place and somehow lift a slab of stone that easily weighed tons. It seemed a futile effort, but it would be Grant's best chance at recovery, and it would add to the number of people who could resist whichever new menace approached.

Brigid reached Grant and Lyta, then stood her ground

behind them as they continued toward the barrier. She had her machine pistol ready as the lights, powered by Charged Energy Modules, began to dim, starting to flicker and sputter.

"Kane, you killed Negari, right?" Brigid asked.

"She's dead," Kane answered. "Why?"

"Because…because things look awful bad," Brigid returned.

Stones started rolling *up* the ramp, toward the blast crater. Brigid knew that whatever was at work drew on the near-limitless battery power of the CEMs, and was assembling something that required a large amount of stone. Her breathing drew shallower as rubble shifted, altered, then cracked apart so as to create more, smaller stones. The figure being formed by the rocks as they stacked atop each other slowly became more and more humanoid, and Brigid's stomach turned. Cold fear threatened to grab hold of her, but she fought the urge to say anything, let alone release the scream building just beneath her diaphragm.

"Negari was a she?" Thurpa asked, grunting as he threw his weight into another effort at lifting the door.

"I'm a copy of her," Neekra answered over the radio. Her voice bespoke of strain as she tried to apply her great Annunaki strength to removing the barrier between the two groups of explorers. "Well, she made the thing that Durga copied me from."

"What?" Thurpa sounded shocked at that bit of information.

Brigid kept track of this conversation, and suddenly the stories of the vampire queen seemed a bit more understandable. One part of her mind recalled the gods of India and how many of them produced avatars—broken-off essences of themselves with complete autonomy—such as Rama and Krishna, who were the superhuman incarnations of the god Vishnu. Neekra, being an avatar of Negari, would have been a formidable mental and physical force, but in the end, she was merely a manifestation, a splinter of the original. Of course, Negari would have constructed a false memory for her copy.

Now Brigid understood why Durga was also so ready to align Neekra with the Cerberus expedition. Even if Neekra somehow resumed her power, or even usurped Negari, Durga would have both mental and physical safeguards within the clone.

As frozen in anticipation of the formation of the stony golem as she was, she was still more than capable of following Durga's machinations. She pitied Neekra but now realized that Thurpa had a sister in the Annunaki clone.

If they survived this growing, solidifying monstrosity before them, Brigid would make it a point to tell the two of them about that.

Now, she braced herself as the head finally formed, and much like the insectile assemblages of canisters, this creature was topped with what appeared to be a hollowed-out boulder with two grim, glowing red eyes floating in omnipresent shadow. Its arms finished assembling themselves, and the two massive fists bumped against each other with the crash of a nearby thunderbolt. The thing stood at twenty feet in height.

She felt the pressure wave given off by the collision of stony fists and knew that the body was made of the same stuff that hand grenades and bullets could not do more than leave smears upon. Shoulder-fired rockets only blew off small patinas of dust.

Brigid lifted her machine pistol, lining up the sights on those burning, hateful firefly eyes. The twin crimson points of fury swiveled toward her and must have deemed her unworthy of a response, even to the threat of a gun at its face.

Instead, it snapped one of its arms out in a powerful jab, but at the end of that lunge, its fist and some of its forearm broke off from the rest, sailing down the corridor in the form of a gigantic missile. Lyta shoved Grant to the ground, stony knuckles missing Grant by a hair's breadth, and Nathan and Thurpa scurried against the walls of the ramp.

But the giant had not aimed at any of the humans. Instead, when the fist landed, Brigid felt the whole universe crash around her.

She knew the reason for this demonstration of limitless power. This was one of Negari's fragments, and it wanted to kill Kane and Neekra alongside their friends. Destroying the group one member at a time would not satisfy the bloody urges of this rocky titan.

You catch on quickly, Brigid Baptiste.

It sounded like Neekra's voice in her mind, but now that the truth was known, there was no mistaking the telepathic message's sender for anyone but Negari, daughter of Enlil.

You are most wise and intelligent, even by Annunaki standards. It is a shame that I shall have to extinguish that intellect, but such is the lot you have cast.

Brigid heard Kane grunt behind her, crawling through the hole shattered in the two-foot-thick stone. Neekra was right behind him, handing Nehushtan through the hole.

Make certain your man is healed. I find hope more satisfying to crush when it's at full strength.

Brigid knew that these thoughts were broadcast to everyone present.

She watched as Kane rushed to Grant's side, motioning for him to hold the artifact.

The Negari golem simply watched and waited.

This time, there seemed to be no way out.

Chapter 24

The twenty-foot giant, an assembly of telekinetically manipulated stones animated by the spirit of the alien goddess Negari, would have to wait for more attention from Kane as he rushed to his friend's side. Brigid stood still, acting as a one-woman line in the sand between them and the monstrous golem looming up the ramp. She'd granted Kane leave to tend to Grant, and unfortunately, his friend seemed worse and worse off.

As Grant touched the shaft of Nehushtan, the ancient artifact, a scepter of kings and a weapon of heroes, blood began to trickle from the injured man's ear and nostrils. The sight of the red slicks pouring down his neck and upper lip, turning his gunfighter mustache into a grisly scarlet tangle, made Kane's stomach lurch with worry.

"Oh God, that feels better," Grant said under his breath, his head rising slowly, even as the blood poured down. "It's like someone jammed dirty laundry in my head, and now they're pulling it out."

Kane calmed some. "You were bleeding inside of your skull. The staff is relieving that pressure."

Grant winced. "Yes. Head still hurts like hell, but I don't feel dizzy or ready to yack up my last meal."

Kane nodded. "Brigid, come over here."

She stood her ground, keeping her eyes locked on the red globes of fire hovering in the middle of the golem's otherwise featureless face. "Negari will not get past me."

"No, but she'll go through your blasted corpse," Kane growled. "We need to have a conference."

Brigid looked back at him. After a moment, she nodded, turning and descending the ramp to where Grant sat, still holding the artifact, still drawing healing energies from it.

Kane nodded to Nehushtan. He hoped that he didn't need to enunciate the need for contact with the artifact, hopefully allowing all three of them some shielding from whatever powers Negari possessed. Brigid smiled slightly, then rested her hand on Grant's shoulder, and all three of them felt *connected,* far more than they had ever been.

The world whited out about them, and it seemed as if they were suspended in the blank, endlessly bright void about them. Brigid nodded with understanding. Grant grunted with surprise. Kane simply looked around. Everything about them was gone—Negari's stone form, the ziggurat, the "kids," as he'd come to refer to Nathan, Neekra, Lyta and Thurpa.

"Brigid?" Kane asked.

"We've been synchronized by the staff," Brigid noted. "This is likely a mental illusion, allowing us the image of the privacy the staff provides."

"Which means what? Sooner or later, Negari is going to get annoyed at waiting for me to heal up," Grant said.

Kane shook his head. "No, because time spent in telepathic contact is compressed. We believe we're speaking words, but we're dumping knowledge into each other instantly. My thoughts become yours, yours become mine. We understand each other completely."

"So we could spend seemingly hours here," Grant mused. "All right. But what about her? When all she had to work with were old recycled cans, her bodies were bad enough. Now, she's a walking avalanche."

"We have an advantage, though," Brigid said. "The staff."

"Yeah. It's powered by the wills of the wielder," Grant added. He looked to Kane. "You knew that and didn't have…damn this telepathy thing is creepy."

Kane nodded. "It's not something you get used to."

"That's why you wanted me in on this contact as well," Brigid said. "By yourself, you barely had the energy necessary to attempt to deal with Negari."

"By the way, one comment. She was an ugly-ass bitch," Grant spat.

"Inside and out," Kane returned.

Grant looked slightly confused. "But if her body was destroyed when Thurpa's venom attacked her system…"

"Negari had a body here in this dimension, but she explored the multiverse," Brigid said. "When Kane and Neekra were battling her, she summoned the splinters she'd sent out, and those splinters put on their battle armor and rushed to her aid."

"And this one is the last fragment of Negari?" Grant asked.

"One, or multiple fragments," Kane answered. "Enough to reconstitute a whole. She'll need a more stable body than a pile of rubble…"

"Neekra," Brigid spoke up. "She'll want her body. Even if she's not the original fragment that Negari sent out, Neekra is still an Annunaki, genetically and physically. She'll become the perfect vessel for the remains of the goddess."

"We cannot allow Neekra to come in contact with that thing," Grant said. "If we can form a circuit just by Brigid touching my shoulder while I hold on to the staff…even a fragment of that stony bastard contacting Neekra might infect her."

Kane looked to Brigid. "Grant's right. Only the three of us should deal with her. The kids are good, and they're brave, but…"

"But they are not a team like us," Brigid concluded. "The three of us have fought side by side long enough. We can *become* a unified front. Kane, you are right. Our three wills, working together to control the power of the staff, will give us enough power to deal with Negari."

"We'll be just like Cerberus," Kane mused, a sly grin crossing his lips. "A three-headed guardian. Except this time, we're not guarding the front door of hell…"

"In a way, we are," Grant put in. "This is Negari's hell. We're not keeping someone out. We're keeping her in."

"Cerberus. So truly fitting," Brigid mused.

"If this doesn't work—" Kane started.

"Not a single doubt, Kane," Brigid cut him off. "It's all or nothing."

She extended her hand. Kane offered his. Grant placed his atop both of theirs.

The three people closed their eyes, feeling the power of the artifact flowing warmly through each of their bodies and minds.

NATHAN LONGA GRIPPED his rifle as he looked up at the horrible menace looming at the end of the corridor. He glanced to the others of this little ragtag group, the young people who had followed the three explorers from Cerberus to this damned little hole in the Earth. His palms were sweaty, despite the environmental adaptation of the shadow suit he'd been lent. Nerves were drawn into taut wires.

All he had seen since coming into the stewardship of Nehushtan, the ancient juju staff, had been a prologue to this moment. He'd thought that after giant winged monsters, reanimated corpses and a naked Annunaki woman, he'd encountered everything under the sun. Now, he faced a goliath made of stone—but not sculpted stone. It was a collection of rocks and boulders, all held in place by some otherworldly glue that allowed it to move and stand like a human being.

He'd watched the thing detach its fist from its arm and shatter a two-foot barrier with a single blow.

And now all he had was one grenade and a rifle full of bullets that wouldn't score so much as a chip off the alien rock it was formed from. His companions were in the same boat. Even Neekra, that naked Annunaki goddess who stood more than six feet tall, was tiny and slender by comparison to the golem.

This was Negari, the creature they'd trekked across miles of jungle to find. And she was huge, angry and unstoppable.

Yet Negari didn't wish to attack. It could easily have pulverized all of them, but instead, it taunted the group, allowing them to heal Grant, the man from Cerberus who had taken an injury to the head. He looked as if he were getting better, despite the runoff of blood from his nose and ear, and the three people knelt, huddled about each other. Nehushtan had blocked telepathic probes before, hidden its wielder from hunters and boosted their strength to battle even the strongest of foes.

Now Nathan wondered if that would be enough. The golem looked as if it were growing impatient, taking smooth, almost feather-light steps for its great bulk and mass. It was agile as well, walking gracefully.

"What can we do against this thing?" Nathan asked.

"Our best," Thurpa answered. "It was an honor meeting you."

"We're not dead…yet," Lyta said, that last qualifier sticking in her throat.

Neekra took a step ahead of the three young people. "Stay behind me. I'll protect you for as long as I can."

Nathan frowned. The woman, when he first encountered her, was an abomination who'd possessed and mutated the body of the man who tried to kill him and the Cerberus group. She had been the definition of monster, but she was very different now. Kane mentioned something about her being a different entity from that blood goddess. She was practically a newborn.

And right now, she was willing to put herself between certain death and them.

Nathan started to edge forward when the air in front of Neekra seemed to suffer three claw slashes, tall inverted triangles ripped in nothing, glowing with an inner white fire, three globes of fire standing atop the seeming shoulders of each angular figure. Stunned, the Annunaki woman reached forward and was pushed back, not harshly, but firmly, her scaled feet scratching on the stone beneath her feet.

"Look! Look at them!" Lyta shouted, squinting and looking between the triangular markings wrought in the air. Nathan crouched and saw that the three people from Cerberus—Brigid, Grant and Kane—were now aglow, fire trail mists swirling in the air, forming a huge quadruped that stepped in front of the wall of light.

"What the hell?" Thurpa asked. "Is that...a dog?"

Nathan blinked as, indeed, a canine seemingly formed from the ether, standing six feet at its shoulder, flames licking along its surface in the form of fur. "What's wrong with its head?"

"Three heads," Neekra interrupted. "Cerberus. They have actually formed a Cerberus out of pure willpower with the staff!"

A growl resonated from a trio of phantom throats, deep

rumbles shaking the air through the energy field that they had set up.

Do the three of you think that just because you have...

That was all that managed to be "said" by the rocky goliath before the elemental force of fire leaped at it, producing a concussive blast that jolted Nathan off his feet, toppling to the ground. Braced on his elbows, Nathan looked through the "bars" of the energy shield that protected him and the others. The three people from Cerberus were still surrounded by an aura akin to the one that blocked off the tunnel, while the stony goliath lashed at the air, red orbs of burning hatred flaring.

No, there's no way you can be that strong!

Neekra knelt next to Nathan, helping him to sit up further. "Yes, they can be that strong. I still have the memories from when Durga and I shared Kane's mind. If there are three wills on this planet that can make that weapon supreme, they are theirs."

The blazing wolf creature lashed out with paws larger than sledgehammers, each swipe turning a rock on the creature's surface into a puff of dust and stone splinters. Negari, however, punched back, managing to hit the flaming Cerberus midtorso. The creature toppled to the ground.

"But Negari, even diminished by the death of her aspect left in this world, is still a strong bitch," Neekra added. Nathan didn't like the sense of defeat sounding in the Annunaki woman's voice.

THE CONFLICT WITH NEGARI, at least the one observed by human and Annunaki in the ziggurat tunnel, was only a small piece of the totality of the battle that Kane, Brigid and Grant engaged in. Nehushtan had converted their wills into the same entity that Negari was, and they were three souls, spread across multiple planes of existence. The flaming three-headed wolf fighting with the rocky goliath avatar of the bloody goddess was merely a shadow, a manifestation of will in the real world.

Negari was before them, in a form similar to Neekra, except this one seemed carved from lightning itself. That lightning, however, was mortal enough to be struck by the "guns" of Kane and Grant, Sin Eaters formed of their own will, firing bolts of force at the pan-dimensional shadow before them. Negari grunted under impacts, but it was clear that, although she felt their effect, the psychic bullets they fired were only hampering her, not causing severe injury.

"How in the hell are the three of you keeping your wits?" Negari growled as she watched her monstrous animate fighting at her feet, jolted by impacts from the two men.

Suddenly, Negari screamed as a spearhead erupted from her chest and red-tinged smoke poured from her elemental chest and into the air. At the other end of the spear's shaft was Brigid Baptiste, leaning into the weapon.

"This is not our first journey across dimensions," Brigid said. "And as we returned to this particular plane of existence, our knowledge returned of our previous…times spent here."

Grant moved in close and punched Negari hard across her jaw. The flash of energy produced by the mighty blow whited out their views of the windows to multiple universes for a moment before Negari snapped the spear from her chest and clawed at Grant in vengeance. The big man backpedaled.

"I was trapped here, only able to exist through shadows in reality," Grant said. "One of my shadows lived in the court of Humbaba for years. The real me was trapped in a place where time had absolutely no meaning."

Kane wove in closer to the Annunaki witch, having

manifested a simulacrum of his combat knife, lashing the blade across her arm, slicing her hand from her wrist for an instant before tendrils of electric current stitched the severed limb back together. Kane paid for that attack with a backhand that hurled him what seemed like miles. When he landed on the ground, the stunned Cerberus man realized that he was above ground and that this was the African countryside, not far from the ziggurat. The world beneath him seemed tiny, almost pitiful.

Grant was at his side in an instant, helping him up. "Don't get distracted."

"Right," Kane answered. Back on his feet now, he launched himself at Negari, remembering how he took flight before while exploring the gaps between universes for Grant. He crashed into Negari with the force of a freight train, flipping the pan-dimensional entity head over heels.

Negari glared after Kane angrily, her eyes red-rimmed and savage. Unfortunately for her, that distraction was more than sufficient for both Grant and Brigid to strike her at once. Grant's chosen weapon was a mental re-creation of his bow and arrow. Brigid simply summoned the biggest rocket launcher she could imagine. Both projectiles hammered Negari violently, swatting her to the ground before she could strike at Kane.

In the meantime, Kane looped back around, blazing away with his Sin Eater. "You remember Neekra's battle with me in my own mind, don't you? You've read her entire existence, just like you've absorbed the experiences of all of your other avatars."

Negari growled and reached up, stretching her arm toward Kane. His guns blazed, blowing massive holes through her ever-expanding hand, making Negari cry out in pain and withdrawing the injured limb.

"Yes, I remember," the hell queen answered.

"Lessons from mine and Brigid's time here between realms," Kane continued. He flipped and landed feet-first against Negari, kicking both of his feet into her head and flipping backward.

The entity growled.

She turned, caught another of Grant's psychic arrows and hurled it at Brigid. The woman grunted, her "will-weapon" disappearing into smoke as she clutched at her pained gut.

"Brigid!" Grant bellowed, rushing to her side.

Kane was distracted by his *anam-chara's* distress and fall. That lapse of focus on Negari lasted long enough for the entity to grab him by the throat. She dragged him from the skies of this battleground and slammed him hard into the African countryside, sending a wave of pain all along his back. Iron-strong fingers closed around his throat.

"You've learned lessons?" Negari asked. "I've *mastered* these powers! I've stalked these back alleys of reality for as long as you stupid little apes have *had* alleys!"

Kane clutched at Negari's arm, feeling strangled by the irresistible force of the blood queen.

Looking to the side, Kane watched as the "Cerberus" that they'd summoned to battle the stone golem was being smashed to the ground by hammering boulders of fists.

Negari leaned in closer to Kane. "You think that you can match me just because you have a little stick?"

"Ahem!" Grant cleared his throat. Negari glanced up and suddenly was face to club with the massive cudgel in Grant's hands. Suddenly Kane could breathe, and he rolled over, gasping to bring fresh oxygen into his lungs.

"Little stick?" Grant asked, winding back with the weapon in his fists. It was more than a cudgel; it resembled a stalactite. He brought the base of the massive object down, but Negari twisted out of Grant's swing.

She kicked up, catching Grant across the side of his head.

"Brigid," Kane said. "We're fighting her on multiple planes?"

"Different realities, yes, I'd say so. Why?" Brigid asked.

"I'm watching our fight inside the ziggurat," Kane answered.

Grant blocked another of Negari's wild, desperate kicks. "Kane!"

Kane pushed off from the ground, leaving behind his view of the battle below, while Brigid knelt to observe both events, below back on Earth and still in this dimensional crossroads. Brigid glanced and saw a flicker of other battles in mirroring universes. This seemed to occur all along the course of history, as well as in different spots in the universe.

Kane and Grant seemed to be represented by different races of men, even aliens, sometimes drawn, cartoonish images.

And Brigid could see herself, also reflected in those realms, in a thousand myriad flavors of self.

She recognized each set of eyes, even if they were the stalks of a mollusk-like variant of her from an Earth wherein vertebrates rose to full sapience and sentience.

Negari suddenly surged forward, hurling Kane and Grant to either side of her and advanced toward Brigid.

"Mewling witch! You'll learn *nothing!*" she cried, reaching out and grabbing Brigid by her arm.

The force of that grip was impossible. It was as if a bear trap had closed on her arm, and her shoulder screamed as if it was being torn from its socket.

Negari lifted her from the ground, tearing her away from the gallery peepholes to countless casements. Brigid hung limply in the deadly grasp of their foe.

But she still managed to rasp out a response to Negari's taunt.

"If there's one thing about us, bitch," she sputtered. "It's that we're *always* learning!"

Negari snorted and hurled her into Kane's lap. The psychic witch summoned a sword of fire as she eyed the fallen three people from Cerberus.

"This lesson will come far too late for you," she hissed.

Brigid took Kane and Grant by the hand, steeling herself for the blood queen's final slash.

Chapter 25

Grant recovered his senses just in time to see the personification of desperation in a bridge between universes as portrayed by three humans and a being whose lifetime was measured in dozens of centuries. Here, where even the Annunaki feared to tread, in the slips between times and places where reality itself could be manipulated with enough will and the right connected technology, he looked up at a towering goddess made of lightning, her hand filled with a sword carved from the fires of suns, raised over Brigid as she spread her arms protectively over him and Kane.

The three people had gotten here by combining their wills behind an artifact that had summoned Kane across the globe, seeking him out via dreams and by implanted thoughts to a young man left behind in Africa. The staff, called Nehushtan according to its resemblance to the biblical walking stick of Moses and King Solomon, had drawn them into the heart of the darkest continent into an ever-unfolding war, specifically between an old enemy of theirs and the entity before them, the reawakened Annunaki psychic Negari. All three of them had formed a circuit with the ancient staff whose mental interface technology had amplified them.

Here, they were beings of pure will, while the staff behind them had assembled a fragment of their essences into a guard dog of elemental fire to protect Nathan and three other friends from Negari's own avatar, a giant of stone and fury. With their three wills combined, they had become immensely powerful, their shadows from Earth's dimension seeming to tower thousands of feet in height, stretching across planes of existence, able to see through windows into other times and places. Despite all that power, Negari had thrashed them, throwing them into a pile and vowing to end this battle in one cruel, brutal stroke.

Brigid, in an act of selflessness, had thrown herself across the tesseracts of Grant and Kane, as if to shield them against Negari's oncoming assault. Yet, in that apparent final act of selflessness, the three human spirits formed a complete circuit. Once more, they were bound together by the powers of their strange artifact, and the deadly, hellish entity brought down her sword only to find it blocked by a length of ebony night. Flames danced off the black shaft as Nehushtan appeared in the grip of a single entity—the combined total of Kane, Brigid and Grant.

No longer was Grant merely, tenaciously connected to his friends by the telepathic circuit bonding them in "the real world"—back in the depths of the ziggurat that Negari had made her home. They were united as a single being. The power of Negari, itself fragments of the Annunaki woman's consciousness seeking a new host body, was blunted by the triumvirate made one.

"There has always been a confluence of possibility when the three of you are involved. Call it luck, call it fate, but you have been able to achieve the impossible," Grant heard Mohandas Lakesh Singh say, as clearly as if he were standing next to him.

"It's an aspect of Brigid's photographic memory," the Cerberus trinity said aloud to itself. "We have all of our aspects, unfiltered by the fragile lenses of our human bodies."

Negari recoiled from her newly configured foes, eyeing them with sudden wariness. "No. No. My intellect has spread across countless realities countless times. I have come within heartbeats of infinite power and potential. How can you match me?"

"Because we have been together across millennia," the Cerberus trinity returned. "You alone are infinite? No. All beings are infinite. All creatures possess mirrors in other worlds in other times. We have always been here to stop you and your greedy kind."

Brigid/Grant/Kane stamped the black juju staff into the "ground" at their feet, creating tremors in this dream space that rocked Negari off of her feet. "We are not alone against you."

The staff rose again, swinging hard to meet Negari's flaming sword, and in a burst of blinding light, the Cerberus trinity shattered her blade of hatred. The transdimensional goddess let the handle of the broken weapon fall away, tumbling into the ether between worlds, and stepped back in dismay.

Back in the ziggurat, Grant saw their flaming canine defender shatter the arm of the telekinetically animated golem seeking to reach Neekra, an Annunaki clone who was Negari's last hope for remaining whole. Neekra was a copy of one of Negari's avatars, one of the entities that Negari had sent out across other casements in search of the proper herald, the proper host body that would make her unstoppable. Kane and the fallen Nagah prince, Durga, had been two candidates for that task, at least in Grant's home dimension.

And it was Durga who knew that there was one group who could have stopped Negari.

Brigid/Grant/Kane lunged, striking against their opponent, and she blocked the embodiment of the staff with crossed forearms. The blow brought her to her knees, however. Eyes of feral hatred looked up toward the three who were one.

"This cannot be," she rasped.

The Cerberus triumvirate looked down upon her, frowning. "Go somewhere else. We don't have to kill you. Find a quiet home, a silent planet…"

"Never!" Negari growled. She raised her hand, lashing out and stretching the limb to reach for Brigid/Grant/Kane's throat. Her assault, however, was cut off. Their own powerful fingers clamped around her wrist, catching her before she could cause harm. Negari's eyes widened in panic, then her brow twisted in fury.

She struggled to get to her feet, but the trinity twisted her wrist, leveraging her back to the floor. Negari's forearm bent and snapped. Blinding pain evidenced itself in the form of a shriek that vibrated through the Cerberus adventurers, sending ripples of discomfort through their collective chest. Even with the power of their wills combined, they had been shoved off balance by that deadly shriek.

Negari moved forward at them once more and was about to strike, her fingers hooked into talons, when she shuddered under a phantom blow. She raised her injured forearm, tucking her eyes into the crook of her elbow. "What sorcery is this?"

Grant looked through one of the windows of alternity, the glimpses of other realities visible in this odd hub of time and space, and noted a bowman in blue-and-purple chain mail firing an explosive arrow into the face of a titanic creature. Another of those windows showed a small woman, perched on the shoulders of another nightmarish aggressor, emptying the magazine of a rifle into its eyes. Grant made an effort to look back to the ziggurat of their world. As the flaming canine was facing off with the granite goliath, their allies jammed the muzzles of their weapons in gaps of the energy field, blasting lead and the last of Grant's FRAG-12 shotgun grenades at the thing's eyes.

His knowledge was instantly the knowledge of Brigid and Kane. The three of them turned back, and drawing upon every iota of might available, rammed their fist *through* Negari's chest. The two tesseracts, suddenly interacting with each other, began burning with untold fires. Brigid/Grant/Kane imagined that this was what the punishments of hell must feel like as the agony poured into their own hearts like acid into an open wound.

Negari howled at the peak of her power, Brigid's intellect informing the trio that this was really more of a psychic phenomenon. There was actually no medium for sound to travel in. All four of them were constructs of pure energy and thus fortunately did not require atmosphere to survive. The pain that speared into the human spirits was the equal of the agony effecting Negari, and she started to blur, her structure diffusing around their fist.

"Together we can endure this," Kane growled. And for Grant's intimate knowledge of his friend, he was at the forefront, absorbing the bulk of the suffering. Even so, though Grant had never suffered a heart attack, he felt the crushing weight upon his chest. Had gravity still held him, his legs would have turned to rubber, strength failing him. Grant tried to feel what was going through Kane, but that contact was closed off.

"I am our intellect," Brigid explained. "You are our strength. But Kane is our spirit. He's the one who is filtering this pain. And nothing will break him, because our spirits are with his, just as your intellects support mine, and our strengths succor yours."

Grant wished he could do more than simply endure. He saw Negari breaking up faster and faster. She grew bright, and her screams vibrated apart, like soundtracks stretched out of shape, losing synchronization with themselves. Cold, black eyes stared from the center of Negari's face, but now they weakened.

"Mercy…"

"We offered it to you," the triumvirate answered. "You rejected it."

Grant's might surged again and he wrenched the arm free of the disintegrating lightning sculpture that she'd taken as her form in this dimension. Murderous pain still racked across the semblance of Grant's nervous system, but the agony ebbed down to a throbbing, dull ache.

The last sparks of Negari's existence flickered and snapped around their combined fist.

THURPA WATCHED, JAW agape as their brief flurry of gunfire had bought the flaming Cerberus entity its opportunity to strike at the heart of Negari's colossus. It plunged its elemental fury into the animated meteor storm that the alien witch had made into her fist of retribution. The heat of the triple-headed wolf, burning as bright as the relentless African sun, caused the massive figure to topple backward. Here, in a place of near darkness, Thurpa had to squint to protect his vision.

The heat licked at their energy barrier, then passed through. Even Neekra's Annunaki flesh seemed to glisten with perspiration. Moisture condensed between Thurpa's scales. The rich, dark complexions of his friend Nathan and the beautiful young Lyta gleamed with beads of sweat that shimmered like gold flakes on their skin.

The stone monster howled horribly, writhing. The fiery orbs of its eyes changed color, actually darkening against its ever-brightening, ever-melting flesh. Against the lavalike backdrop, those eyes turned into blackened pits before the burst and pop of magma bubbles swallowed them forever.

The sizzling stone began to move and pulsate, spreading out into a rough approximation of what the ramp above them used to be, allowing them to get up the incline back to the landing, back toward the surface.

And with that, the rubble cooled, settling into place as the fiery energies dissipated.

The barrier between them and Brigid, Grant and Kane also faded. Their glowing aura dimmed. The three people, having sat motionless encased in their shield of light, now collapsed to the ground, appearing unable to move.

"Pick them up!" Neekra commanded. She rushed toward the edge of the slope and bent, obviously feeling as if the stone were still too hot to walk safely upon. Nathan helped Kane up as Thurpa, larger and stronger than Nathan, put his size to good use on the heavier Grant. Lyta worked to get Brigid back to her feet.

"It's safe to walk up," Neekra told them. She looked around the landing and picked up as many magazines as she could. They'd expended almost all of their reserves of ammunition in holding off Durga's last-ditch assault on them, but they were under little illusion that Durga had exhausted his forces.

Neekra changed out magazines in her empty weapon.

"They made this ramp perfectly for us," Nathan said, helping the groggy Kane climb the slope.

Kane let out a low groan. "Well, it's not as if we could climb up the mess."

"You can talk already?" Nathan asked.

Kane nodded. "And walk, too."

"Where is the staff?" Brigid asked.

"What staff?" Lyta countered.

Grant butted in. "Nehushtan. The artifact…"

"Wait, none of you have it?" Neekra asked.

"You didn't have anything other than your regular gear," Thurpa mentioned. He blinked, showing confusion. "I think I remember something about a walking stick…"

"Brigid?" Grant called to the woman. They walked up the seemingly endless ramp, following its spiral from landing to landing with relative swiftness. There was no telling if the ziggurat was going to maintain its structural integrity, or if some other threat was going to come after them.

Negari was finished.

Nathan knew what the others were talking about, but his memory had grown fuzzy about its exact details, where it had gone, what had happened to it. The last he'd known…

"Nehushtan's deleting as much of the information about it that it can," Nathan said. "It's been displaying its power overtly, but now it's just reaching out."

"But where is it?" Brigid asked. She closed her eyes. "We did not have it when…we awakened from our trance."

"What happened to you?" Thurpa inquired. By now, Kane, Grant and Brigid were running under their own power as they accompanied the others up the ramp. Spare magazines were tossed so that each of the members of this escaping expedition had at least one full weapon. It might not have been much, but at least they would have some teeth.

"For the life of me, I can't explain it," Kane said. "There was a fight. And it wasn't here."

"We were sitting ringside to a pretty terrible-looking battle," Lyta said. "You don't remember the flaming three-headed dog?"

"I remember calling on the symbology of Cerberus, the mythical guardian our redoubt was named for," Brigid stated. "After that…oh dear."

"If Brigid can't recall what happened, there's no way

in hell anyone can remember anything," Kane grumbled. "Just like when we went looking for you, Grant, when you were lost in time."

The big man nodded. "You step into the time scoop, and the next thing you know, I'm piggybacking your body when you come out of the ether."

"You think we left the stick behind in that…ether?" Kane asked. "We took it with us, and now that it's gone, it's fading from human memory?"

Brigid shrugged. "It's as good a theory as anything. Right now, our main concern should be escaping this structure."

"You're certain that the big bad witch is dead, though," Lyta spoke up.

"I don't think we'd be having this conversation if she was still intact," Brigid answered.

Kane saw the entrance to the surface, actually the roof of the ziggurat, which was a half a mile above the surrounding area. The last time they had seen daylight, ranks of Durga's cloned soldiers were standing at attention up there. He didn't know what kind of forces had attacked Brigid, Grant and the others, but given the smears and body parts strewn about, he did not have a good feeling about their odds should they exit.

As they approached the top, a blip resounded in his Commtact.

"You survived. The world is still here, and it's not threatened," Durga spoke over the radio waves. "Congratulations."

"Where are you, worm?" Neekra growled.

"Ah. She found out the truth about herself," Durga chuckled. "You're upset with me?"

"My life is a lie," she responded.

Durga snorted. "Oh. Yes. You're so upset that you're not

a she-demon responsible for thousands, if not millions of deaths across thirty centuries?"

Kane jogged to the top lip of the ramp. Their truck was still there, untouched, right where the flight of Kongamato monstrosities had set it down. It stood alone. The rest of the top of the ziggurat was empty.

"You have burdened me with everything that bitch ever did," Neekra snapped loud enough to make Kane wince as he continued scanning for signs of an ambush. The caldera about them had seemingly cooled. Wisps of steam still rose from cracks in the blackened obsidian, but no bright orange lines of naked lava showed in the flattened volcanic crater about them.

Kane almost felt disappointed having to rush to the surface, when the deadly moat seemed to cool down.

"I also gave you a chance at a life without guilt, darling Neekra," Durga said.

"And me?" Thurpa asked. "What about me?"

"You are a proof of concept for the creation you see before you," Durga answered. "By the way, you two are now brother and sister, in case you ever worry about being alone in this world."

"Thurpa won't be alone," Lyta snarled.

"No," Nathan added. "They won't be alone."

Kane looked back to see Nathan reach out and take Neekra's hand in a show of solidarity. The ragtag bunch had been the ones who distracted Negari, that much he could recall. They had formed a family, a bond forged in danger and adversity. Nothing solidified such a union like a common enemy, Kane noted. Baron Cobalt was one such galvanizing force in his deep unity with Brigid Baptiste. That struggle had even given him respect for Mohandas Lakesh Singh, the founder of the Cerberus redoubt whose meddling had at first irked Kane, but they eventually reconciled, becoming partners in the return of Earth to a better state.

"Durga, I'm going to guess that you're gloating from a good safe distance," Kane spoke up. "Maybe Alaska, if you didn't lie to Neekra, but I doubt you're there. You wouldn't tell her anything that would lead us to your scaly ass."

As Kane challenged Durga, he noticed a ramp they could drive down, the steps of the ziggurat having a winding road around the base. The caldera looked better now, and despite vents of steam, it looked like they could navigate the cooled lava flow.

Grant walked to his side, the scowl on his face evidence of his distaste for the gloating creep haranguing them over the radio. He nodded to Kane, who came back from the top of the spiral to the surface. "The truck has been refueled from fresh jerry cans in the back. And there are four brand-new rifles with plenty of ammunition for each in a trunk. Handgun replacements for them, as well."

"Four?" Kane asked. He looked back to the group, who stood united in the face of Durga's taunts. "Enough for them to carve out a new life and existence here."

"That's what Brigid surmised, too," Grant said.

Kane tilted his head. "Surmised?"

Grant shrugged. "Our feminine compatriot's lexicon is literally infectious."

"Durga, you never told me what you got out of this," Kane said, rolling his eyes at his friend's silliness.

"Not enough," Durga responded. "Your annoying partners still live. Yet who knows how much easier my conquest of Africa would be with four adventurers like my son and daughter, Nathan and Lyta, dealing with disruptions of order such as the militias."

"The Panthers of Mashona being the first to drop," Kane said.

Kane could *feel* Durga's grin of smug self-satisfaction across the airwaves. "Amazing coincidence, that?"

Brigid was on a different frequency, Kane could see. She called to Cerberus redoubt. Naturally, Negari's ziggurat would correspond to a parallax point, a crossroads of magnetic energy where reality could be more easily opened up for wormhole matter transmission. Sure enough, the interphaser materialized in a puff of plasma waveform mist. Domi was there, standing alone, a genuine smile on her face as she saw her friends again after this long African journey.

"All this trip. Destroying the militia. Destroying Negari's fragments. Destroying Negari herself," Kane said. "You used us to accomplish your goals."

"Would you not have done the same without such manipulation?" Durga asked.

Kane and Grant frowned to each other. "Yes."

"Then my invitation was well sent," Durga concluded. "Fare thee well, heroes of Cerberus."

Those last words were meant to be a sneering insult. Kane shared a smile with Grant and Brigid at that mention.

Durga continued. "The next time we meet, I will know your measure, and you shall not have a mighty artifact from the annals of history to protect you."

They heard a burst of static, then silence on the line.

"I'm going to love turning that prick into a pair of snakeskin boots," Grant grumbled.

The three of them turned back to the small assembly, which seemed to have picked Nathan as their spokesman. It made sense to Kane. After all, he was the oldest of them. Neekra was mere days old, and Thurpa was only weeks old.

"It is time for us to part, I guess," Nathan said, nodding toward Domi and the interphaser.

Kane nodded and held out his hand. "Somewhere in

the past, we were brothers by blood. This adventure just shows that we never truly parted ways."

Nathan shook Kane's hand, smiling. "The staff won't be here to bring us back together."

"You have the radio headsets," Kane told him. "Cerberus satellites will keep their ears open if you ever need help again."

"Besides, Durga was the one who manipulated the staff," Brigid explained. "He used Austin Fargo to interface with the device to bring this all together. That much I could gather from his mention of his 'invitation.'"

"It figures," Nathan said. "Of course, this means that he might know where the staff is now."

"We'll handle that when we run into him again," Kane answered.

Thurpa frowned. "Make sure to invite me to that party."

Kane smirked. "If we have enough warning, Thurpa. So, you're not going back to India?"

"I never *was* in India," the young Nagah man said. "And there's a lot more for me here."

He glanced back to Lyta, who was saying her good-byes to Brigid.

Kane looked and saw Neekra buttoning up a shirt. Another gift from Durga?

"It's going to be a shame to cover up that tall, naked body," Nathan mused.

Kane gave the younger man an elbow. "Take care."

Nathan opened his arms, and the two men embraced like long lost brothers.

With that done, Nathan and his companions got into the pickup truck. The Cerberus exiles watched their new friends drive down the ramp.

"Safe journeys," Kane whispered.

Domi knelt and entered the return code into the interphaser, waiting for Kane to step into range so they could mat-trans back home.

Home, Kane thought. *I might never remember what we did to end Negari, but there's one thing I hope I never forget.*

He walked into the perimeter of the interphaser's transmission sphere. Brigid and Grant took his hand. Domi, on the other side, joined hers with theirs.

I'll never forget my friends.

With that, the four people winked out of existence atop the ziggurat, sliding through a wormhole back to the redoubt.

Epilogue

Durga sat in his personally built headquarters. Austin Fargo had left it behind when he'd disappeared.

The Nagah prince had accomplished about half of his goals. He could walk again. He'd eliminated the Panthers of Mashona as a potential rival in Africa. He'd ended the existence of Negari.

His schemes had succeeded against incredible odds. Yet…

Durga was alone in his office. All he had in the facility about him were clones, mindless drones he'd created to serve as his army, as his minions.

The one who was actually sentient, Thurpa, was now far away in Africa.

Durga felt happy for his "son," yet he was more than a little jealous. That young man had fallen into a quickly forged set of friendships.

Durga had drones and beasts in his employ.

Hell, even Austin Fargo would be preferable to the numbing solitude he now lived in.

Durga wiped the top of his desk clean. The only thing actually on the surface before him had been a crumpled note, and the wad of paper bounced partially into the hallway as he headed to the doorway.

Nehushtan, the artifact that Durga had initially manipulated to gather the pieces of his "chess game" against

Negari, was not in his possession. Austin Fargo had vanished without a trace. His ability to make clones had been deeply tapped. Stores of biomass and other supplies had been used up in the creation of his army, the Kongamato themselves proving quite resource intensive.

The artifact was what stung the worst, in Durga's opinion. It was a focus of power. It had been instrumental in tearing down a god between dimensions, and Durga had learned from Kane's memories of another such traveler—Colonel Thrush.

Without the ancient staff, Durga would not be able to conquer Thrush and rob him of his dimension-spanning ship.

The wad of paper lay between Durga's feet. Even crumpled, Fargo's message was a mocking slap in his face.

"Durga, the staff does not belong to you. You will never be allowed to find us," it read.

Us. As if Fargo were now some holy warrior, equipped with a religious artifact, defending it from the serpents that infected Eden.

Durga narrowed his eyes. "Of course Nehushtan truly was worshiped as a holy symbol. I stumbled right into that unfortunate thought."

"Sir? Are you in distress?"

Durga looked up. It was one of his servitor drones.

With a swipe of his foot, he kicked the garbage into the corridor before him. "Pick that up, and leave my presence."

The clone nodded and picked up the wad of paper.

Durga watched it walk away. He returned to his office and closed the door tightly behind him.

Somewhere, in the memory banks of this facility's computers, there would be a key, a clue that would give him the power to return to Garuda and sit on *his* rightful throne.

"You only have delayed the inevitable, Fargo. I will get what is mine."

His words echoed hollowly in the quiet office.

* * * * *

ALEX ARCHER
CELTIC FIRE

The theft of a whetstone and the murder of a curate seem like random crimes, but the troubling deeds are linked by a precarious thread...

Annja Creed, archaeologist and host of television's *Chasing History's Monsters*, is in the U.K. when her mentor, Roux, interrupts her sojourn with news of the thefts. He's certain that the thirteen Treasures of Britain are wanted for their rumored power. Roux tasks Annja with locating and protecting the treasures before the wrong person finds them. Meaning she must stand against a woman fueled by madness and the fires of her ancient Celt blood—and a sword as powerful and otherworldly as Annja's own.

Available September wherever books and ebooks are sold.

GOLD EAGLE®

GEI3